ALL THAT
GLITTERS

Other Nick Polo cases reported by Jerry Kennealy

Beggar's Choice
Vintage Polo
Special Delivery
Green with Envy
Polo's Wild Card
Polo in the Rough
Polo's Ponies
Polo Anyone?
Polo Solo

ALL THAT GLITTERS

A Nick Polo Mystery

Jerry Kennealy

ST. MARTIN'S PRESS

NEW YORK

A THOMAS DUNNE BOOK.
An imprint of St. Martin's Press.

Library of Congress Cataloging-in-Publication Data

Kennealy, Jerry.
    All that glitters : a Nick Polo mystery / Jerry Kennealy.—1st ed.
        p.   cm.
    "A Thomas Dunne book."
    ISBN 0-312-15049-0
    I. Title.
  PS3561.E4246A79   1997
  813'.54—dc20
                                                                96-27307
                                                                CIP

First Edition: January 1997

10   9   8   7   6   5   4   3   2   1

For my editor, Ruth Cavin.
I love Ruth. In fact, once I wrote her a love letter.
She edited it and sent it back.

ALL THAT GLITTERS

CHAPTER 1

Alexander Rostov's shop looked as if it belonged on the back lot of Warner Brothers movie studio, circa 1940. Dusty floors, the walls lined with pictures—timeworn oils and watercolors of landscapes, seascapes, and undistinguishable portraits—hung so closely together that it was impossible to make out the color of the walls. You had to turn sideways to move through the endless clutter of tables that were crammed with a variety of small statues, lamps, and brass boxes, some barely the size of a matchbox, others big enough to hold a loaf of bread. Ancient daggers in fancy scrolled sheaths, vases in the shape of flowers, animals, and naked men and women. Books with worn, faded leather covers, teapots, cookie jars, metal toy banks, tobacco tins, and the clocks—birdcage clocks, tabernacle clocks, mantel clocks, drum clocks, all in various stages of disrepair. A glass display case held shoe boxes filled with baseball trading cards, coins, and a variety of military medals, American and foreign. In other words, junk. But of course Alexander referred to them as antiques. There were some real antiques. They were secreted away in the back room, where they could not be handled by those whom Alexander referred to as "the great unwashed, who think a tin of Log Cabin syrup is an antique."

Alexander Rostov was a bit of an antique himself. He was in his late seventies, with tissue paper skin stretched over the hawklike bones of his finely molded head, which was topped by a full crop of creamy white hair long enough to curl over his collar. He wore an old camel-colored wool cardigan with leather patches at the sleeves over a yellow turtleneck sweater and baggy cords.

Hidden under the sweater was a holster holding a pearl-handled .38-caliber revolver. Like most everything Rostov owned, the gun was an antique. Manufactured by Smith & Wesson in 1887, it was still in working order. At least it had been a few years back when I pried it from Alexander's shaking hands. A young tough had mistakenly thought Rostov and his wife, Ester, would be easy pickings. He had come into the shop brandishing a gun, swatting Ester over the head with the weapon just seconds before Rostov reached for his .38 and killed the would-be robber.

The man died from his wounds, and, unfortunately, so did Rostov's wife. The blow to her head wasn't fatal, but the resulting heart attack was.

Now Rostov gave me a small smile and flipped the envelope-sized sign hanging on the front door from OPEN to CLOSED.

"Come, Nick, I've something to show you."

I followed Rostov through the narrow maze to the back room, where he kept his quality line of merchandise. No more than half a dozen oils in hand-carved frames dotted the saffron-colored walls.

The rug on the floor was a genuine Ravar Kerman, and the clocks atop the Cuban mahogany dining table were seventeenth century and ticked away in perfect working order. Another glass display case, this one filled with velvet-lined tablets holding rare coins, and three-ring binders with valuable stamps carefully preserved between thick plastic sheet protectors.

A palm-leaf ceiling fan whirled in endless circles, fighting a losing battle with the smoke from the cigarettes that Rostov constantly puffed on.

We've all heard those reports about the possible dangers of secondhand smoke, but watching Alexander smoke was a show in itself. He did it the old-fashioned way, putting Humphrey Bogart to shame—an almost unnoticed inhale, and then smoke spurted from his nostrils and billowed from his lips as he talked. He was also a very good storyteller. This one could have started out, "Long, long ago and far, far away." Listen in.

"Nick, do you know anything about the Mongol Empire?"

"Not much," I admitted. "Genghis Khan, that's about it."

"Chingis Khan," Rostov corrected. "Born in 1162, died in 1227." He opened the top of a beautiful bird's-eye maple rolltop desk to reveal a sepia-colored map that was spread open and anchored at each end by round brass ingots, of the type once used to weigh postage. "At one time, the Mongol Empire extended from the coast of Korea all the way to Hungary. They controlled everything in between, including Russia and India. All of eastern, central, and western Asia."

Alexander had long, slender fingers, with gray hair sprouting from the knuckles. He ran them across the map as if he was playing the piano. "Chingis Khan's son Ögödei, took over after the Great Khan died, and only Ögödei's death saved Europe from the Mongol army that surely would have reached the shores of the Atlantic."

Alexander plopped down into an overstuffed chair, removed one of his fur-lined slippers, and massaged his arch. "Ögödei had a bit of a womanizing and drinking problem, like many of the Khans. They lived high on the horse, you might say. Tough, cruel. The Devil's Horseman. The greatest calvary ever, Nick. You've no doubt heard of the American pony express."

"Yes. That I've heard about."

"Amateurs compared to the Mongols," he responded, waving his slipper toward the map. "The Mongols had thousands of miles of territory, and, in addition to a first-class army, they had a great intelligence system. Imperial posts, or *yams,* strung out every twenty-five miles or so, according to Marco Polo's accounts." He paused, his forehead furrowing into deep crevices. "Marco Polo. Have you ever traced your family history, Nick? Is there any chance that—"

"Sorry Alexander. He was a Venetian. My folks came from a little farther south. Sicily."

He sighed deeply, as if this news greatly disappointed him, then continued with his story. "The Khan's elite were the Imperial Messengers. Bound up in thick clothing and leather belts studded with bells, they rode their horses up to a hundred and twenty-five miles a day." Alexander crisscrossed the butt end of his cigarette into an ashtray shaped like an upturned turtle, then immediately popped another one between his lips, firing it up with a well-worn rolled-gold lighter. "When the stationmaster at the post heard the sound of those bells, he'd have a fresh horse waiting for the messenger. If at any time during his journey the messenger needed another horse, food, clothing, whatever, the populace was obliged to give it to him."

Alexander put his slipper back on and sighed. "All the messenger had to do was show his *paitza,* a sort of a badge of honor, and he was given whatever he asked for. In turn, he'd give his benefactor a token, or perhaps a coin. Like one of these."

He arched his back and dug a hand into his trouser pocket, then handed me a coin. It was the size of a quarter, a distorted circle, worn around the edges, the center a blur of unintelligible shapes. The opposite side showed a man on a horse.

"That is a bronze coin of Mongke," Alexander said, a mushroom of smoke oozing from his lips. "It dates back to about 1220. 'There is no god but Allah alone. He has no associate.' That's what is written on the coin in the Uighur language."

I hefted the coin in my palm. "Is it valuable?"

"Certainly. It's very rare."

I passed the coin back to him. "How much is it worth?"

"I paid seven thousand dollars. As you can see, it's not in good condition. Look under the map."

I lifted the edge of the map. There were three Polaroid photographs. I slid them free. One showed a photo of a coin similar to Alexander's Mongke. The coin in the photograph appeared to be silver, and in mint condition.

"What's this one worth?" I asked him.

"Oh, between sixty and seventy-five thousand, if the patination is as good as it appears in the photo. It's made of electrum, a natural mixture of gold and silver. But look at the next pictures, Nick. Look at them."

The other Polaroids showed an oblong gold-colored object

with some of the same type of lettering that was on the coin.

"That, Nick, is a *paitza*. Five and an eighth inches long, and an inch and five-eighths wide. See the hole drilled in the upper portion? A leather thong went through there, then around the messenger's neck. Usually, a *paitza* was made of bronze, but this one appears to be gold, doesn't it?"

"Yes," I agreed. "You haven't actually seen it?"

"No," Alexander said, shaking his head sadly. "I have not. The inscription on this side is the standard one: 'There is no god but Allah. Muhammad is the messenger of God.' But the other side—here, hand me those."

I passed the pictures to him and he tapped a fingernail against one. "This tells us who the messenger was. Very unusual. As I say, from what we know, the *paitza* were usually bronze, or even crude iron, but this one is gold for a reason."

He paused dramatically, waiting for me to respond. I obliged. "And that reason is?"

"His name is there. Ögödie, who was Chingis Khan's son, and who later became Khan himself. Ögödie at one time was thought of as a savior by Pope Innocent IV, who tried to induce the Mongols to help the Christians in their war against the Muslims."

"Ah," I said, trying to sound enthusiastic.

"Nick, I haven't been able to contact the person who sold me the coin and brought me those pictures."

"What's his name?"

"It's a she. Anna."

"Her last name?"

"That I don't know. I asked, but she wouldn't give it to me."

"Where does she live?"

"That I don't know."

"Her phone number?"

Alexander pulled a piece of paper from the sleeve of his cardigan. "That I have." He handed me the paper. "It's an answering machine. No message. The machine just comes on so that you can leave a message. I've been calling for days, Nick. I've got to talk her. The *paitza*. I've got to see it. It's . . . it's . . . invaluable."

He pushed his half-smoked cigarette into the ashtray and snuffed it out, breaking it in half in the process.

" 'From each according to his ability, to each according to his work.' Do you know who said that?"

I was getting a little tired of Alexander's history lessons. "No, I don't."

"The old bastard himself—Stalin. Well, even Stalin couldn't control the country now. The Mafia, *boyeviks,* are running everything." He dug another cigarette from his sweater pocket and lit up. "Drugs, looting, fires, assaults, rapes. The police are spread very thin. And they are as corrupt as *boyeviks.*"

"So what you're telling me is that this *paitza* was stolen."

Alexander shrugged his slender shoulders. "It has no doubt been stolen many times, perhaps dozens of times since Ögödie Khan wore it around his neck. I've done some research. Two hundred years ago, it was known to be in Istanbul. Somehow the Germans came into possession of it; one story has it that Hermann Göring gave it to one of his favorite dancing boys. Then the Russians got control. It was definitely in the Oruzheynaya Palata, the Armory Palace, the oldest and richest museum in the Kremlin. It's where they keep the royal treasures and the Fabergé eggs.

"Rumor has it that Khrushchev traded it to a German arms manufacturer in 1969. It was reportedly kept in a safe-deposit box in Switzerland. It was offered for sale by a Swiss dealer in 1974. Then it went back to Russia, reportedly purchased by a banker in St. Petersburg. The banker and his whole family perished in a fire at their summer home in Pushkin, just south of St. Petersburg. That was seven years ago. The *paitza* has not been seen since. It has gone underground."

"And now some good soul decided it was time to bring it all out for some fresh air."

Alexander confirmed the conclusion with a pleased grin. "A good Samaritan, you could say."

"You could say that, Alexander, but I'm not so sure the police would."

"Police? What police? The Turkish police? The German police? The Swiss police? The Russian police? Think of it as capitalism, Nick. Whoever freed the *paitza* from its dark, dreary hiding place in Russia has done a great service. They have brought a work of art, and history, back to the people of the world."

I used the back of my hand to paddle away some of the cigarette smoke. "Meaning that if I can find this woman Anna, and she can deliver the *paitza,* you've got a buyer for it, right, Alexander?"

He let some more smoke pour through his teeth in a luxurious hiss. "Capitalism, Nick. That's what it's all about, isn't it?"

CHAPTER 2

Capitalism is a little like God. Both get a lot of praise, and blame, for things that they're not really responsible for.

"Are you sure that this Anna has the coin and the—"

"*Paitza*," Rostov interjected smoothly. "I have no reason to doubt her. She sold me the bronze coin. She said she had more merchandise. She asked me to find out how much the *paitza* would bring."

"And you have found out, haven't you?"

He coughed into his hand. A chest-rattling smoker's cough. "I have made inquiries. There is a some interest."

"How much interest?" I asked.

"A great deal. There is no set price on such an object. The negotiations in selling something like this are very troublesome. The people who buy such items don't just open their wallets or charge it on plastic."

Meaning he had more than one buyer. I threw a few more questions at him, but Alexander was keeping the details and the value of the *paitza* to himself.

"How many times did Anna come to see you?"

"Twice only. Once to sell the coin I showed you, then again with the photographs."

"Why did she pick you, Alexander? Or did she shop the photographs of the coin and the *paitza* around?"

He squared his shoulders and pushed out his toast rack chest. "She came to me because I have a reputation as a dealer, Nicky. The people know me. Know I am honest, and that I will give them a good price. And I speak Russian."

"Did she speak English?"

"Yes, and quite well. But she preferred Russian."

"What does she look like?"

A smile ruffled his face into a thousand wrinkles. "Beautiful, Nick. Like a Madonna. Long dark hair, soft brown eyes. Tall. A real Russian figure." His hands did a shaky version of an hour-glass.

"Was anyone with her when she came into the shop?"

"No. No one."

"Did you see how she arrived? By car? By taxi?"

He shook his head. "I did not notice. Nick. The *paitza*. It's what I've waited for all my life. Every day you think, you hope, that someone will come to your shop with a *cokpobiiiie,* a trea-sure. A real treasure. They come in with old jewelry, paintings, coins, statues. All hoping that the grimy portrait found in grandma's attic is a Rembrandt or a van Gogh. And I hope along with them, but it has never happened. Until now. This is my trea-sure."

Alexander Rostov leaned back in his chair, like an old man on a porch watching the traffic go by. "Find out where this telephone number is. You can do that, can't you?"

"Yes, I can do that."

Alexander Rostov's shop was located on Clement Street, in the fog-shrouded Richmond district of San Francisco. When I joined the San Francisco Police Department, my first assignment had been Richmond Station. Then, the area had been mostly a French and Russian enclave. Now it was a wonderfully eclectic mix: There were still a good many Russians, quite a few recent arrivals from the former Soviet Union, the ones Rostov was no doubt doing business with. The French community was slowly moving out; the newcomers were Cambodian, Chinese, Japanese, Korean, Thai, and Vietnamese. Clement Street was the main shopping spot, and I used to know most of the merchants by their first names.

There had been bars, mom-and-pop grocers, small family-run

clothing stores that didn't know then that they could raise their prices 15 or 20 percent simply by calling their shop a boutique.

French and Russian restaurants, coffee shops, and bakeries had also abounded. Now the sidewalks were lined with produce stands and fast-food outlets pushing everything from dim sum to sushi to go. Youngsters peddled baseball-sized garlic bulbs from small produce boxes hanging around their shoulders, somehow reminding me of one of those old movies—the nightclub scene with the pretty girl in a short flared skirt wandering through the tuxedoed crowd, cradling a tray and chorusing, "Cigars, cigarettes, chewing gum."

I was pleased to see that my favorite Russian bakery was still in business. The plump, rosy-cheeked woman behind the counter could have been the same person who had served coffee to that young uniformed officer who used to be me. She hadn't changed all that much. I hoped she would say the same about me, but there was no sign of recognition. Just a polite smile and an accented, "Can I help you?"

I ordered a puffy cream-filled pastry and a cup of coffee, found an unoccupied chair near the window, and thought about Alexander Rostov.

Like most people, Alexander was a bit of an enigma. He could be very tight with a dollar, and at other times very generous. Years ago, a well-liked district station sergeant had been diagnosed as having terminal cancer. He was only forty-two, and he didn't have enough time in the department to qualify for a pension.

I visited Rostov and the other merchants with hat in hand, looking for a small donation. Rostov sent me away empty-handed. The next day, he handed me an envelope containing a money order in the amount of five thousand dollars. He had put a finger to his lips and whispered, "No one must know."

He was there with donations every year for the Police Athletic League, the Firemen's Toys for Tots programs, and I knew he helped out the local Russian community with similar silent contributions.

What he wanted me to do was a simple-enough assignment.

If the telephone number the mysterious Anna had given him was listed, all I had to do was check a reverse directory. But a beautiful woman hawking photographs of a rare coin and a priceless gold tablet once worn by a Mongol Khan was hardly the type to have a listed number.

An unlisted number, or nonpub as they're called in the trade, really wasn't a problem, either. Rostov had given me a check for two hundred dollars, more than enough to get an address for the phone number and do a little background investigation on the mysterious Anna X.

I didn't know just how much of Rostov's history lesson was true, but the story of the *paitza* disappearing in Russia had me worried. Maybe he was right and the damn thing had been stolen over and over again during the last few centuries, but somehow the police always seemed to focus on who had it last—and how they had ended up with it.

I licked the pastry crumbs from my finger and walked down Clement Street to one of life's little pleasures—a used bookstore. The Bookmonger had its overflow paperbacks in wooden bins on the sidewalk. I went inside and asked a studious-looking clerk where I could find a history book on the Mongol Empire. He pointed me in the right direction.

The bookshelves extended all the way up to the ten-foot ceiling, which was where I found just what I wanted. I used the library ladder to climb up and fetch it, hanging from the rungs à la Henry Higgins in *My Fair Lady* as I thumbed through the book. It didn't take me long. The index listed *paitza*. There was a drawing of the chocolate bar–sized tablet, looking much the same as the one in the photographs the mysterious Anna had given to Alexander Rostov.

I replaced the book, climbed down, and then browsed awhile, ending up with an armful of novels, cookbooks, and one of those coffee table–sized epics featuring *The Wildflowers of Italy*.

I put the books in the trunk of my car and made another stop. More books. This time, a public library on Ninth Avenue. The librarian at the reference desk was a tired-looking woman wearing a floral-print dress and granny glasses. Her pinched facial features suggested that she thought that life itself was one long-overdue book. She wouldn't release the reverse directory to me until I handed her my driver's license. She bounced her eyes from me to my DMV photo several times before sliding the powder blue–jacketed *Haines Reverse Directory* across the counter.

The number Alexander Rostov had supplied me with—555-2626—was not listed.

I used the library's pay phone to call my contact at the phone company, and in a matter of minutes I was fifty dollars poorer, but I had the name and address for 555-2626. D. Jones—304 Cole Street, number 6, San Francisco, which put it in the Haight-Ashbury district, just a mile or so from the library.

The Haight, birthplace of the so-called flower children. The flowers hadn't bloomed for very long, if, in fact, they had ever seen the light of day. All the dreamy-eyed hippies searching for love and peace had been quickly devoured by the freeloading hard cases who had picked their pockets, their purses, then their veins as "less harmful than martinis" marijuana trips detoured down the LSD-heroin-speedball highway.

Not that the Haight didn't have its charm. I remember a fun-loving beat cop, Bogus Bob McCard, who had patrolled the Haight at its peak, telling me about a pot bust that had turned into a rooftop chase, the chasee bounding gracefully from build-ing to building. He was finally cornered atop a pitch-roofed Vic-torian by a squadron of red-faced, out-of-breath cops. They thought they'd captured a cat burglar or a Ringling Brothers trapeze artist. He turned out to be an artist, all right. Rudolf Nureyev. "Hell of a nice guy," McCard conceded. "He signed au-tographs for all of us at the station."

The fog had given way to a blue sky spotted with popcorn clouds. I circled Cole Street twice, looking for a legal parking spot, finding none, ending up where I usually did, in front of a fire hydrant—a hundred-dollar ticket should a meter maid swoop by.

My car, a two-year-old chipped and dented tan Ford sedan had one saving grace—it looked amazingly like an undercover police car: blackwall tires, whip antenna, and spotlight. For good measure, I placed one of my old San Francisco Police Department Inspector business cards on the edge of the dashboard.

Three-oh-four Cole Street had once been a magnificent three-story Queen Anne Victorian with towering chimneys, an onion-domed turret, bay windows, and a gabled roof with swallow nest stucco work under the gables. The pearl-drop shingles covering the house were painted gunboat gray. The north side of the building had a view of Golden Gate Park's Panhandle, an area that had given shelter to the victims of the 1906 earthquake. Now it was a magnet for the homeless and drug dealers.

The Faded Lady's front entrance was littered with bicycles—battered, streetwise bikes. The varnish on the weather-pitted front door was peeling and there were scratches around the weather-pitted doorknob.

Rusting black metal mailboxes hung on the wall on each side of the door—each box marked with hand-painted numbers from one to six. Boxes one and two belonged to the Mercury Messenger Service, which explained the presence of all the old bikes.

There was no name listed on the mailbox marked 6. The top of the box made a squeaky sound as I lifted it. I flipped through the half-dozen third-class mailings, all of which were addressed to Occupant.

There was a bell plate positioned under the row of mailboxes. There were no names in the slots other than that of Mercury Messenger Service.

A crude penciled note was taped to the wall, advertising the fact that units three and five were vacant. "See Manager." There was no indication as to just where the manager could be seen. I pushed the button marked 6 and waited a couple of minutes. No response.

The entrance door was ajar. I shouldered it open and stepped inside, finding a small foyer and more bikes. A grainy-skinned kid with a Mohawk-style haircut, the broom-stiff ridge of hair dyed emerald green, exited the messenger service, bumping into me as he reached for one of the bikes.

"I'm trying to contact the people in apartment six. Jones. You know them?"

He shrugged his shoulders. "Nah." He twitched his head toward the door labeled MERCURY. "Maybe Leo will."

Leo turned out to be a slope-shouldered, hatchet-jawed man with an "I'm busy, don't bother me" look chiseled into his features.

He was sitting behind a desk with four telephones and foot-high stacks of notepaper. "Yeah, what'd you want?" he bellowed.

"I'm looking for the building manager."

Two of his telephones rang at the same instant. He picked one up, put his hand over the receiver, and said, "Next door. Patel."

Patel is an East Indian name that literally means "innkeeper," and the Patel families were major landlords throughout the city.

I went back out to the foyer. A frayed, odorous carpet runner covered the staircase risers and treads. The balusters and handrail had been painted landlord brown. There were two units per floor.

Number six was on the third floor, down a musty hallway at the rear of the building. I leaned my head next to the door, stepped back, and knocked lightly; then in a few moments, I knocked again, this time with more authority.

No response. No noises from within. I tried the doorknob. You never know. Sometimes they're unlocked. Just like in the movies. But life is seldom like the movies. One of the first things you're instructed in at the Police Academy is how to slip a lock, so you can help kids who have locked themselves in the bathroom, or grandma stuck in her bedroom, or tenants who had lost their keys and couldn't find a locksmith at three in the morning. By now, everyone has seen a TV burglar extract a credit card, wedge it in the crack above the door lock, shimmy it down, and spring the latch bolt. And it can work that way. It can also work out that the credit card snaps in two and you've left your name in the doorjamb. I've experimented with several different tools and found that the plastic-coated California private investigator's license in my wallet works the best. Not this time. The door was swollen tight to the frame and wouldn't budge.

I trooped back downstairs and over to the property next door, another sad-faced Victorian. Mr. Patel was listed as residing in unit A. I rang the bell and was buzzed in.

A beautiful little girl, no more than seven or eight years old, was waiting for me. She had bright button eyes and straight black hair that was parted in the middle and reached to her waist.

"Hi, is your mommy or daddy home?"

She nodded her head slightly, then closed the door. It was banged open moments later by a middle-aged man in a stained T-shirt, his belly hanging over his belt buckle. He had the same dark eyes as the little girl, but the brightness had dimmed a long time ago. His egg-shaped face was darkened by a two-day stubble. He was wearing rubber beach sandals. His feet were tea-colored, his toenails painted red.

"What do you want?" he asked in a tired voice.

I wasn't sure how to play it until I saw him. Hard or soft. Straight or bent. I decided on bent.

"I'm looking for an apartment for my . . . niece. She's going to school near here and I want a quiet spot where I can visit her once in awhile. I was next door, saw you had some vacant units."

He squinted his eyes and ran a thumbnail across his chin. "My places are not completely furnished. Just a refrigerator, a bed, a few pots and pans."

"That's all right. We'll manage."

He digested this slowly, then smiled knowingly.

He held up a finger to signal for me to wait, then closed the door, coming back a minute later with a thin black-jacketed ledger in hand. The little girl was alongside, hanging on to his belt.

"You are in luck. Unit five is available. So is unit three, on the second floor. Fifteen hundred dollars a month."

Fifteen hundred dollars. I winced inwardly. My one and only tenant, Mrs. Damonte, was paying less than a third of that for the full five-room flat below mine. "Those face the park. It might be noisy. Who's in unit six? Is it occupied? I'd be willing to sign a lease. For a year, say."

Patel pushed the dog-eared ledger at me. "Mr. Jones rents month to month." He gave another toothy grin. "He is seldom there, I think."

The ledger listed little information. D. Jones. First and last months' rent as well as the cleaning fee paid in advance—in cash.

"Maybe he'd be interested in switching apartments. Maybe if I talked to him. What kind of work does he do?"

Patel retrieved the ledger and slapped it against his leg. "Who knows?"

Who knows? Who cares? "Give me the passkey. I'll look at both vacant units and let you know."

He unclipped a key from his belt and gave it to the little girl. "Maya will show you."

CHAPTER 3

Little Maya skipped ahead of me, her Barney the Dinosaur dress blowing in the wind as she gracefully dodged the bicycles blocking the entrance to 304 Cole Street.

I followed behind as she dutifully opened the door for apartment three and then apartment five. I gave both units a cursory look. One room, plus kitchen and bath.

Maya was hopping from one foot to the other when I asked her to use the passkey to open unit six.

"That's not for rent," she replied in a soft, cuddly voice.

"It may be soon."

She scrunched up her nose. "I like ice cream," she said, raising her hand, the tiny fingers forming a cup.

I reached into my pocket and came out with a handful of change. Her nose unscrunched as she deftly plucked three quarters and a dime from my palm. Ah, she was going to be a great landlady when she grew up.

She used the passkey on the door to unit six, those buttonlike eyes bright with mischief.

"Thanks, Maya. Go tell your daddy I'll come and see him tomorrow."

Feeling slightly tacky for bribing a seven-year-old kid, I watched her run down the hallway.

The Jones unit wasn't much to look at. Hardwood floors, warped and uneven. Bare walls of yellowish plaster with random amoeba-shaped stains. A single mattress on the floor, the sheets notched back on one corner, a gold-and-black plaid blanket neatly folded under the pillow. A small metal folding table shouldering a black plastic answering machine, a telephone, and a shadeless lamp with a single lightbulb hovered next to the mattress.

The closet was empty—not even a clothes hanger.

The kitchen had a rusty sink, the porcelain worn down to metal in spots. I opened the cabinets, but, just as in Old Mother Hubbard's kitchen, the cupboards were bare. Under the sink was an empty plastic garbage pail and a spray can of roach killer. The refrigerator was an ancient shoulder-height Frigidare. I opened the door cautiously, my nostrils pinched shut, but it was as empty as everything else in the place. I popped the small freezer drawer. Bingo. Two frosty shot glasses and a bottle of booze. I edged the bottle out. Stolichnaya vodka, the contents down to the label.

The bathroom was closet-size: sink, toilet, a fiberglass shower stall with no curtain.

The answering machine was a Sony digital model. The message indicator showed the number 1. I pushed the play button and a mechanical voice advised me, "You have one message."

Then a man's voice. A foreign language—Russian probably—ending with a snatch of English. "Soon, darling."

The message rewound automatically, and I pushed the play button again, planning to stop the machine when the call was back on line; then suddenly, the damn thing rang, startling me.

Four rings, then the machine clicked on. There was a series of three beeps, before the message started rewinding. Someone was using the remote function, calling in for messages. I unplugged the cord connecting the machine to the telephone.

The caller tried four more times, letting the phone ring a dozen times each call. When they finally gave up, I reattached the cord to the phone, settled the answering machine back the way I'd found it, then wiggled the connector just barely loose, so that it was still attached, but not in working order.

Maya had left the door to unit five across the hall unlocked. I decided to wait and see if the caller showed up.

I spent almost an hour gazing out at the festivities in the Panhandle. Frisbee players, a couple of football tossers, a few garbage can treasure divers, and at least a dozen quick transactions between a young man with a Dutch Boy haircut and the drivers of cars ranging from Mercedes sedans to ancient VWs. After every deal, Dutch Boy would walk a few feet down to a bird guano–speckled van and pass something through the van's window to an accomplice I couldn't see.

The sound of clicking heels on the hallway floor brought me from the window to the door. The heels came to a stop and I cracked the door open an inch.

A tall dark-haired woman in a black raincoat was inserting a key into the door of unit six. Her profile showed high cheekbones and a well-cut nose. As the lock clicked open, she glanced down the hall and I got a full front view of that face: broad, arching brows, slightly pointed chin. Alexander Rostov had described Anna as beautiful, "a Madonna." This lady fit the description.

She entered the apartment and slammed the door shut behind her. I could hear her heels clattering. Then a word. Just one word—a foreign language. It sounded like a curse.

I hurried down the stairs and out to my car, digging a 35-mm camera from the trunk before settling behind the wheel.

I had the camera loaded with film and the zoom lens adjusted by the time the woman I hoped was Alexander's Anna came out the front door of 304 Cole Street.

She hesitated briefly on the stoop, sweeping her eyes in both directions.

I didn't think she could spot me with the sun visor pulled down, so I got off half a dozen snaps before she hit the street. She walked north on Cole, turning right on Oak Street.

I kicked the motor over and throttled down to loitering speed as I turned onto Oak. She was in a hurry—shoulders back, head up, arms swinging rhythmically, as if she was prepared to break out in a jog at any moment. She stepped off the sidewalk, then came to a halt alongside a maroon-colored sedan. I had no choice but to cruise by as she got into the car. I pulled headfirst into a driveway and watched as the sedan raced by, the left blinker light flashing as she maneuvered into the far lane on the one-way street. The car was a Volvo. I could see only the first four digits of the license plate.

I jammed the gear lever into reverse and backed out into traffic, flinching at the sound of honking horns.

A guy in a mud-splashed pickup truck waved at me, one finger sticking straight up in the air. You didn't have to be a lip-reader to get the gist of his thoughts about my driving technique.

The maroon Volvo had turned left on Masonic. I was trapped by a red light, and by the time I was onto Masonic myself, I had to be two minutes behind her. Luck came my way for a change. The Volvo was stopped for the red light on Fell Street.

When the light went to green, the Volvo took a left onto Fell Street, flowed onto Kennedy Drive, then into the mouth of Golden Gate Park.

The park was jammed with traffic: cars, motorcycles, bicycles, joggers, and strollers. I was one car back of the Volvo, tucked behind a station wagon filled with fidgety kids in baseball uniforms.

The Volvo motored west, past the white-glassed Conservatory of Flowers, Rainbow Falls, Spreckels Lake, and the Buffalo Paddock. A tour bus had traffic bottled up by the Chain of Lakes and the joggers were making better time than the internal-combustion chariots.

The woman in the Volvo got impatient and leaned on her horn, drawing no-no looks from the joggers and hikers.

We started moving again. We were getting close to the west end of the park and the Pacific Ocean.

The Volvo pulled to a stop near the Dutch Windmill. I went by, taking a turn onto the Great Highway. The sky was now molten gray, the air thick with salt, and I could hear the breakers hitting the beach as I parked and hurried back to the windmill, which dated back to the beginning of the century and was once used to pump water from an underground river that runs beneath Golden Gate Park. The usual thing happened. The city government bought the water company in the thirties and let the windmill fall apart. Some good citizens got together twenty years ago and restored it to its original glory and added the Queen Wilhemina Tulip Garden to the landscape.

An army of red, pink, and yellow tulips were at full attention. There were upward of sixty people threading their way slowly through the carefully manicured garden, many, like me, with cameras dangling from their necks. I dry-shot pictures of the tulips and windmill while keeping an eye out for the Volvo's driver, finally spotting her snuggled in among a grove of wind-tortured cypress trees, their branches interlocked like arthritic-knuckled fingers.

I took several pictures of her, then wandered toward the Volvo, taking a photo of the car and jotting down the license plate.

Anna was watching the road as if waiting for someone. She didn't have a purse. She dug a cigarette from her raincoat pocket and lit it with a match. She held the cigarette in the European manner, with the palm of her hand facing upward, the cigarette pinched between her forefinger and thumb.

She went through the first smoke in a hurry, chain-lighting another one. I could envision her and Alexander Rostov blowing clouds of smoke at each other.

A smile came to her face and she dropped her cigarette to the ground, grinding it out with her toe; then she started running. A man exited a Yellow Cab, leaned in to pay the driver, then started moving toward her. I wasn't in position to see the cab's number or license plate. The scene was almost like one of those dopey TV commercials: two lovers running to each other, embracing, kissing, telling each other how wonderful their hair looked and that they owed it all to Sexy Shampoo.

The man was tall, thin, with flaxen-colored hair that streamed in the wind. He was wearing a dark green knee-length parka, the hood dangling down the back. They hugged each other, then kissed passionately, the man coming up for air and looking over his shoulder. Wrong shoulder. I was on the opposite side.

Then he turned my way and I got a better look at him: mid-thirties, with a bony, strong-featured face. They embraced again;

then he draped his arm over her shoulder and guided her toward the road.

Love in bloom, and Polo playing voyeur.

They strolled to the maroon Volvo. The woman whispered something in his ear. He nodded his head and she handed him the key. He opened the passenger-side door for her, getting a peck on the lips for his chivalry.

CHAPTER 4

◄►

The Volvo streamed by within ten feet of me. The two lovers were chatting away, paying no attention to anyone but themselves.

Flaxen Hair took a short left turn and pulled to a stop in the open parking area that gave a view of the white-crested ocean waves pounding into the surf-smoothed beach.

It brought back more memories of my early days in the police department: as a bored young patrolman trying to stay awake on the midnight watch, with nothing better to do then aim a flashlight beam into the cars parked along the Great Highway, disturbing the occupants, mostly teenagers, grappling in the backseat of dad's borrowed sedan.

More times then I liked to remember, I'd found a suicide victim. A "wave watcher" was the way one veteran sergeant had described them. Poor souls who had somehow found that the rhythmical action of the tide gave them the impetus to put the barrel of a gun against their temple. Or swallow that last glass of gin spiked with a lethal dose of sleeping pills.

One early-morning hour, I'd come across a man who ended his particular nightmare with a double-barrel shotgun. I didn't know the sex or age of the person when I first shined the flashlight into the car's darkened interior. It took a minute to realize that the spattered gore had once been a human being.

Mysterious Anna and her boyfriend were acting more like teenagers—their heads merging, then sinking out of sight behind the Volvo's headrest.

I used the car phone to call the Department of Motor Vehicles in Sacramento and check the Volvo's license plate number.

Ever since that well-reported incident where a private eye sold DMV records to a stalker who ended up slashing a young Southern California woman to death, the Department of Motor Vehicles had been very cautious about letting address information out. If you were a licensed private investigator, and if you paid a three-hundred-dollar sign-up fee, then posted the necessary bond, and if you promised that the reason for your inquiry had to do with the legal serving of a subpoena, they would sell you everything: name, address, legal owner, registered license transactions.

Abuse the system and they got nasty and fined you big bucks and suspended your license.

I had two accounts with DMV: one that gave me the owner's name and address information—the one they monitored extensively—and another that released the register name only.

Over the phone, they would release only vehicle registration info. To get the details on a driver's license, you either had to deal directly with the DMV by mail, which was too slow in most cases, or go through a third party—a database that would flash the information to your computer in a matter of seconds.

So far, this wasn't a case worth stepping on DMV's toes, so I went for the name only on the Volvo. It was registered to something called WLFR.

I checked with telephone information. There was a business listing for WLFR on the 1600 block of Van Ness Avenue.

A woman with a heavy European accent answered my call.

"Is Anna there?"

"Who is this?" she asked in a husky voice.

"A friend."

"Give me your number and I will have her contact you."

"I'll call back," I responded, then pushed the disconnect button.

I killed ten minutes trying to put words to the WLFR letters, my eyes wandering from the Volvo to the slick wet-suited surfers braving the frigid, foamy waves for a short, choppy ride into the gray sand beach.

Anna's head popped up, followed by Flaxen Hair's. Their two

profiles stared at each other. Even from thirty yards away, I could see that true love was having a bumpier ride than the surfers.

Flaxen Hair got out of the car, slamming the door after him. The mysterious Anna soon gave chase. She had doffed the black raincoat. A beet red sweater and skirt outfit confirmed that old Rostov's hourglass description of Anna's figure was right on target.

Her jiggling chase caught the attention of the driver of a sporty blue convertible, who skidded to a stop and beeped his horn.

Anna ignored him and began running after Flaxen Hair. She finally caught up to him, grabbing his arm, tugging him to a halt. Flaxen Hair swung around, his hand raised over his shoulder as if he was about to strike out at her.

I rolled the car window down, but I couldn't hear what he was saying. Whatever it was, it got the veins on his neck dancing.

Anna extended her arms in a pleading gesture. Flaxen Hair just shook his head, then whirled around, loosing his balance for a moment, and stalked off.

Anna yelled at him. "Jonathan!" Then her shoulders dropped and she headed back to the Volvo, her chin pointing at her chest.

The driver of the convertible pulled up alongside her, but she ignored him, sliding behind the wheel of the Volvo and barreling off in a scream of burning rubber.

I had a couple of choices. Chase after Anna, follow her to her destination, or have the photos developed and report my findings to Alexander Rostov.

The Volvo made an abrupt ninety-degree turn onto Fulton Street. I decided to let her go. Following someone, especially someone who is mad as hell and in a hurry, is difficult. The only way to pull off a one-man tail job is to stick close to your quarry. Sometimes you have to ride their bumper. That old "duck behind a few cars" and "drop back a quarter mile" stuff looks good on-screen, but if you catch one or two red lights, your target is gone.

But, you ask, if you're riding your target's bumper, won't they spot you? If they're expecting to be tailed, yes. Otherwise, almost never. Try it next time you're out for a spin. How often do you look in your rearview mirror to see who or what is behind you? I once tailed a jewelry salesman whose boss thought he was fencing stolen property from San Francisco to Eureka and back, some six hundred miles. We stopped for gas at the same stations, had coffee at the same shops, slept in the same motel. I was probably never more than fifty yards away from the guy for two days. He looked through me half a dozen times, but he never saw me.

People just don't bother to look at who's behind them. Including me, as it turned out.

I cruised past Jonathan as he stomped off into a chaparral of cypress trees, muttering to himself. What was it that had bent cupid's arrow?

It was the following morning and I was back in Alexander Rostov's private office. He was all smiles when I handed him the packet of photographs. As he examined them, his handsome head bobbed up and down, like a robin tugging at a worm.

"Yes, yes. This is Anna. This is her." He crooked his neck and looked up at me. "Did you talk to her, Nick?"

"No. I traced the phone number she gave you. It led to a flat in the Haight. A mattress, a refrigerator with a bottle of vodka in the freezer, a telephone, and an answering machine. Anna was driving a Volvo, Alexander. It's registered to a business on Van Ness Avenue called WLFR. I haven't checked it out yet. How far do you want me to go on this?"

Rostov answered my question with one of his own. He tapped a nicotine-stained finger on one of the photographs.

"Who is the young man?"

"I don't know, Alex. Your Anna called him Jonathan. He arrived in a cab. He could have been the voice on her answering machine. There was just one message. It sounded like Russian, except for the send-off—'Soon, darling.' "

"It could have been this man? This Jonathan?"

"It could have been anyone, Alexander."

"She did not see you? Anna? The young man did not see you?"

"Nobody saw me, Alex." It wasn't a lie—at the time anyway.

Rostov lit a cigarette from the dog end of his old one, then looked at me through a veil of smoke. "The young man, Jonathan. Can you find out who he is? Maybe he has something to do with the coin and the *paitza*."

"Maybe, but the only way I could pick him up would be by staking out Anna. Do you want me to do that? It will cost you, Alexander."

He picked up one of the photographs and held it under a brass gooseneck lamp. "Let me think about this." He pulled the photo closer to his eyes. "Beautiful, isn't she? A Madonna. Just like I told you."

I put the Rostov case out of my mind and concentrated on a couple of insurance-fraud cases and cleaning up my flat. Jane Tobin, a lady whose last name I had been unsuccessfully trying to change to Polo, was coming home in a few days.

Jane, a reporter for the *San Francisco Bulletin,* had wangled an assignment on board one of those cruise ships that sail out of Miami and tour the Caribbean. Sun, fun, and financial seminars on the stock market by those gurus who spout their stuff on public television. That way, the fiscally concerned passengers could write the whole package off. Jane had booked herself a three-way deal with a travel magazine, a financial journal, and her newspaper editor, convincing them all that a story on how the asset-conscious absorb buy low/sell high theories while slurping daiquiris was just what readers wanted to know.

I was at the computer, putting the finishing touches on a report when the doorbell chimed.

A skinny kid with a do-rag tied around his scalp handed me a small package, then a clipboard. "Special Delivery for Nick Polo," he said between smacks of gum. I signed for the packet, carried it in to the kitchen, and used a boning knife to slice through the cardboard envelope.

Inside was a videocassette with a stick-on note attached—a typewritten message. "Can we talk?" No name.

I cranked up the TV and inserted the cassette in the VCR. A familiar scene: the Queen Wilhelmina Tulip Garden at Golden Gate Park. Me wandering around with the camera around my neck. Then me taking pictures of Anna and Flaxen Hair.

At one point, the lens zoomed in on a close-up of my face. It was so close, I noticed I hadn't done a very good job shaving that morning.

I washed my hands and waited for the phone to ring. It didn't take long.

CHAPTER 5

"How'd you like the video?"

The voice was male, young, cocky. I flicked on the tape recorder attached to the phone. "A little too dark. You should use a faster film when the weather is gloomy."

A light chuckle. "Cut the bull, Mr. Polo. I just wanted to thank you for leading me to her."

"To who?"

The chuckle again. He was having a lot of fun. "And her boyfriend. Now that was nice. You should have followed her home. You want to know where she ended up?"

"Desperately."

"Tell me about your interest in all this and maybe we can play ball."

"I love playing ball, but only when I know the other players. Why don't you stop by and we can have a face-to-face chat." I threw out a pitch. "We private eyes have to stick together."

Home run. There was a trace of ironic applause in his voice. "Good guess. I think there's a lot of money in this. A whole lot. We should at least discuss it. So, who are you working for?"

"A rich man. A very rich man."

The chuckle was back. "Me, too. The trouble with rich men is that they don't like spending their money, Mr. Polo. That's how they got rich in the first place. Think it over. I'll get back to you tomorrow."

He severed the connection before I could respond. Don't you hate it when they do that?

The phone company in California was one of the last in the

nation to put caller ID into operation, where the number of the person ringing you shows up on a small screen attached to your phone.

Of course, anyone intending to play games on the phone could pay the phone company a few dollars more to place a block on their number so it couldn't be transmitted.

Chuckles was one of those game players.

The phone company had another service that helped you get around the block: call return. If you wanted to get back to those annoying people who hung up as soon as you picked up the phone, all you had to do was press star 69 on your touch pad and his or her number was automatically dialed from your end.

The telephone company wouldn't provide you with the next service I was to make use of. I dug through the desk drawer, found the soap bar–sized gadget called a tone decoder, loaded it with fresh batteries, and hooked it into the microphone connection on the tape recorder.

I made sure the spools on the tape recorder were twirling, then punched the star 69 buttons. The autodialer went to work and the chirping of the phone numbers came in loud and clear. I hung up before the first ring.

I then rewound the tape and ran it through the tone decoder. The numbers of the phone that Chuckles had called from showed up on the small plastic screen. I thumbed through the "Customer Guide" section in the front of the phone book. The exchange was a San Francisco one.

I dug out the Yellow Pages and flipped to the section listing private investigators.

When I threw out that line about private eyes sticking together, Chuckles hadn't denied he was a member of the profession. It was hard to believe that an investigator with any moxie at all wouldn't know about the callback system, but the longer I stayed in the game, the more incompetent the investigators I stumbled across.

Chuckles was making it too easy. The number was listed to a Thomas Dashuk, with an address on Polk Street. Are you sitting down? This is hard to believe. The matchbook-sized ad read:

THOMAS DASHUK
THE THINNER MAN INVESTIGATIONS

Process Serving, Fugitive Recovery
& Confidential Countermeasures.

Foreign Languages a Specialty.
We Follow Anyone Anywhere.

I checked the residential listings. T. Dashuk, an address on Turk Street—the same telephone number as listed for his office.

The doorbell rang again while I was trying to figure out my next move. It was Mrs. Damonte, my downstairs tenant. Mrs. D was a five-foot, ninety-pound octogenarian who had resided in the downstairs flat since my parents first bought the property, well before I was born. They had both been killed in an airplane accident some years back. I inherited the flats, the normal scheme of things to most people—but Mrs. D was not one of those people.

She was wearing her everyday getup of a black dress that covered her from her neck to the tip of her Nikes and carrying a cake platter in her small, sinewy hands. *"Zuppa inglese,"* she said with a smile. A real smile. I could actually see her teeth. Her usual smile was a quick twitch of the cheeks.

"Thank you, thank you." I took the platter and invited her inside.

Mrs. D understood English. She kept her speaking of the language down to a minimum, usually getting by on just three words: *Nopa,* her negative response to almost everything; *shita,* often tacked right on to *nopa;* and, her favorite, *bingo.* She much preferred Italian, and since I had a hard time keeping up with her, she threw a mixture at me—a little of her particular brand of English, spiced up with Italian.

I placed the frosty chocolate rum custard cake in the refrigerator. When I turned around, she was lifting the lid of the pan on the stove.

"Linguini with clam sauce," I explained. I had long ago learned the old bachelor trick of cooking up a big pot of something that could last for three or four meals.

She stuck her nose to the pan, inhaled deeply, then said, *"Ottima."*

Excellent. Something was wrong here. Mrs. D didn't pass out *ottimas* unless she wanted something. The cake—it certainly wasn't to celebrate Jane Tobin's return. Jane was not a favorite of Mrs D. She saw any woman I dated as a threat—someone who might marry me, have my children, and take control of what she considered "her flats."

"Can I fix you a drink?"

"Si, a solito."

As usual. Usually when Mrs. D had a drink, it was once a day, and that once was at eight in the morning. Her preference was a Manhattan—no cherry. Maybe she was worried about the calories.

I went to work fixing her cocktail, keeping a wary eye on her as she skimmed her hands over the table, the chairs, the countertops.

I poured myself a glass of wine and handed her the Manhattan.

We raised our glasses and made our customary toast. *"Cent' anni."* Sort of an abbreviated version of "May you live to be a hundred." There was no doubt in my mind that Mrs. D would do that and more. There was no doubt in her mind, either.

She slugged a third of her drink down without batting an eye and gave me another *"Ottima."*

I started to sweat. What had I forgotten? It wasn't her birthday. Her rent wasn't due for a couple of weeks. Her entire flat had been remodeled and repainted after a fire months ago. All her kitchen appliances had been replaced. What the hell was she up to?

I dug the book on the wildflowers of Italy from a drawer and handed it to her.

She first flipped the jacket open to check on the price tag, no doubt wondering where she could return it for cash, then nodded her acceptance. She tucked the book under her arm, then knocked back the rest of her drink and carefully placed the glass in the sink. When she turned around, her eyes were twinkling. "Carla. Yousa not forget?"

Mesa forget? "Of course not," I said with a forced smile, and then it came back to me. Carla. One of her unending supply of nieces was arriving from Italy in a couple of days. I'd have to pick her up at the airport.

"*Divertitti,*" she gushed. Enjoy yourself. While you can, she might have added.

I waited until she was gone and the door firmly closed before groaning out loud. Mrs. D's nieces all came from northern Italy—sweet, smiling, "butter wouldn't melt in their mouths" young women who didn't like the local crop of husband material in Italy.

The girls were usually pretty desperate by the time they got to San Francisco, and Mrs. D would have a lineup of young *paesanos* from North Beach waiting for inspection.

But before they were put through the matchmaking routine, I was put on the grill.

The fact that I was too old, too ornery, and too *"Americano"* for the girls made no difference. I had the flats! If I hooked up with one of her nieces, Mrs. D wouldn't have to wait for me to die in order to take over officially.

I said a silent prayer for Jane to hurry home and save me.

The best thing you could say about Thomas Dashuk's address was that it was within walking distance of city hall, the federal courthouse, and the main library, places that private investigators visited frequently in the normal course of their business.

The building—six stories of dingy gray cement—squatted on the corner of Polk and Turk streets. The street-front tenants included the subtly named Lickie's Tanning Salon, a coffee shop, an adult bookstore, and The Thinner Man Investigations.

Dashuk's sign was made out of black stick-on letters that had been glued on the window by someone with an unsteady hand.

Curtains covered the fly-specked windows. The residential lobby entrance to the building was around the corner on Turk Street. The mailbox nameplates showed a T. Dashuk resided in apartment 3J. Dashuk had a nice short commute to work—just out the door and around the corner. I rang the bell several times. When the door buzzed open, I rang it again, then headed for the coffee shop. It was an old-fashioned joint with wood-backed booths and cracked red vinyl stools, the stools patched with duct tape. The kind of place that existed because of the loyalty of a small band of regular customers who had nowhere else to go. A Buddha-bellied man in a white T-shirt and a Giants baseball cap worn backward was working the grill. There were half a dozen customers who glanced up when I entered, saw I wasn't a regular, and went back to their morning newspapers. The waitress was a buxom brunette whose forehead was hidden by thick ringlets.

I took a booth that gave me a view of the street and ordered a cup of coffee.

"You can't sit in a booth unless you order more than three dollars' worth, sir," she advised me in a tired voice.

I handed her a five-dollar bill, which disappeared quickly into her apron pocket. "A gentleman named Dashuk lives upstairs. Does he ever come in here?"

She glanced up at the wall clock. "Every morning. Right around nine. Orders the same thing—a short stack. Makes the same pass. All he gets are the pancakes."

It was twenty minutes to nine. "What's he look like?"

Her fingers went to her apron pocket. I could almost hear them crinkling the five-dollar bill. "Tall, skinny. He tries to look like Elvis, but it don't work. You want something besides the coffee?"

"How are the pancakes?"

"Great."

I placed another five spot on the table. "I'll try them, and I'd just as soon Dashuk didn't know I was asking about him."

"About who?" she said, snatching the bill between thumb and forefinger.

The pancakes were as good as advertized and the coffee was a strong French roast. A few minutes past nine, a lean, lanky man in his mid-twenties, his brown hair sprayed in a pompadour, pushed his way into the shop. He was wearing khaki chinos, a yellow, knit shirt with an upturned collar and a black Members Only jacket.

"Hey, Judy," he called out to the waitress. "Today could be your lucky day, baby."

Judy pursed her mouth in a gesture of contempt: then, in a voice louder than necessary, she asked, "You want your usual pancakes, Mr. Dashuk?"

I nodded a thank-you in her direction. She was giving me my ten dollars' worth.

"Mr. Dashuk? Kind of formal this morning, ain't you?" He wrapped his long legs around a counter stool, then twisted around, scanning the sparse crowd. He did a theatrical double take when he saw me, almost falling off his seat.

CHAPTER 6

I fanned my face with the videocassette Dashuk had sent me. He got to his feet, his face dropping into a hound-dog look that Elvis would have appreciated.

"It was the phone call, wasn't it?" he asked as he settled down across from me. His gooped-up hair was a cinnamon brown color. He had quick-shifting blue eyes shuttered by long, silky lashes. His skin was smooth, wrinkle-free. A boyishly good-looking face. Somewhere between twenty-five and thirty was my guess.

"How long have you been licensed, Tom?"

"Four months."

He pulled out his wallet and handed me a business card, his hand remaining open until I deposited one of my cards in it.

If you ever consider a career as a private investigator, the best place to go is the Centennial State, Colorado. Have some cards printed up, put a sign on your door, an ad in the phone book, and you're in business. It's that old rugged western tradition, I guess.

In California, you had to work for a licensed investigator for six thousand hours—three years' worth of hours—then pass a state test, post a bond, and be sponsored by a licensed investigator. I asked Dashuk whom he had worked for.

"Uncle Sam," he responded with a sly grin. "Military intelligence."

Ah, that explained it. The ever-present loophole. The state would waive the six-thousand-hour regulation if the applicant was an investigating police officer from any legitimate local, state, or federal agency.

Military intelligence—the oxymoron of all time. That explained why he didn't know about the callback system. "When did you get out of the army?"

Dashuk scratched the area under his nose as though he were using his thumbnail as a razor. "Last year. I was stationed over in Oakland. I decided to set up shop here in Frisco."

I shuddered to think what military intelligence was investigating in Oakland. I had done a brief stint in MI during my hitch in the army. We were glorified military police for the most part. I fingered the videotape. "What did your client say when he saw this?"

Dashuk smacked his lips as the waitress put a platter of pancakes in front of him.

She topped up my coffee and gave me a wink.

Being a regular customer had its benefits. The pat of butter on Dashuk's plate was the size of a golf ball. He dribbled syrup on his pancakes and said, "I didn't tell him about it, or about finding the girl, Mr. Polo. Yet."

"Isn't that what he's paying you for, Mr. Dashuk?"

He began sawing away at his short stack, first cutting the cakes in half, then quarters, then eighths, then into bite-sized cubes. His face had an "I know something that you don't know" look on it. I decided to wipe it off.

"Dashuk, you can lose your license for something like this. Did you know that?"

He grinned, showing me a mouthful of pancake-smeared teeth. "I reckon you're the expert in losing your license, ain't you, Mr. Polo?"

Well, well, well. He was showing his cards, starting with an ace. I had left the police department when my parents died in the airplane crash. The airline had paid off the death claims with what was to me, at the time, a small fortune. Between that money and the flats, I figured I was set for life, so why work?

A stockbroker had shown me how to change a small fortune into long-term debt. I'd had to go back to work, and investigating was about all that I could do.

I'd started out on the wrong foot, then ended up putting the other shoe in my mouth. I was given an assignment to find a certain individual. I did. In a motel room, dead from a self-inflicted drug overdose. My attorney-client assured me that the man had no family, no loved ones, and would not be missed by anyone on God's still partially green planet. There was a suitcase alongside the body, filled with currency—a half a million dollars in cash. All that money. Give it to the feds and they'd just waste it on something stupid like nuclear submarines. He had a better idea. Split it down the middle and not tell a soul.

I kept my part of the bargain, but when his client's disgruntled business partners started pounding on the attorney's door, he went right to the cops and cried his heart out. He got a thank-you and a pat on the back; I got handcuffs, a kick in the butt, six months as a guest of the federal prison system, and the loss of my PI license.

I was able to get the license back, but I still wake up in a sweat some mornings thinking I'm back in that cold gray cell.

Dashuk was enjoying himself. He shoveled another wedge of pancakes in his mouth and between bites said, "You were a policeman, too, wasn't you?"

"You did your homework, didn't you, Tommy?"

He took a sip of coffee and squished the liquid around in his mouth before swallowing. "I saw the cop card on your dashboard. It scared the hell out of me. Then I figured maybe it was a scam. Guys in MI used to do that. Get some cop's business card and put it on their dash so they wouldn't get a ticket. I called the phone number on the card. The guy who answered laughed and told me you quit the department years ago and were working as a private eye. Later, I went down to the library and ran your name through their computer that gets you the newspaper stories. I found out all about you, Mr. Polo. I figure if we put our heads together, we could make a good team."

If we put our heads together, I'd end up with pomade all over my hair. "What did you have in mind?"

Dashuk slouched into a comfortable position. "I know there's big bucks in this. I mean really big bucks." His eyes darted around the room, then came back to me. He batted those long lashes and grinned. "What do you say? We gonna cooperate on this one?"

"What makes you think there's a lot of money ripe for picking?"

He gave me a sly wink. "My client didn't want to put me in the picture—you know what I mean? He wanted to keep everything to himself, but I have ways of finding these things out—you know what I mean?"

"Finding what out?"

"Come on, Nick. You know what's involved. I know you do."

I figured I better give him something, or he'd walk out. "The coin."

"Yeah, yeah. The coin. But what else?"

I pulled a napkin from a dispenser and folded it in the approximate dimension of the *paitza* in Alexander's photographs.

"You mean something like this?"

"Yeah, man. I went to the library and checked them out; then I called some other rare antique guy. He almost went ape when I mentioned those items to him. I figure there's probably a lot of those coins. Who knows what else? A guy I know in MI told me that they're smuggling everything out of Russia except old Lenin's body. My client was paying me to stake out the apartment—around the clock. There's got to be a gold mine somewhere."

"That's where you picked me up? On Cole Street?"

Another flurry of eyelash batting and a chuckle. "Yeah. Like I said, you scared the hell out of me at first. Then I saw you taking pictures of the girl, so I figured maybe we're after the same thing. What do you say?"

I didn't tell him what I felt like saying. Instead, I asked, "How did your client find you?"

Dashuk shrugged his shoulders. "I guess it was my ad in the phone book. And the fact that I can speak Russian."

"You're fluent in Russian?"

He ran a finger across his forehead, pushing away an errant strand of hair. "Yeah, sure. Russian, German, Polish. I was an army brat. I lived in Germany when I was a little kid. Dashuk is Russian. That's why they wanted me in military intelligence." He mopped up the remains of his pancakes, then dug out his wallet and carefully laid four one-dollar bills and two quarters on the table. "I figure if we're going to make this work, we have to move fast."

"How many people do you have working for you?"

"Just me. I'm a one-man shop right now, but I plan on expanding soon as I get some steady clients."

"The apartment on Cole Street—did you search it?"

"Sure. I checked it out good. Nothing in there, just that answering machine."

"How did you know the woman would show up?"

"My client had the phone number." He gave me a patronizing smile, then said, "It was unlisted, but I've got connections. He also gave me a photo of Tanya, though it's not much of a photo. So I just had to sit there and wait for her to show up."

Tanya? I came with in a minisecond of repeating the name. "I'd like to see that picture."

His eyes narrowed. "So far, I'm doing all the giving here, partner. When are you going to start contributing?"

I took a swallow of coffee. I wanted to get into Dashuk's office. To see how he operated, and possibly to get a peek at his file.

"Show me Tanya's picture."

"Why? You already know what she looks like." He pointed his coffee cup to the videotape at my elbow. "I saw you taking pictures of her out at the windmill."

"The man I'm working for said the woman at the windmill looks a little different from the one he's interested in."

He didn't like it. He chewed on the inside of his cheek, then nodded. "Okay. It's in my office."

When Dashuk stood up, his jacket flapped open, revealing a

leather shoulder holster and the butt end of a semiautomatic pistol.

His office was just a square room. Industrial gray carpeting, the walls raw Sheetrock, taped at the seams but not painted. A black steel desk with chrome legs, the top littered with folders, an electric typewriter, notepads, a desk caddy jammed with pens and pencils. A six-foot wooden stepladder leaned against the back wall, along with a three-drawer filing cabinet. The only artwork was a *Sports Illustrated* swimsuit calendar. The calendar was two months behind. Maybe Dashuk just couldn't bear to turn the toothsome blonde riding a bicycle over to next month's beauty.

It wasn't so much what was in the room that gave me a good look into Dashuk's operation; it was what wasn't there. No computer. No fax machine. A private investigator working without a computer was like a carpenter without a hammer. You might get the job done, but it was going to take a long, long time.

"I know it's a mess," Dashuk said apologetically, "but I'm getting ready to move. I need a bigger place. You know how it is."

I didn't know, but I had an idea. My bet was that the filing cabinet was just about empty. Dashuk had to be desperate to have contacted me in the first place. Make that in the second place. He had to be stupid to have contacted me in the first place.

He rummaged around the folders on the desk, extracted one, then turned his back on me as he flipped through the file. When he swiveled around, he batted his eyelashes and said, "Here you go."

Dashuk was right. The photograph wasn't very good. A crowded street scene. A dark-haired woman in a dark coat stood on a sidewalk curb, looking as if she was waiting for a break in traffic before crossing the street. You could make out the back of her head, her right ear, the barest glimpse of her cheek. It appeared to have been taken from a height of twelve to fifteen feet above street level, through a window. The very bottom portion of a string of gold-rimmed black lettering showed in the upper corner of the photo. A dozen or more unsuspecting people, going about their business, had been caught by the camera's lens. They all appeared well dressed. One woman in a sweeping fur coat was carrying a blue Tiffany shopping bag.

"Your client must have gotten this as Tanya was leaving his office," I suggested. "It could be the same girl, I guess."

"Yeah. It's got to be the broad from Cole Street. Now, what do we do about her?"

"Forget about her is my advice, son."

Dashuk placed his hands on his hips, opening his jacket wide in the process, giving me a full view of his shoulder holster. "That don't make much sense to me."

"Send your client a full report. Tell him everything you know; then forget about it. Forget about her."

"Sure," he snorted. "And leave everything to you. You think I'm stupid?"

"Yes."

His right hand started to move toward the gun, then froze in place, as if he was about to recite the Pledge of Allegiance. "You're just screwing me around, ain't you, Polo? Get out of here. I tried being nice to you. Now you just stay out of my way—you hear?"

When a man had a gun within inches of his hand, my hearing was damn near perfect.

CHAPTER 7

Anna. Tanya. What other names was the mysterious beauty using? There were several things I could do, but first on the agenda was following the advice I'd given to young Mr. Dashuk: Consult the client.

I was careful this time, checking my rearview mirror constantly, driving in short speed bursts, then pulling over to the curb. It was downright embarrassing being picked up by someone with the investigative experience and skills of Thomas Dashuk.

When I got to his shop, Alexander Rostov was waiting on a gaunt silver-haired man who wanted desperately to purchase a cookie jar. The ceramic jar was in the shape of a short, fat, dumb-faced dog.

They were haggling over the price. I knew from experience that Alexander enjoyed haggling as much as politicians enjoy taxpayer-financed junkets.

I wandered around the shop, searching through the myriad of merchandise, when I came across something I had always wanted—a Shirley Temple water pitcher. A legend had arisen about the use of this blue glass vessel sporting a picture of the former child movie star—it supposedly harbored the secret of a perfect martini. You used Shirley's smiling face to get the measurements just right: Load it up with ice and pour in gin to her chin and vermouth to her shiny eyes.

Alexander had puffed through two cigarettes and had finally worn his adversary down, the humbled, vanquished customer reaching into his wallet and slapping a total of ten twenty-dollar bills on the counter.

"Two hundred bucks for that goofy cookie jar?" I said in amazement after the gentleman had left the premises with his trophy in hand.

Rostov managed a wintery smile. "I picked it up at a garage sale for much less. People are crazy." He eyed the pitcher in my hand.

"How much?" I queried.

"For you, Nick, fifty dollars."

"Fifty dollars! You probably picked this up for a buck, Alexander."

He went into a long, practiced speech about the value of collectibles, and how he was giving it to me for cost. "You just can't find those anymore, Nick. Think of it as an investment."

I'm a terrible haggler. I ended up paying forty-five dollars for the damn thing.

Rostov took my cash; then his voice turned serious. "Let's go into my office."

He put the CLOSED sign on the front door and I followed him to the back of the store.

"I've got bad some news, Alexander. Someone else is interested in your beautiful Anna. She also uses the name Tanya."

Rostov's face was wreathed in cigarette smoke by the time I'd finished updating him.

"The private investigator made a couple of dumb moves. He bragged to me that his client hadn't told him about the coin or the *paitza* but that he'd found out anyway. My hunch is that he either broke into his client's office or bugged the place. Dashuk is young, dumb, and dangerous. He said he called some other rare antiques dealer and told him about the merchandise, so his client is probably in the rare coin business.

"Dashuk wouldn't tell me his client's name, but he did show me a photograph of the woman the client claimed was Anna. I think it was taken when she left his office. The woman could have been Anna—it really didn't show her face. The area looked like downtown San Francisco to me. One woman was carrying a

Tiffany shopping bag, so it was probably around the Union Square area. The photo was taken from the second floor of a building—no higher than that."

Rostov's face turned a bright red color. "Joseph Vallin, the bastard! Vallin has a shop on the second floor at Two-oh-six Post Street."

"Is Vallin in the rare coin business?"

"Vallin," Rostov said scornfully, then went into one of his coughing spells. I got up to pat him on the back, but he waved me away. "Vallinstowski is his name, but he said it was too long. He sells anything, but he specializes in antique coins and weaponry. He has a big ad in the phone book," Rostov added, as if this was an unworthy thing.

"Well, it looks like your Anna is shopping her wares around. What did you do with the information I gave you? Did you call her at the work number?"

Rostov shifted uneasily in his chair. "No. I didn't want to frighten her. If she thinks I'm spying on her, she may go elsewhere. The other number—the one I had you check—it's been disconnected." He rattled off a string of harsh Russian, then said, "If I get in a bidding war with that prick Vallin, I will lose, Nicky." He got to his feet and plucked the Shirley Temple pitcher from my hand. "You know, this one has a little crack. Did you notice that? And poor Shirley—you can barely see her lips. Did you notice that? I know where I can get one that is in mint condition, Nicky. Mint. Worth several hundred dollars." He waggled his bushy brows at me. "Go see Vallin. Find out if he has the *paitza*. We'll call it a trade. The pitcher for a little of your time. Is it a deal?"

I started haggling. The pitcher and a two-hundred-dollar retainer. I ended up with the promise of the mint Shirley Temple and the forty-five dollars in cash I had paid out for the one with the "little crack."

I made a silent vow to bring Mrs. Damonte along with me the next time I got into a deal with Alexander Rostov.

"Don't let Vallin know about me," Rostov warned as I was leaving. "He mustn't know."

Before confronting the coin dealer, I decided to check out Anna/Tanya. The license plate on her Volvo was listed to WLFR on Van Ness Avenue, which I had to pass on the way to Joseph Vallin's office.

Van Ness Avenue was the widest street in San Francisco. One hundred and twenty-five feet from gutter to gutter, and it made a ruler-straight two-mile line from Market Street to Beach Street. Van Ness had been used as a firebreak during the great earthquake of 1906. Twenty years later, it became an elaborate auto row with huge marble-columned temples put up to show off Dusenbergs, Cadillacs, Packards, and the like.

The highlights along the way were Davies Symphony Hall, city hall, and the opera house. From then on, it was stacked with the usual urban sprawl—a boxlike Holiday Inn, the disastrous Cathedral Hill Hotel, an array of fast-food emporiums and electronic supermarkets, a movie theater that looked like a pile of ice cubes just dumped from a tray. If you were in the mood for a steak dinner, there was Ruth's Chris, or Harris', with the nod definitely going to Harris'. The Hard Rock Cafe always had a line waiting to get in.

The address for WLFR was located at the corner of Van Ness and California, near the turnaround for the California Street Cable Car line. It was a bland four-story brick-veneered building. The lobby was nothing more than a lineoleum floor and two elevators, the doors sheathed in imitation walnut paneling.

A glass-enclosed building register showed that WLFR occupied suite 409.

Although I was the only passenger, the elevator insisted on stopping on every floor, the doors groaning open to an empty hallway.

The wall-to-wall carpeting on the fourth floor was a murky green color, with lumpy bulges everywhere, giving it the look of a lake on a windy day.

The top half of the door to 409 was frosted glass. Neatly stenciled letters spelled out the name: WITH LOVE FROM RUSSIA.

A woman with improbable red hair was sitting behind a kidney-shaped desk. She rose to greet me, offering her hand. She had heavy shoulders and a zaftig figure, encased in a cream-colored dress. The short skirt swished around her thighs as she walked over to me. She had smooth ivory skin. Her eyebrows were a thin line, making me wonder if they were tattoos. Her lashes were as thick and long as Tammy Faye Bakker's. Her eyes were bright green—too bright. Contact lenses?

"Ah, you are the gentleman who called a short time ago?" she asked in a soft, husky voice, one hand going to my elbow.

"Well, no. Actually, I called the other day, but I . . ."

"There is no reason to be embarrassed," she assured me, steering me to a pool table–green leather couch across from her desk. She settled down gracefully and patted the cushion next to her.

"Most of our men are nervous on their first visit, but once you've seen our program, and our videos, I'm sure you will be pleased. Shall we get started?"

"Yes," I said, not knowing just what I was agreeing to.

"Did you want to see our catalogs or the videos?" She asked, shifting her weight and smoothing her skirt.

"What do you suggest?"

Her lips formed a pout for a moment. "The videos. You men always seem to be most interested in the videos." She stirred an index finger under my nose. "We can't fool you that way, right? Come with me."

She picked up a clipboard with a pen attached to it by a metal chain. I followed her through an unmarked door in to a small, bedroom-sized room. There was a couch that was a duplicate of the one we'd just vacated and a big-screen TV set, on top of which was a VCR.

"I didn't catch your name," I said as the redhead slid open the drawers of a smoke-colored acrylic cabinet alongside the TV.

"I am Svetlana Bakarich." She turned and flashed a radiant smile. "And I did not get your name."

I dug out a card with just my name and phone number on it. Since I dealt primarily with attorneys and insurance companies, I had long ago taken my private investigator ad out of the Yellow Pages, so if she tried looking me up in the phone book, all she would find would be my name—no address, no occupation. She pinched the card between long, brightly enameled fingernails. "Polo. That's Italian, isn't it?"

"Yes."

"Ah, such romantic people the Italians. We have found it to be a wonderful combination."

"Combination?"

She slotted a cassette into the VCR. "Yes. Romantic and passionate." She twisted her head and flashed another smile. "We Russian women are passionate. You know that, don't you?"

"Yes. I've heard that. . . ."

"There is no need to be shy, Mr. Polo." Her eyes gave me a quick once-over from scalp to shoe leather. "You are still a young man, so I have selected a tape of young women for you. Sit. Relax. Smoke if you wish. I'll be back in a few minutes." She handed me the clipboard. "Be sure and mark down the ones who interest you."

She punched the TV and video play buttons, gave me yet another enormous smile, and then left the room.

The first part of the video was a soft sales pitch, a beautiful raven-haired woman explaining that With Love from Russia had been in business five years and during that time had united "hundreds of men with beautiful, sympathetic, fun-loving young Russian women.

"The women you are about to see are just a recent sampling of the many who are interested in meeting American men," the face on the screen told me in a voice so soft, I had to lean forward to pick it up. "If you do not find the woman of your dreams on this tape, do not despair. We have many more tapes available. Now, sit back and enjoy."

I sat back. An assortment of women, none looking to be over thirty, paraded across the screen. They wore dresses, T-shirts, formal evening gowns, tennis outfits, and sweaters and jeans.

The two- or three-minute individual videos were taken in parks, around swimming pools, in houses, apartments, and one at a zoo, with an elephant standing in the background.

Each of the ladies gave a short spiel, which included her name, her educational background, her hopes and dreams. The predominate dream was to come to America and meet a man. The most sought-after mates were those who fit into the categories of kind, understanding, loving, value-minded, polite, and intelligent. The women spoke broken English and all of them smiled wistfully at the camera.

Before it was revealed as a terrible male chauvinist attitude, there had been a rating system those terrible male chauvinist animals used in evaluating the opposite sex—a scale from one to ten. Bo Derek had starred in a movie titled *10,* due to her supposedly representing the pinnacle of that particular mathematical scale.

None of the ladies on the video would have dipped below a seven.

Number four on the tape, in order of sequence, and the only one definitely in those Bo Derek double digits, was Alex Rostov's Anna, and Dashuk's Tanya.

Only now she used the name Irina. She was leaning against a stark white adobe wall. She wore a yellow spaghetti-strap dress, scooped low in front, and black leather high-heeled shoes. Her pitch was much like the others, but her eyes focused on the camera lens as if it were her dream lover. She liked dancing, hiking, sports, movies, and "having fun."

Svetlana must have had the video length down to a science. As soon as the last girl had finished with her self-description, the door opened and Svetlana peered in.

"Did you see anyone who interested you?"

I cleared my throat before responding. "Yes. Irina, number four, looked very interesting."

She gave me a knowing smile. "Ah, yes. You have a good eye. She is very beautiful, is she not? Come to the office and we can go into more details."

CHAPTER 8

JOSEPH VALLIN, LTD. The brass lettering was polished so brightly, it shined like gold. The door was lacquered ebony. A miniature TV camera dangled over the door frame. I smiled up at it, then pushed an ivory button. After a few moments, the door was opened by a uniformed rent-a-cop. He was potbellied, with a drinker's badge of a nose, and there were flakes of dandruff on the shoulders of his dark blue jacket. A Sam Browne–style leather holster girdled his waist and confirmed that he wasn't there just for his good looks.

He gave me a forced smile and pulled the door fully open.

The floor was the same lacquered ebony as the door. The walls were sponged to look like parchment. A glass-topped counter stretched the length of the room and displayed gold and silver coins, rings, bracelets, and ancient weapons. The barrel-vaulted ceiling's recessed lighting illuminated a series of four paintings, all featuring the same dark-skinned, dark-bearded man wielding his curved sword at a variety of opponents—men on horseback, in armor, and one with a fire-breathing dragon.

A man with a high, sunburned forehead, a long, narrow nose, and neatly brush-cut brown hair was standing behind the counter. He was wearing a beautifully tailored dark blue suit. His eyes were a slick gray color.

"How do you do, sir?" he asked, as if he was really interested.

The ball was in The Thinner Man's court. If Dashuk had actually told Vallin about me—given him my name—or had shown him the photographs from the garden in Golden Gate Park, then my little act wasn't going to get very far. But I figured I didn't have much to lose.

"Joseph Vallin?" I asked, knowing from Alexander Rostov's description that Vallin had some thirty years on Blue Suit.

"No, sir. My name is Nathan Felder. Is there something I can help you with?"

"I'd like to talk to Joseph."

His smooth forehead creased in consternation. "Mr. Vallin is not available right now. Perhaps if I knew your interest." He spread his hands out like a merchant at a bazaar. "As you can see, we have some beautiful items in stock. Or, if there is something in particular you're after, I'm sure I can assist you."

I glanced along the coins under glass. They were individually boxed, cushioned in burgundy velvet, and all appeared to be in mint condition.

"I have a . . . principal who is interested in a rather unique item. A *paitza*. A gold *paitza*. Do you know what that is?"

Nathan's forehead creased again and his eyes narrowed, making crow's-feet.

"Yes, I do. Perhaps I could make some inquiries. Your name is . . ."

"Polo. Nick Polo."

His eyes flicked over to the uniformed guard, sending a signal of some kind. The guard walked around me, then behind the counter, disappearing through a back door.

"Are you in the trade, Mr. Polo?" Nathan asked, his fingers drumming on the countertop.

"Not directly. I'm sort of a consultant. People hire me to look for certain items."

"Really, that's interesting. You must—"

The back door slapped open and a man with a shaven head and a close-cropped beard came through, followed closely by the rent-a-cop. He was at least six feet tall and walked in a stiff-backed, shoulder-straight manner that made me think of a military man. His caterpillar-thick eyebrows were the same inky black color of his beard. A cream-colored, sapphire-eyed Siamese cat was cradled in his arms.

His chalk-striped charcoal suit had a white carnation in the buttonhole and made Nathan's look as if it had come off the rack at Sears.

"Ah, Nathan. Get us some tea. I'll handle the gentleman." He set the cat on the ground, then extended a well-groomed hand. "Joseph Vallin, sir. What brings you to my humble establishment?"

"He's looking for a gold *paitza,* Mr. Vallin," Nathan informed him.

"Are you now?" Vallin beamed. He turned his attention to Nathan. "Tea."

Nathan did a quick about-face and hurried to the back door.

"A golden *paitza.* Good Lord, what an amazing request."

I dug another one of those cards with my name and telephone number only from my wallet.

Vallin studied it carefully, rubbing it between his fingers as if to see if the ink would rub off.

"Why would you come to me for this item?"

"You have a reputation, Mr. Vallin. If anyone would have such a treasure, I assumed it would be you. Or that you could put me in touch with the right party."

"Right party? Hmmmm. If I were to come across such an item, the expense could be quite formidable."

"My principal realizes that."

Vallin dropped my card in his coat pocket. "Does he? Or she?"

I nodded my head. "Yes."

Apparently, Dashuk had been telling me the truth about holding out on his client. The rent-a-cop moved off to the far end of the room, leaning his bulk against the wall.

Nathan came back, balancing a silver tray crowded with an elaborate porcelain teapot and two dainty-looking cups and saucers embossed with climbing red roses.

Vallin waved me around the counter and into his private office, an ornately furnished room. A collection of paintings and etchings of nudes by various artists covered the walls. We walked past a massive Renaissance desk with a burgundy leather writing surface and moved over toward the window. Two upholstered club chairs bracketed a round oak table with brass claw feet.

"Cream or sugar?" Vallin queried, pointing me to the chairs.

"Just plain, thanks."

The uncurtained window gave a view out to Post Street. The black lettering rimmed with gold stretched across the glass. It read: RARE COINS & ANTIQUITIES.

"Sit, sit, please. Make yourself comfortable, sir," Vallin urged as he sank into one of the chairs. "Your principal wouldn't by chance be interested in something like that, would he, sir?"

I followed his manicured finger over to a wooden and metal contraption that appeared to be some type of a coatrack.

"A medieval washstand," Vallin explained. "It dates back to the Crusades. An iron basin hung from one rung, a soap dish from the other. Muslims used them, of course. The Crusaders weren't much for bathing." He laughed lightly, then said, "I could let your principal have it at a substantial discount."

Nathan gently settled a cup down in front of me as if it contained nitroglycerin. "I'll let my principal know, but our interest is in the *paitza*. Can you help me there?"

The cat rubbed against my leg and began purring softly.

Vallin sampled his tea. "Tiara likes you," he said, nodding at the cat. "She usually doesn't take to strangers. It's odd your coming in here now. Someone was in the other day making inquiries about the same item."

"Is that right? What did you tell him?"

Vallin frowned, causing his caterpillar eyebrows to connect in a straight line. "I didn't say it was a him, Mr. Polo."

"Him, her—I'm sure my principal doesn't care. Was she buying or selling?"

"Fishing, I think." He drained the remains of his tea. "What do you think?"

"If she was fishing, she was doing it in expensive waters."

Vallin leaned over and looked out the window, gazing down

at the pedestrians like a general inspecting his troops. "Look at them. So ordinary-looking, aren't they? Businesspeople, shoppers, deliverymen, insurance salesmen, actors, actresses, perhaps undercover policemen." He turned around and locked his eyes onto mine. "You can't tell what they are from here, can you?"

I got to my feet and walked to the window. "Sometimes you can't tell when you are standing right next to them. I don't want to waste your time. If you don't know where I can find the item I'm looking for, I'll just have to look elsewhere." I studied the people below casually; then the sun came out from behind a cloud and I got a glimpse of something shiny in the center of the Q of ANTIQUITIES.

"Look elsewhere. Just where is that, sir?"

I edged closer to the window to make sure. There it was. A small patch of honeycombed plastic. "I was hoping you could tell me. Of course, my principal would be willing to pay you a handsome commission."

"Would he? Or she?"

"I'll be sure and mention the washstand. You never can tell."

Vallin leaned down and swooped up the cat. "That is the most interesting thing you've said, Mr. Polo. You never can tell."

Take away all the hype, noire-glamour, and celluloid stereotypes, and a private investigator turns out to be nothing more than a businessman—usually, a small businessman.

Like any businessman, the investigator has to keep up on the latest goings-on in the trade. One way of doing this is to attend seminars, trade shows, conferences.

Another reason for attending such activities is that they're usually held at some jazzy resort: Jamaica, Las Vegas, Palm Springs.

Still another reason for attendance is that they are a tax write-off. While you're supposed to be attending those often-boring speeches and equipment displays, you can actually be off at the beach, or around the casino tables.

A year ago, Jane Tobin and I took advantage of a seminar up in Lake Tahoe. We spent most of our time sailing the lake, lying in the sun, and gambling. I did meander around the conference area, looking at all the latest electronic wonders coming on-line.

One of the most exotic was a laser bug, though it isn't a very impressive-looking instrument: a tripod, a small rectangular black box, on top of which sits another black box with a distinctive cone-shaped tip for zeroing in on the target. "Making concealment and transportation a simple operation," the salesman informed me. "You can focus in on your target from up to a half a mile away, though, of course, the closer the better."

The laser shoots a reflecting beam onto the street side area of a window.

Any conversation taking place on the inside area of that window sends minute vibrations off the glass. The laser picks these up and feeds the data into a demodulator, which in turn is fed into a tape recorder. Bingo. You're recording the conversation.

The only hitch is that the beam will leave a visible dot on the target. To negate this dot, the salesman showed me a clear honeycombed patch filter that when placed on the target window soaks up the beam and makes that dot virtually invisible.

The patch also enhances voice transmission. He gave me the last bit of his sales pitch with a straight face. "All that for only thirty-seven thousand dollars." Thirty-seven grand. Not in the price range of most private investigators, including Thomas "The Thinner Man" Dashuk. The salesman admitted that most of their clients belonged to the government—as in military intelligence. Had Dashuk taken a little souvenir with him when he left the army? If so, he could have parked his car across the street from Joseph Vallin's shop and listened away to his heart's content.

For the sum of fifty dollars, Svetlana Bakarich, the redhead at With Love from Russia, had let me take the videotape with Anna/Tanya/Irina the Mysterious and her friends home with me.

I had gone through the procedure of filling out their "Confidential Questionnaire," which asked the usual personal questions about the prospective client: profession, address, telephone number, marital status, children, if any.

I fibbed my way through the questionnaire, including the "profession" box. Take my word for this. If you're ever in a situation where someone questions you about what you do for a living and you don't want the interrogation to go very far, tell them this: "I sell life insurance." End of questioning.

The fun part was the page listing personal traits. There were fifty-six individual boxes to be checked, the choices ranging from "adventurous" to "sensitive."

I filled in the boxes next to "fun-loving," "sensual," and "humble." What the hell, it was only a game.

WLFR had several ways in which I could hook up with the girl of my dreams. For three hundred dollars, they would arrange a correspondence between us. For six hundred, they would film a video of me, "which will show you at your very best," Svetlana assured me, and send it to the lady, who would then send me another video in return.

If things went well, Svetlana was all set to fly back to Russia with me and meet with the lady face-to-face. There was no mention of the final financial figure here. "It depends on the travel costs of course, Mr. Polo, but we have an agency that gives us special discounts."

Finally—again the pricing was vague—they could arrange for the lady to fly here to San Francisco. "We handle all the paperwork. There will be no headaches."

The ballpark figure that was floated around was five thousand dollars. Here, Svetlana went into the hard sell, assuring me that it usually worked out better if the lady flew in from Russia. "You will see her in your own setting. You will have a few days together, to really see if you both want to go further. We have an apartment that we use just for these purposes, though, of course, if you hit it off right away, then perhaps the two of you . . ."

She had let me fill in the perhaps in my own dirty old mind.

"But do not waste too much time," Svetlana had pleaded. "It would be a terrible shame if the lady you picked was spirited away by someone else. Remember, the lost heart stiffens."

The lost heart stiffens. It sounded familiar, either a country-

and-western song or an old poem. I dug out my Bartlett's *Familiar Quotations.* Sure enough, there it was—a line from T. S. Eliot's "Ash Wednesday." "And the lost heart stiffens and rejoices/In the lost lilac and the lost sea voices/And the weak spirit quickens to rebel/For the bent golden-rod and the lost sea smell."

I was willing to bet a lot of money that most of WLFR's customers had more than their "golden-rods" bent by the time Svetlana and her crew were finished with them.

I whisked the video through my VCR, rerunning the sequence on Anna several times. There was no doubt it was the same girl. What about the others? Were they crunching their feet through the frozen streets of Moscow, or were they all here in San Francisco, sharing an apartment with Anna, just waiting for to be sprung on some poor unsuspecting, horny sucker.

Horny had popped in my mind at the same moment the phone rang. I reached for it eagerly, hoping to here Jane Tobin's lovely voice.

Instead, I got Alexander Rostov's nervous rasp.

"Nick, Joseph Vallin called me! He asked about the *paitza.* Did you talk to him? Did you give him my name?"

"Yes and no, Alexander. I did talk to him. I definitely did not give him your name."

"God, I was so nervous, I thought that you—"

"Vallin is probably calling everyone he can think of who may have knowledge of the *paitza,*" I assured Rostov. "How many of you can there be?"

"Well, there are the museums, of course, and the universities, but dealers—maybe a dozen who really know their stuff."

"So Vallin is probably calling all of them."

"Perhaps," Rostov said, unconvinced. "It just is so worrisome, Nick. Maybe it wasn't a good idea for you to confront Vallin."

"It was your idea," I reminded him. "And I didn't confront him. I said I had a buyer, that's all. We've obviously shaken his cage. He did admit that someone had come into his shop asking about the *paitza.*"

"Anna? It was Anna?"

"Vallin wouldn't say. And regarding your Anna, I found out just what WLFR is."

I told Rostov of my visit and the videotape. "I was just watching it now. Anna calls herself Irina. She's supposed to be in Russia, but for the right amount of money, she'll fly over here and meet with a prospective suitor."

I could hear some wheezing and I imagined Rostov sucking deeply on a cigarette. "The young man in the pictures you took. Jonathan. Do you think that's what he was? A prospective suitor?"

"They were going at it pretty hot and heavy in the Volvo before they got into a fight."

"A fight. Perhaps over the coin. And the *paitza*. That's what worries me, Nick. He might be part of it. Maybe he works with Anna. We have to find out."

"So far, I've made two hundred dollars on this case, along with the promise of an old glass pitcher, Alexander. If you want me to dig deeper into this, I'm going to have to be paid—in real money."

"All right, all right. How much?"

"A thousand-dollar retainer, Alexander."

"And the Shirley Temple pitcher?"

"Yep."

There was a loud sigh, a hissing sound. I held the phone away from my ear, expecting to see smoke pouring through the tiny holes in the receiver. "All right, Nick. More sighing and hissing. "What if I was to give you cash? Say five hundred dollars. And Errol Flynn's cigarette case."

CHAPTER 9

Jane Tobin finally called early the next morning. She was in Florida. There was something about the tone of her voice that told me problems were on the horizon.

"I'll be staying a few extra days in Miami, Nick."

No explanation as to why. We had a sort of unwritten agreement that when one of us said he or she wasn't available, the other was to ask no leading questions.

"How's the weather?" I said inanely, groping for something to say.

Her voice cheered up a bit. "Oh, warm and wonderful. I'll be back in a few days. Take care."

Take care. No "I miss you; I love you; I can't live without you."

Jane had had one major concern about the trip.

"I hope you didn't get seasick," I said, my voice cracking.

"No, no. It was . . . very smooth. I'll see you soon."

I had barely hung up when the phone rang again. I jumped for it, thinking it was Jane, ready to apologize for being so abrupt, ready to—

"*Sei pronto?*" demanded Mrs. Damonte. Are you ready?

"*Perchè?*" I roared back. What for?

"Carla!"

Oh God. Her niece was due in at the airport in three hours. Which meant we had to get there two hours early. *Non si sa mai.* Just in case. In case there was an earthquake, in case terrorists dropped an atomic bomb on the city, in case it snowed in San Francisco for the first time ever in May, or—Mrs. D's worst fear— in case I got lost.

Usually, I could easily kill a couple of hours at the airport. It's a great place for people watching, but this was not one of those times. I kept looking at the pay phones, thinking of Jane. The fact that I had no idea where she was—or worse, with whom— didn't stop me from looking at those stupid phones.

Carla's United flight from New York was late of course, so that gave us almost another hour to kill.

Mrs. D sat primly in the airport lounge chair, her eyes straight ahead, fastened on the flight-arrival monitors.

She was great at waiting. No food, no drink, just that long-suffering look on her face, catching the attention of flight attendants, airport security people, and good-hearted tourists who wandered over and asked if there was anything they could do for her. They felt sorry for the little old lady who was continually being abandoned by the nervous-looking man making the rounds of the bar, the coffee shop, and the newsstands.

There had been a time when airport newsstands had a world-weary glamour about them: newspapers and magazines from all over the world and thousands of paperback books. Now there were just a few papers. There were still thousands of books, but now they were divided up into a hundred copies of a few best-sellers. I suppose they had to make room for all those wonderful T-shirts, sweaters, and hats bearing the latest travel slogans.

The nearest bar had one of those mechanical pouring devices that dribbled out small measures of Jack Daniel's at five bucks a pop.

I checked my answering machine every fifteen minutes, hearing nothing but my own dull voice advising me to leave a message.

I settled down next to Mrs. D with my sixth cup of coffee that morning.

Her eyes brightened and she bounced to her feet. *"Che viene."* She's here.

The flight had indeed arrived and now the passengers streamed into the terminal. The first person to come into view was a slender, long-legged woman with stylishly feathered dark brown hair. She was wearing a fawn-colored dress piped in white and was carrying an expensive-looking leather purse. She held out her arms to Mrs. Damonte, clutching her to her chest while she peered over Mrs. D's head at me. She had clear olive skin. Her dark eyes had a slight lavender tint. Her lips were sinfully full, slightly protruding. She was, by any man's, woman's, or child's definition, a knockout.

She smiled at me, those swollen lips parting, to reveal a full range of snowy white teeth. "Hi, you must be Nick. I'm Carla Borelli."

"Yes, I know," I responded, wondering how those Romans ever let her out of Italy.

"How do I know this is Errol Flynn's cigarette case?" I asked Alexander Rostov skeptically.

It was silver, with a striped Art Deco design on the outside case. Inside was an inscription: "To Errol. You were wonderful!!! C.C."

"It came from his estate auction," Rostov assured me, waving his arm in a circle. We were back in his private office. "Somewhere in here I have the Christie's auction certificate."

"Who was C.C.?"

Rostov gave me a wolfish smile. "That, I do not know, Nick. But it is a beautiful case, is it not?"

C.C. Claudette Colbert? Cyd Charisse? I wished that Jane was here. She's a whiz at movie trivia.

He took the case from my hands and polished it with a jeweler's cloth. "An investment, Nick. Collectibles are coming back, believe me. In a few years, you'll be able to sell this for a thousand, fifteen hundred. Who can tell?"

"All right. It's a deal."

Alexander smiled brightly as he loaded the case with some of his cigarettes. He handed me the case, then dug down into his pants pocket, coming out with a wad of money, from which he peeled off five one-hundred dollar bills. He peeled them off so slowly, you'd think they were made of Velcro. I checked the money. The solemn face of Ben Franklin stared back at me.

"Help me, Nick. Help me find my treasures."

CHAPTER 10

I was sitting at the kitchen table, the *World Almanac* in hand, digging through the list of noted entertainers, trying to come up with more names that would fit the C.C. initials on Errol Flynn's cigarette case. I was not having much luck—outside of Coco Chanel. Of course, there was Carol Channing, but somehow I just couldn't imagine Flynn saying "Hello, Dolly" to Carol. A dual gift from Cher and Charo? Cher? Too young. Charo? Ditto. Though age never seemed to be a barrier for Flynn. The ringing of the phone brought me back to the real world.

"Mr. Polo," the low, throaty voice purred. "This is Svetlana at With Love from Russia. How are you?"

"Just fine."

"I have wonderful news. Irina is here. In America!"

"That is wonderful," I agreed.

"Yes. In Seattle. Irina came to meet a man who visited our office there. And"—she paused a long moment—"they were not compatible. Isn't that wonderful?"

"Not for the man in Seattle."

"Ah . . . you have a sense of humor, Nick. May I call you Nick?"

"Certainly. So what are Irina's plans now?"

"That is up to you, Nick. You do want to meet her, don't you?"

"Well, I liked all of the ladies in the video, but she is the one who caught my eye."

"Exactly! I can arrange it so that she comes here, to San Francisco. She could be here by tomorrow."

"Ah . . ."

"And this will save you so much money, Nick. Since Irina is

already in America, all we have to charge you for is the airfare and our introduction fee. A thousand dollars. A thousand dollars and you can meet the girl of your dreams, Nick."

"Well, I don't know. I haven't really had a chance to think everything through, and—"

"I spoke to her about you, Nick. I told her what a handsome man you are. I read your application to her over the telephone. She seemed charmed. I would hate to see her fly back to Russia without seeing you."

"Hmmmm. I would have to get to the bank and move some money around. Would she be in San Francisco by, say, five to-morrow afternoon?"

"That could most definitely be arranged. She is waiting for me to call her at this moment. Shall I tell her to come? Come here? For you?"

"Well, if you think . . ."

"She will be here," Svetlana promised. "I feel it in my heart, Nick. The two of you were meant for each other. Five o'clock. And you will bring a check?"

Anna. Tanya. Irina. How did she keep the names straight? How many more was she using? And how mad would she and Svetlana be when the check bounced?

There were still parts of the North Beach area where you could go and feel as if you were somewhere in Italy—the people, the food, the language, the customs, including a dozen or so places where bocce was treated like a religion. The game I was watching was located in Dino's on Vallejo Street, just a few blocks from my flat.

Bocce supposedly originated in Egypt around 4000 B.C., give or take a century or two. Alexander the Great liked it enough to spread it around his conquered territories. It was so popular in the Roman Empire that Charles II forbid his soldiers to play because it was interfering with all their killing, sacking, and loot-ing.

It's a pretty simple game, really. The clay-floored court is fifteen feet by ninety-one feet. The ball weighs a little over two pounds. You roll the bocce ball at a smaller target ball, called a *pallino,* and the team, usually four members, who gets their ball closest to the *pallino* scores points. The first team with twelve points wins. Of course, there are subtle variations from game to game.

Luckily, it's not too strenuous, because the majority of the players were well into their seventies, all crusty male *paesanos,* most with gnarled Toscano cigars clenched between their teeth.

It is very rare that a woman is invited into the game. Mrs. Damonte was an exception, of course. Tonight, there was another exception: Mrs. D's niece, Carla Borelli.

Mrs. D had arranged a dinner in Dino's private dining room, and troops of younger men came streaming in to meet Carla.

Mrs. D had picked the menu, and she spent some time in the restaurant's kitchen making sure everything was done to her satisfaction: *minestrone verde,* an all-green soup loaded with vegetables and a pesto sauce; *pasta con le sarde,* spaghetti with fresh sardines, olives, anchovies, and saffron; and *animelle al prosciutto,* sweetbreads with ham.

Carla seemed amused by the whole procession. I was having a tough time figuring her out. She seemed too sharp to get caught up in one of Mrs. D's matchmaking efforts.

She smiled graciously at all the would-be suitors, and she winked her eye at me often enough to let me know that I was not forgotten.

After dessert, *torta di riso,* a chocolate rice cake from the nearby Danilo bakery, we moved to the bocce courts.

Carla was wearing a pair of second-skin jeans and a cranberry-colored T-backed knit top that had the old-timers dribbling cigar ashes down their flannel shirts every time she leaned over to toss out the *pallino.*

I sat at the bar, nursing an Amaretto and enjoying the spectacle.

A heavy hand patted my shoulder. I turned, to see my uncle Dominic.

He placed his fingers to his lips and blew a kiss toward the bocce court. "That is one very beautiful woman."

"Yes. Mrs. Damonte's niece, Carla."

Uncle's eyebrows raised up toward his hairline. *"Lei? Ma non mi far ridere."*

A loose translation would be: "Are you kidding me?"

"No, Uncle. Carla Borelli. I'm sure Mrs. D will introduce you sooner or later."

"Sooner would be much better," Uncle said with a grin. For a man in his profession—Uncle Dominic was a bookie—he grinned quite a bit. His closest friends were allowed to call him "Pee Wee." He hadn't gotten the nickname because of his size— he was broad-shouldered and six feet tall—but because his brother, my father, had been six foot three.

He nodded to the bartender, then circled a finger over his head, indicating that he was buying a round for the entire house.

This brought a loud cheer, almost drowning out the Pavarotti aria on the jukebox, and the bartender hurried about his duties as Uncle strolled over to pay his respects to Mrs. D.

Carla wormed her way through the crowd and slid onto the empty stool next to mine.

"Are you having a good time?" she asked, smoothing a wisp of hair from her damp forehead.

"Yes. How about you? Made a selection yet?"

She smiled, showing off her dazzling set of teeth.

"Angelica is so sweet, isn't she?"

"Angelica?"

The teeth flashed again and she raked her fingers across the back of my hand. "Mrs. Damonte. She means well." Her fingers stopped and her nails did a little flamenco on my wrist. "I do want to talk to you. Alone. Later, all right?"

Carla was confident enough not to wait for an answer. She bounced to her feet and hurried back to the bocce court. I sat stunned while Mrs. D took Uncle Dominic by the hand and for-merly introduced him to Carla.

Angelica. Little Angel. I'd never known Mrs. Damonte's first name. Never thought about it. Since I could crawl and gurgle, she'd been Mrs. Damonte. Mrs. D for short. But never to her face. Angelica? Biblical creatures came to mind when I thought of Mrs. D, but they certainly weren't angels.

The sudden pressure of something jabbing my kidneys brought me out of my musings.

"You're a real son of a bitch, Polo."

I craned my neck around far enough to see the scowling face of Thomas Dashuk.

"Let's go," he said between clenched teeth, then added, "I don't want to embarrass you in front of all your friends."

"What are friends for, Tommy?" I patted the warm stool that Carla had just abandoned. "How the hell did you find me here?"

The pressure on my kidneys increased. Something hard was being pressed into my camel hair sport coat.

"I just started checking out the local dago joints. Outside. Now!"

The bartender slammed down the drink Uncle Dominic had ordered, spilling Amaretto onto the already-damp mahogany.

"*Fucile,* Dino," I said in the manner of a toast, then smiled at Dashuk. "I can't leave now. I just got a fresh drink. Stop acting like an idiot and sit down."

The pressure eased off, but Dashuk stood his ground. "You went to see my client, Polo. He didn't like that. He thinks that maybe I told you about him."

"You did."

I arched my back when whatever it was Dashuk had in his jacket pocket jabbed into my kidney. "Bullshit."

"The photograph of the girl. It gave me the location. Post and Grant streets. Joseph Vallin was the only person in the area who would be interested in what the girl was selling. I spotted your laser patch on the window. Very clever."

Dashuk's eyes were bouncing around the room. There was a sudden roar from the bocce court. Carla was jumping up and down, her arms raised over her head. She had scored some points—both in the game and in the eyes of the men riveted on her writhing figure. She walked over to Uncle Dominic and gave him a big toothpasty kiss on the lips.

Another jab in the back, harder this time. "Let's go, Polo. Outside."

I shook my head and slowly stood up. "I thought you were a linguist, Tommy."

"Yeah, you thought—"

"That thing that you're feeling in your back now is a *fucile*— a sawed-off shotgun. It makes a hell of a mess, believe me."

Dashuk feigned a smile. "I picked up a little Italian, but not enough, I guess."

"It's strictly a Sicilian word," I said to console him. I peeled the gun from his right hand.

Dashuk stared at me icily during the disarmament.

"You're making a real mistake, Polo."

"*Grazie,* Dino. I think he'll be a good boy now."

The bartender gave me a curt nod, then scuttled back behind the bar, the shotgun hanging down alongside his leg.

Dashuk was rocking back and forth on his heels, like a fighter waiting for the bell for round one to ring.

Uncle Dominic sidled up toward him. "Trouble, Nick?"

"No. Not anymore, Uncle."

Dashuk gave him a hard look. "Get out of here, old man." His head snaked back at me. "And I want my gun."

Uncle gave a short, curt whistle. Suddenly, two tall men in dark suits had Dashuk bracketed. They each grabbed one of his arms.

"*Disfarsi di lui,*" Uncle said sharply.

Dashuk started to protest, then found his feet were being lifted off the ground.

Uncle Dominic waited until Dashuk was deposited outside, then signaled for another round of drinks. He pointed to Dashuk's pistol, asking me seriously, "Why do you stay in this crazy profession of yours, Nicky?"

Didn't I tell you North Beach was like Italy?

CHAPTER 11

When I got back to my flat, I found that there had been no calls, from anyone—especially Jane Tobin.

I removed the clip and set Thomas Dashuk's gun down on the kitchen table. It was a compact, wicked-looking blue metal semi-automatic, some eight or ten inches in length. The troubling aspects were the fact that there was no manufacturer's name on it and the throated barrel tip was threaded. The only logical reason I could come up with for that little added feature was for screwing on a silencer. What the hell was I going to do with the damn thing? Give it back to Dashuk and wait for him to shove it in my ribs? Or somewhere more delicate?

Dump it in the bay? Turn it over to the cops? For all I knew, Dashuk was at a police station making out a report, swearing that I'd stolen the gun from him.

Dashuk. He seemed crazy enough to come storming back with a bigger weapon in his nervous little hands.

The doorbell chimed. Dashuk, already?

Carla Borelli's almond-shaped eyes stared back at me through the peephole in the door.

"Hi," I said once the door was open.

Her goose-pimpled arms were folded across her chest. "You left too early. We didnt' have time for a dance."

"Something came up. Come on in. You look like you're freezing."

She nodded and shivered at the same time. "It is cold here. Not like at home." Her eyes roamed the room. "You have music? A cigarette?"

"Sure." I waved her into the front room and pointed at the shelves groaning under the weight of the records and CDs. "Find something you like. I'll get you a glass of red wine and a smoke."

When I came back with the drink, she had dozens of the CDs spread across the couch. "No Pearl Jam? Bon Jovi? Michael? The Smoking Popes?"

Her radiant smile dimmed with each negative nod of my head. "Sorry. How about some jazz?"

I rummaged around for an early André Previn album, all the time wondering if there really was a group called The Smoking Popes.

Carla was still in her second-skin jeans and thin T-shirt outfit. Her slim, elegant feet were encased in leather sandals. She placed the wine on the coffee table and held out her arms for a dance.

I managed not to step on her toes during Previn's rendition of "I Remember You." She dragged me to the couch when the song ended, her lips nuzzling my ear.

I pulled back and Carla rolled her eyes at me questioningly. "Nick, you are not . . ." She paused, her arm making a rocking motion. "Ah, *frocio,* are you?"

Frocio gay, homosexual. "No, Carla, but there is someone. A woman that I—"

She put a finger to her lips and made a shushing sound. "No, that I can respect. She is a lucky lady." She sipped the wine, then asked about her smoke.

I proffered the case Rostov had given me and a book of matches. She extracted one of the cigarettes and lit up, snapping the case open and closed.

"This is beautiful."

"It belonged to Errol Flynn."

Her face remained blank.

"Errol Flynn. The old swashbuckling movie star."

Her face beamed. "Movies. You know movie people? You know this Mr. Flynn?"

"Ah, he died a long time ago, Carla."

She frowned, then licked her lips. "Do you know any of his friends?"

"No, 'fraid not."

"Your uncle. He is a *giocatore,* no?"

"A gambler. Yes, you could say that." I searched my mind for the right word for bookie. *"Allibratore."*

That information seemed to please her. "Ah, a bookie. He is successful?"

"Very."

She began to ask questions about Uncle Dominic, which I parried as best as I could. The phone rang, causing Carla to bounce to her feet and head for the door. "Your woman, I hope," she said, winking and flashing a smile.

I hoped, too. But it wasn't Jane Tobin. A male voice—a dry, nervous voice.

"Nick Polo?"

"Speaking."

"This is Detective Rickard, CID, United States Park Police. I wonder if you would mind coming down to Fort Mason. We have a problem you might be able to help us with."

"What kind of problem?"

"I'd rather not mention it on the phone, sir. I could send a car for you."

Carla was leaning against the doorjam. She blew me a kiss, then exited.

"Listen, Detective, I don't know who you are or what your problem is, but if you don't give me some specifics, I'm going to bed."

"We have the body of a man we believe is Thomas C. Dashuk. He was murdered in his van, here on Fort Mason property. He had one of your business cards in his wallet. I was hoping you could make a positive ID, sir."

Fort Mason had started out as Punta Medanos, or Black Point, an army battery in 1797, to defend the Bay in case the invaders got past the long guns at the Presidio, which guarded the entrance to San Francisco Bay.

The army built some homes on the land in the mid-1800s, and they built them right, for a few were still standing, including the Officers' Club, which was open to the public and had a bar and restaurant with one of the better views of the Bay from its wrap-around windows.

The waterfront piers, numbered 1, 2, and 3, saw a lot of action during World War II, shipping our boys off to the Pacific.

Now most of the area had been turned over to the Golden Gate National Recreation Area, part of the National Park System, and the piers and warehouses featured numerous crafts shops and the Zen Center's famous vegetarian restaurant, Green's.

I pulled into Fort Mason's Bay Street entrance. Detective Rickard hadn't given me any specific instructions, and they weren't needed. A cluster of twirling red lights blinked steadily through the low-lying fog.

I parked down the street and made my way toward the police vehicles.

Two young men in full army gear, including rifles across their chests, stood guard near the vehicles.

"I'm looking for a Detective Rickard," I told one of the soldiers. "My name's Nick Polo."

He snapped to attention, shouted out, "Moment, sir," did an abrupt about-face, and marched off in the direction of a group of ten or twelve men huddled around a primer-spotted white van.

A large floodlight, powered by a gas engine that made a loud humming noise, bathed the area in glaring white light. The doors to the van were open. Every once in awhile, the popping of a camera's flash unit threw even more light onto the van.

The soldier tapped the shoulder of a man in a black raincoat. He twisted around to look in my direction, a hand going to his forehead to reduce the glare from the floodlight.

The soldier came back moments later and informed me that Detective Rickard would be with me shortly.

Shortly turned out to be fifteen minutes. That much about the army hadn't changed. Hurry over and then wait.

The man in the black raincoat signaled to me by waving his flashlight in my direction. I weaved my way through a tangle of electrical cords.

"Sorry to keep you waiting, Mr. Polo. I'm Detective Rickard, CID."

CID. It sounded so impressive. Criminal Investigation Department. He was of stocky build, with linebacker shoulders and an oval face. His eyes were pale blue, gabled by shaggy brows. A weedy mustache sat under a pug nose. He looked to be about Tom Dashuk's age. Maybe the mustache was supposed to make him look older. If so, it wasn't working.

"I called the San Francisco Homicide detail and spoke to an Inspector Robert Tehaney."

Tehaney was a good man. I told Rickard so.

"Yes. He says he knows you, that you were once a policeman," Rickard said, looking somewhat uncomfortable. He coughed into his hand. "He said you've been working as a private investigator for some time now. Would you mind telling me how you came into contact with Dashuk?"

I silently thanked Tehaney for not telling Rickard about my jail time. An ambulance sirened its way into the area. Rickard went over to direct traffic. While he was talking to the stewards, I sidestepped over to the Dodge van. A soldier with sergeant's stripes was taking photographs.

He saw me peering over his shoulder, looked up, and asked, "You CID?"

"Just a visiting cop," I said.

The answer seemed to satisfy him and he went back to taking pictures.

"Move please," a voice said, and I turned, to see the ambulance crew coming by with a carryall gurney.

Rickard's face showed his displeasure when he saw me peering into the van.

"You through, Sergeant?" he asked the photographer.

"Yes, sir. Here and with the body."

Rickard gave me a worried look, then asked, "When you were in the police department, did you work Homicide?"

"For a while."

He tapped his foot on the wet pavement, then made his decision. "Come with me, please."

It was a short trip—a few feet to the Dodge's front door. Fragmented pieces of glass glittered like diamonds on the damp asphalt. The door was wide-open. Slumped on the driver's seat was the remains of The Thinner Man, Thomas Dashuk. His head was tilted back and there was a gaping gash running across his neck, starting below his left ear, moving downward across the midline, then upward again, ending under his right ear.

Rickard turned on his flashlight and gave me an unrestricted view. *Gaping* was the right word. No matter how sharp, or thin, the weapon's blade, the wound itself started out very narrow, then widened as the pattern progressed, then narrowed again. The depth sequence was much the same—first shallow, then deep, then shallow.

The front of Dashuk's shirt and suit coat were saturated with blood. You forget just how much blood the human body holds, until you see it spilled like this.

"Do you recognize the body?" Rickard asked formally.

"That's Tom Dashuk," I confirmed.

"We believe he was killed right here. We had to break into the vehicle," Rickard said, trailing the flashlight beam around the Dodge's interior. "Apparently, someone sitting behind him grabbed him by the hair and slit his throat."

"Yeah, that's how it looks," I said, noticing that the keys weren't in the ignition, then turning my head away. I'd seen more than enough. "I still don't know why you bothered calling me."

"I ran the van's license plate. It's registered to Dashuk. He had business cards in his wallet showing he's a private investigator, Mr. Polo. You're a private investigator. He had your card. So calling you made a great deal of sense to me."

One of the ambulance stewards bumped me with the gurney. They were getting ready to lift Dashuk from the van. I backed away. Rickard came right after me.

The backlight from the beams of the floodlight dissipated the fog and gave him an eerie, ghostlike image.

"Did you notice Dashuk's shoulder holster, Mr. Polo? It was empty. His gun was apparently taken away from him before he was killed."

"Apparently," I agreed.

"Exactly what was your connection with Mr. Dashuk?" Rickard asked impatiently.

"Exactly why should I answer your questions? Am I a suspect? If so, let me know and I'll contact my attorney. If not, be polite, or I'm going back home to a warm bed."

Rickard inhaled and straightened his shoulders as if he was about to issue an order; then he exhaled sharply. "It's cold. Can I buy you a drink?"

We hiked less than a block to the Officers' Club. It had a warm, homey atmosphere: beautiful hardwood floors, a cloakroom, a fireplace, antique furniture. The bar and restaurant were in the rear. The dining room was closed. The bartender was busy going about his business, putting away glasses, swabbing down the bar.

"Brandy all right?" Rickard asked, and when I nodded in agreement, he pointed to a table by the window. "I'll bring it over."

The fog had thinned a bit and I could make out the murky lights of the hook-shaped Aquatic Park pier and the outline of the Maritime Museum, which was worth seeing on nights like this. The three-story structure had been designed to look like the upper decking of a luxury liner, with tapered ends and porthole windows. It was built back in the thirties. One of the original propositions was to use it as a gambling casino, but the city hall movers and shakers couldn't push that through the governor's office, so it became a bathouse. The idea had been for the populace to take a swim in the Bay, then come inside for a hot bath.

Whoever had thought that one up had never taken a dip in those icy waters. Now it was a museum, but it didn't require much of an imagination to see it as an ocean liner, stranded in the fog, searching for safe waters.

Rickard handed me a balloon snifter, then settled down in the chair across from me.

"Cheers," he said, sipping from a bottle of Evian water.

Detective Rickard, CID, United States Park Police, looked like a man watching his boat sink under him—a man who couldn't swim.

The United States Park Police had taken a lot of heat over the discovery of Vincent Foster's body in Fort Marcy Park, Washington, D.C., including being blamed for a lot of the FBI's screwups. They were convenient scapegoats. Their main function was patrolling government parks, rousting overnight campers and the like.

A homicide investigation was not an everyday occurrence. I wondered if Rickard had ever handled one before.

"Detective, I met Mr. Dashuk at his office yesterday morning. He wanted me to help him out in an investigation he was working on. I declined. He did tell me he had been in the army—military intelligence."

Rickard started to say something, then hesitated. He seemed to hesitate a lot. That was either the gesture of a cautious man or one who was confused and didn't know what to do next.

"Yes. There were some items in his van, cameras, recorders, and a notebook. The book had his old military ID cards and some phone numbers. One of the numbers belongs to a Colonel Colby of army intelligence, in Oakland. The colonel's card was in Dashuk's wallet also. I spoke with him. Colonel Colby seemed quite . . . concerned. He indicated that he wanted to be involved in the investigation."

"And you didn't object?"

Rickard inhaled sharply. "No, sir. I . . . I'm not exactly an expert in homicide investigations."

I didn't doubt that. Rickard probably had done a tour of duty in the army, navy, or marines, taken a civil service exam when he was still in uniform, then gone right to work for the Park Police when he was discharged. I remembered from my time in the department that the San Francisco Homicide inspectors used to "cooperate" with the Park boys—in fact, take charge of the investigation. But they had to be invited in first.

I mentioned that to Rickard. "What about Inspector Tehaney? He's good. I'm sure he'd lend a hand if you asked him."

"I had intended to do just that, sir. But Colonel Colby strongly suggested that I hold off."

"Where's this Colby now?"

Rickard pushed back his raincoat sleeve and looked at his watch. "En route. From Oakland. In fact, I expected him half an hour ago."

"Do you have any idea what brought Dashuk here? To Fort Mason?"

Another hesitation. "No. I spoke to the bartender. He saw Dashuk earlier. Dashuk came in and had a drink at the bar." Rickard took a small notepad from his raincoat pocket and flicked the pages. "That was at approximately twenty-two-thirty. He had two drinks. Bourbon and water."

I tried to figure out the military time without counting on my fingers. Twenty-two-thirty would be 10:30 p.m. I glanced at my faux Rolex. It was pushing two in the morning. Uncle Dominic's friends had kicked Dashuk out of Dino's around eight o'clock.

Rickard drew in a patient breath. "The bartender said that Dashuk appeared to be waiting for someone. Someone who apparently never showed up. A couple from Sausalito who had dinner here at the club discovered the body when they returned to their car, which was parked next to Dashuk's. The woman became quite sick, I'm afraid."

The bartender was clinking glasses, slamming drawers closed. He wanted to go home. So did I.

"What kind of case was it that Dashuk wanted you to help him with?" Rickard asked.

"Sub rosa. A surveillance case. It's not my specialty. He didn't give me a lot of details."

Rickard sipped at his Evian and stared at me. "Did you notice anything unusual at his office?"

"Unusual? No. I was there only a short time. I told him I wasn't interested in doing business with him and left."

Rickard took a ballpoint from his shirt pocket and snapped it a few times. "Where were you this evening, Mr. Polo. From—"

"You must be Detective Rickard," a loud voice boomed out.

Rickard almost jumped out of his chair.

A man in a putty-colored trench coat introduced himself. "Col. Jack Colby."

Colby wasn't very big—five seven or five eight. He wore his brown hair in a fringe-cropped crew cut. His eyes were close-set, and his elongated face tapered down to a square, dimpled chin. His eyes were gray, a gray so light, they looked almost without pupils. It was the face of a man you wouldn't want for a boss. Wouldn't want to be even one grade or rank higher than you in the service.

Rickard, I guess out of habit, gave Colby a salute.

"Who's he?" Colby asked, jutting his chin in my direction.

"This is Nick Polo. I mentioned him to you on the phone."

"Ah, the snooper." He held out his hand. "Nice of you to drop by."

His gloved handshake was rock-hard. He looked me straight in the eye as he squeezed, his mouth bending into a smile.

"You worked with Tommy, eh, Polo?"

"No. I just met the man. Barely knew him."

"He was good, Tommy was. Damn good."

"At what?" I asked, drawing an icy stare from Colby.

"Black-bag stuff. Electronic surveillance. I trained that boy my-self. Damn shame, him getting it like this." He reached for my brandy snifter. "You through with this, Polo?"

"Haven't even touched it yet."

Colby sampled the brandy. Apparently, it met his qualifications, because he took a long sip.

"The body's been taken to the morgue," Rickard informed the colonel.

"Yes. I know. What about Tommy's office? Have you been there yet?"

"No, sir."

Colby finished off the brandy. "Well, let's take a look. You ever been there, Polo? To Tommy's office."

"Just once."

"Well, come along, maybe you—"

Rickard broke in. "Dashuk's keys were missing from the van, sir." He held up a jangling key ring. "We found these in a toolbox in the back of the van."

Colby smiled and slipped his hand into the slash pockets of his trench coat and came out with an identical-looking key ring. "Not many locks I can't get by with these, gentlemen. Let's go."

CHAPTER 12

There were a couple of things that were bothering me about Thomas Dashuk, besides, of course, the fact that the poor devil had been brutally murdered.

First, he had snookered me. The laser patch on Joseph Vallin's shop window should have been proof enough. But now Col. Jack Colby was bragging about Dashuk's military service, and his "black bag" electronic expertise, which meant that Dashuk had called me from his office on purpose, waiting to see if I was smart enough to trace the call back to him. He had gone into that "Aw shucks" routine of his at the coffee shop, and all the time he was ahead of me, playing me for the big sucker that I thought he was.

Dashuk had told me that he was a one-man outfit, but he'd also said that he had staked out the Cole Street address around the clock. That was not easy to do. Either he'd had help or he'd had the place wired, an alarm of some type that alerted him when anyone entered the premises. I tried picturing Anna's apartment. There must have been a trip wire somewhere.

I checked the rearview mirror. The lights of Rickard's white sedan were right behind me. Colby was riding shotgun with Rickard. Obviously, neither of them knew much about the city, since they asked me to lead them to Dashuk's office.

I cut across Van Ness, took a right on Polk Street, and drove straight to Dashuk's place.

There were only a few stragglers left on the streets. I parked in a bus zone while Rickard turned the corner.

A chalk-faced, cadaver-thin man wrapped in an overcoat, his old-fashioned felt hat pulled down over his forehead, exited

Lickie's Tanning Salon, bumping into me in his haste to get to his car. His eyes met mine. There was a brief flash of fear, then a shudder of relief.

A few years ago, Lickie's would have been called a massage parlor, but the city passed an ordinance that masseuses had to be registered and licensed by the city. Of course, 99 percent of the customers who frequented these establishments weren't really looking for a legitimate massage. And an equally high percentage of the masseuses had rap sheets that would disqualify them from becoming licensed. So someone came up with the tanning salon idea. Entrepreneurs, free enterprise—you've got to love this country.

The door to Lickie's opened a couple of inches. A hand appeared; then the door widened and an attractive Asian girl slid a long leg out. She was wearing a white nurse-style uniform, cut short enough to show the top of her white stockings and the black tips of a garter belt. Her hair was done up in twin ponytails, each dangling over one of her ears. Her lipstick was a brilliant red.

"Hey, handsome. Don't be shy. Come on in. You'll have a good time."

"Sorry, I'm working. Do you know Tom Dashuk? The private eye next door?"

She shook her head sadly. "No. But I want to know you. Come on. It's late. I'm all alone. I'll give you the closing time special price." Those bright red lips made kissy sounds. "Please."

The cracking of Rickard's and Colby's heels on the sidewalk drew her attention. She gave me a "You don't know what you missed" look and eased the door shut.

Colonel Colby pulled out his ring of break-in keys and began fiddling with the door to The Thinner Man's office.

It didn't take long. The third key turned the lock.

Rickard waved a flashlight beam around and found the light switch. The overhead fluorescents blinked on.

Rickard slipped on a pair of white funeral-type cotton gloves and closed the door behind him, shaking it to make sure that the lock had caught.

Dashuk's office was pretty much the same as when I'd last seen it, except that the drawers of the desk and file cabinet were all gaping open.

The lid on the typewriter was in an upright position. The ribbon had been removed. Whoever had been there before us was a very thorough individual.

Colby drop-kicked a metal wastebasket across the room.

"Shit. We've been had," he swore angrily. "You should have come over here right away," he said to Rickard accusingly.

Rickard didn't back off. "I was tied up with the body, Colonel. I didn't have anyone to send."

"Maybe it's time to call in the San Francisco PD," I suggested.

Colby walked over to me and stuck his finger in my chest. "We'll make the decisions, Polo. Were you ever in the service?"

"Just long enough to regret it, Colonel."

"Polo was a San Francisco cop," Rickard advised. "He says he worked homicide cases."

The recommendation didn't seem to impress Colby.

"Did you now? Why'd you leave the job, Polo?"

"I couldn't stomach it anymore. Doughnut poisoning."

Colby stared at me for a full minute before the light went on. "Very funny. Very funny."

Apparently, the indoor lighting wasn't bright enough for Rickard. He was shining his flashlight beam into each desk drawer.

Colby stretched his arms over his head and yawned. "This looks like a waste of time now, Rickard. The killer obviously came over here and got what he wanted."

"What do you think he was after?" I said, moving toward the wall where the *Sports Illustrated* calendar hung.

"When we know that, we'll know who killed him," Colby responded dryly.

I said, "Did Dashuk have any family? A wife?"

"No. His parents are dead. Tommy never married."

Rickard joined the conversation. "Is there anything missing, Mr. Polo? Anything different? Outside of all this mess."

I glanced around the room, trying to remember it as it had been the day before. "No. He didn't have much. That typewriter. The file cabinet. I don't even remember a Rolodex. There were some manila files on the desk."

"This is waste of time now," Colby muttered, peering at the typewriter, noticing the missing ribbon. "The killer took what he wanted."

Something else *was* missing. "A ladder. A wooden stepladder. About six feet high. It was leaning against that wall."

"A ladder," Rickard said in a puzzled voice. "Why would the killer bother taking a ladder?"

Colby marched over to the door and yanked it open. "You can go now, Polo. We'll be in touch."

I edged over to the wall with the *Sports Illustrated* calendar. There was something wrong about the calendar. It certainly wasn't the gorgeous long-legged blonde straddling the bicycle seat.

It was too high. Dashuk would have needed that ladder to hang it on the wall. Why place it so high? I took a handkerchief from my pants and tugged on the edge of the calendar. It was taped to the wall. I tugged harder and it came away with a soft, sticky sound.

Rickard swiveled around at the noise, his flashlight pointed at the blonde's fanny.

"What the hell . . ."

I kept pulling and the calendar fell away, revealing a cavity in the wall—a rectangular shaped cutout, slightly smaller than the calendar. There was nothing but the two-by-four wall studs and the back of the Sheetrock, which I figured must lead to Lickie's Tanning Salon.

Colby wheeled Dashuk's chair over and almost fell while climbing up on it. I steadied the chair as he made a second attempt.

"Umm-hmmm, Ummm-hmmm," he mumbled before jumping back to the floor.

"Ummm-hmmm what?" Rickard asked.

"A hole. A small pinhole." He wiggled his thumb and forefinger. "It was covered with this piece of tape."

Rickard climbed up on the chair to take a look.

Whoever had raked Dashuk's office over had yanked his file cabinet away from the wall. There was an outline in the carpet where the cabinet had originally stood. Directly behind the cabinet was a patch of Sheetrock, some four feet high by three feet wide. All the other slabs of Sheetrock were the standard four-by-eight-feet sheets. Maybe the contractor had pieced this portion in to save some money. Maybe, but this section wasn't taped. And there were smudge marks around the edges.

Colonel Colby glared over my shoulder as I wormed a pocketknife along the seams, then began pounding along the edges. The Sheetrock popped free. Colby pushed me out of the way, then dropped to his knees, a small flashlight in hand, and crawled into the hole.

I dropped down behind him. He worked his way inside, struggled to his feet, and announced, "There's a light switch."

He snapped it on, and I had a good view of his shoes and the raw cement floor. I scuddled through the opening; Rickard followed behind me. Not exactly the Temple of Doom that Indiana Jones worked so hard to find. Just a narrow room, stretching out some ten feet in length.

The case of the missing ladder was solved. It was leaning up against one wall. Like the area behind the calendar, the wall was nothing but studs and the back sides of Sheetrock panels. On the opposite wall were rows of pine shelving that held boxes of videotapes and camera equipment.

Colby climbed up the first few steps of the ladder, his head bumping on the raftered ceiling. There was a metal bracket screwed into the studs. Attached to the bracket was a tapering finger-sized black plastic gizmo. Attached to the gizmo was a thin black electrical cord.

"You know what this is?" Colby asked, his voice a whisper now.

"A spike microphone and pinhole video lens, I presume."

Colby didn't seem to like my presumption, but I knew I was

right. What the hell else could it be? Dashuk was using all that expensive military training to spy on a whorehouse.

Colby hopped down from the ladder and began rumbling through the video equipment, shaking his head from side to side as he did so.

"God, this is awful," Rickard moaned while examining an expensive-looking black box coupled to a palm-sized camcorder.

I said, "Colonel, it looks like your boy Tommy took away a few souvenirs from the army."

He gave me a noncommittal grunt, then ran his palm across a neatly stacked row of videotapes.

I was dusting off my knees and wondering what Colby's next move would be. I didn't have to wait long.

"I suggest you leave now, Polo. We will be contacting you shortly."

"Doesn't this change the lineup now, Colonel? If Dashuk was filming the fun and games next door, he wasn't just doing it for his personal amusement. He was probably following the customers to their cars, then to their homes. Blackmailing them. Are you going to notify the San Francisco Police Department?"

"We'll make that decision, Polo." His hand grazed over my shoulder. "I know we can trust you to keep quiet about this. Dashuk was one of my men. I'd like to handle it in-house. I'm sure Detective Rickard feels the same way. You can go now. I'll be in touch."

"Maybe I should—"

The veins on Colby's forehead were sending out a Morse code. "You can go, Polo," he said in that crisp military manner I remembered so well. "Now!"

CHAPTER 13

◄►

I arrived at the Hall of Justice bright and early the next morning. The receptionist at the Homicide detail was new, at least to me. She was a frizzy-haired blonde who had a phone cradled between her neck and shoulder, while her hands clicked away at a desktop computer.

I said, "Bob Tehaney." She jerked a thumb over her shoulder and continued to concentrate on the computer screen.

There were a few familiar faces among the fifteen or so desks in the next room. It seemed that every time I journeyed down to the Hall of Justice, I encountered more and more new ones.

Morale was about as bad as I had ever seen. It had started plummeting years ago; no one knew exactly why, or how. Worse, no one seemed to know how to stop it. When I first joined the department, there had been a camaraderie, a "good guy versus bad guy" attitude. There were rules, and everyone knew them, including the bad guys. When the handcuffs finally got snapped on their wrists, they realized that was the way it was. A shrug of the shoulders, a shake of the head, a silent look that said, You got me.

If the bad guy wasn't a jerk, or a drug-saturated sadomasochist, as all too many of the current crop were, the cuffs weren't ground tightly into his flesh. If he had a wife or girlfriend he wanted to give one last kiss, or perhaps a little bit more, the cuffs might be removed and the cop might wait in the next room for a few minutes.

Or, if there was no lady in waiting, the gentleman on his way to the local crossbar hotel might be given the opportunity to take a final nip or two from the nearest bottle of booze.

My old partner, Paul Paulsen, and I once cornered a con man, Dale Frazier, who specialized in defrauding commercial real estate financiers. He had an amazing line of phony ID, and we chased him up and down California, finally finding him holed up in a plush suite at the Mark Hopkins Hotel.

I had my hand raised, ready to knock on his room door, when it swung opened. Frazier, a dapper, pint-sized, dark-haired guy in his fifties, was standing there, his arm around the waist of a statuesque blonde who towered over him. He took one look at Paul and me and knew exactly who we were.

"Gentlemen, I've been expecting you," he had said, as if we were business associates. He rose up on his toes, gave the blonde a farewell kiss, and cordially invited us into the suite.

"Listen," he said as Paul was digging the arrest warrant from his coat pocket, "I don't know how you guys found me, but you did, and that's that." He reached out for the phone. "Would you care to join me for lunch before we leave? Room service is great here. It may be the last good meal I get for a long time."

He was right. Room service was great. We dined on champagne, French Bordeaux, shrimp salad, and rack of lamb.

The department wasn't like that anymore. The latest chief was a puppet of the mayor, a man of charm and vitality who just didn't happen to like cops. The current district attorney had started his campaign by proposing to legalize marijuana and prostitution so he could concentrate on "real crime." The fact that he bungled the first two "real crime" cases he took to court had added to the weight of gloom.

The city itself, the Great Gray Lady, was struggling to get her makeup on straight. San Francisco had always been the unquestionable *it* of the Bay Area: the best of everything. Those who had reluctantly moved away always came back—to work, to eat, to go to a show, to a favorite saloon, a favorite coffeehouse, to picnic in Golden Gate Park.

Now all too many of those former lovers found that it wasn't worth the trip: the traffic, the parking problems, the crime, the continuous line of beggars—no, you couldn't call them beggars anymore, and not just because that wasn't a politically correct term. They didn't beg; they demanded: "Give me some money." And if you didn't comply with their wishes, they added a few descriptive adjectives to the next request, along with a stream of saliva.

The in crowd was getting the outgoing message. Well-known restaurants were opening branches on the Peninsula, in the East Bay, and Marin County. Top-rated chefs were quitting and starting their own places in those much-maligned suburbs.

Small businesses, the backbone of any real city, were abandoning ship, fed up with the spaghettilike maze of regulations and taxes.

And a number of cops were practicing that age-old civil service canon: Don't do anything and you'll never get in shit.

Inspector Robert Tehaney was leaning back in his chair, his hands locked behind his neck. He's was craggy-faced Irishman, his sandy hair almost all gray now. He had put on some weight since I'd last seen him, all around the middle.

He was in shirtsleeves, his red-black-and-green-striped Royal Irish Regiment necktie riding high on his tummy. Usually, there was an unfiltered Lucky Strike dangling from his mouth. Now there was a toothpick.

Other than the police department, his main interests in life were the Notre Dame football and basketball teams.

He spotted me and waved me over. "What's doing, Nick? Somebody called me about you last night."

"Right. Detective Rickard, CID, United States Park Police."

Tehaney worked the toothpick from one side of his mouth to the other. "Yeah, that's the man. He called again about fifteen minutes ago. He's not going to rope me in on that one-eighty-seven out at Fort Mason. He wants to handle it himself."

One-eighty-seven was California's penal code designation for homicide. Tehaney patted a stack of manila folders on his desk. "Good thing, 'cause I've got more work than I need now." He ran his eyes around the room. "We all do. What's the deal? Rickard told me some private eye got killed."

"Right. A young guy by the name of Thomas Dashuk was murdered in the front seat of his van. Knife wound—ear to ear."

"What kind of guy is this Rickard?"

"He seems like a nice kid. But he's just a kid. He's got no experience at all, Bob."

Tehaney deposited his toothpick in the wastebasket and replaced it with one from a shot glass on his desk. "Then why doesn't he want to tap in on my valuable expertise?" he said jokingly.

"Dashuk got out of the army a short time ago. He worked for military intelligence. His former boss, Col. Jack Colby, who's still with Uncle Sam, is pulling Rickard's strings. He wants to keep the investigation in-house."

"Well, may God bless that sweet man also." Tehaney rapped his knuckles on his desk. "Did the victim have any knock?"

Knock—power, pull, juice, connections. "No. And no living family members."

"So what's your interest in the lad, Nick?"

"A job. I was hired by Alexander Rostov. You know Alex."

"The junk dealer out in the Richmond district? What the hell is that old bandit up to?"

"A woman came into his shop, with pictures of an old, very valuable Mongol coin and something called a *paitza,* a sort of ID tag. Alex hired me to locate her. I did, and I found that Dashuk had been hired for the same purpose. By someone else."

"So? You guys got together to compare notes?"

"Dashuk wanted to do just that. I didn't. He made a mistake. I was able to figure out who his client was."

"Did Dashuk know you're working for old Alex?"

"No. I don't think so. And I don't think he was telling his client much of what he had developed. Dashuk came into Dino's last night. He got a little excited. He was armed—a semiautomatic. No manufacturer's name on it, and a barrel grooved for screwing on a silencer. I took the gun away from him. All he had was an empty holster when he was killed."

Tehaney held up his hands like a traffic cop. "Whoa, Nick.

Don't tell me nothin' more. If this Rickard kid and the army gent want to handle the beef themselves, they're entitled. Fort Mason is government property."

"Yes. But Dashuk's office is on Polk Street. Rickard called me down to Fort Mason to identify the body. Colby showed up. We all went over to Dashuk's office. I found a little spy room. The entrance was hidden behind a file cabinet. There were all kinds of expensive surveillance equipment: spy cameras, recorders. My hunch is that Dashuk took them, and his fancy gun, with him when he left the army. Dashuk's shop is next to Lickie's Tanning Salon. Dashuk was filming the customers through a hole in the wall."

Tehaney snapped the toothpick between his teeth.

"Lickie's Tanning Salon? How original." He used both hands to pick up the files on his desk, then slammed them down hard. "I've got five gangland killings, three liquor store owners gunned down for the cash-box till, a guy who did an O.J. on his ex-wife and her boyfriend, and another moron who got tired of yelling at his upstairs neighbor to turn down the stereo, so he sends six rounds from his shotgun through the ceiling, killing the neighbor and his eighty-four-year-old mother. I don't need to add some bent private eye to the mix."

"What about Lickie's? Dashuk was filming right through a peephole in the wall."

He reached for another toothpick, holding it between his fingers like a cigarette. "You're sure he was filming the customers?"

"I saw the camera setup, and there was a boxful of videos."

"Did you see the videos?"

"No."

"Well, Rickard didn't mention them to me. If your buddy Dashuk was playing hidden camera, there's no telling how many people he filmed. They'd all have to be possible suspects. I'm glad it's not my problem. And I don't want you volunteering my services. But get to the point, Nick. What do you want? Other than to cover your ass by unloading all of this crap on me."

"I was hoping you'd check something for me."

"And why would I want to do that?"

"Old times' sake?"

Tehaney's features creased in exaggerated pain. "Old times' sake my ass. Okay. What do you want?"

"Col. Jack Colby—I'd like a little background on him."

Tehaney picked up a pencil and began doodling on the back of one of the folders.

"What's your interest in Colby?"

"Colby told me that Dashuk was a black-bag man, a surveillance expert. I'm thinking that—"

"Enough already," Tehaney growled. "I'll run Colby for you, but that's it. It's Rickard's case. I'm not interfering. Understood?"

"Understood."

"Give me his stats," Tehaney said.

"Colby's white, early forties, Bob. He works out of military intelligence in Oakland. That's all I've got."

He gave me a surly look. Running a background check on someone without their date of birth or Social Security number was a difficult task. You had to go through a number of checks to obtain that information before you got to the good stuff.

"Thanks for not mentioning my jail time to Rickard."

"What are friends for?" Tehaney responded acidly, reaching for another toothpick.

"How long since you gave up smoking this time?"

He patted his stomach. "About fifteen pounds ago," he said disgustedly.

I wandered down the hall to the General Works detail to look in on my old partner, Paul Paulsen. I wanted him to check out the offices of WLFR on Van Ness to see if there were any reports on file. I also needed him to get a DMV on Svetlana, the redhead.

The receptionist informed me that Paul had left the day before for New Orleans to pick up a prisoner.

"He's not due back on duty until Saturday," she informed me.

I used the pay phone in the lobby of the Hall of Justice to check my answering machine. Two calls: one from Detective Rickard, the other from Joseph Vallin.

I called Rickard first.

"Mr. Polo. I'd like to get a formal statement from you, sir. What would be a convenient time?"

"I'm not interested in supplying a formal statement, Detective."

He seemed surprised by the statement. "But this is a homicide case. A man has been murdered."

"Yes, I noticed that. Is Colonel Colby in charge of the investigation now?"

Rickard coughed and cleared his throat. "No. But he is assisting."

"Did you view those videotapes you found in Dashuk's peek-aboo room?"

"I did, but I'm not at liberty to discuss what was on those tapes. I'm sure you can understand my position."

"And I'm sure you can understand mine, Detective. I will tell you this. I saw Dashuk last night. Around eight o'clock. He came into a North Beach restaurant, Dino's, and acted foolish. He was armed. I took his gun away from him. I have it at home. You're welcome to it."

"Why didn't you tell me this last night?" Rickard protested.

"I didn't get much of a chance to talk to you. Colby kicked me out, remember?"

"You could have told me about the gun when we were at Fort Mason," he protested logically.

"Yes. Maybe it was the sight of all that blood."

"Blood? You're an ex-policeman. You told me you worked Homicide!"

"I didn't say I was any good at it. I spoke to Inspector Tehaney this morning. He's a good man."

"I don't doubt it, but I don't need his assistance. I want that weapon. Right away."

"How about a swap? The gun for a chance to look at those videos?"

"I'll be here at my office for an hour. I expect to see you before I leave."

"Do we have a deal?"

There was a long pause. I had a vision of Rickard placing his hand over the phone and talking to someone. Colby.

"All right," he said when he came back on the line. "But get over here right now."

I pushed the disconnect bar, dropped in another quarter, and dialed Joseph Vallin's number. His man Nathan Felder answered.

"Joseph just slipped out the door, Mr. Polo. He'll be back in an hour or so."

"Do you know why he called me?"

"Yes. We were wondering if you had any luck in your quest for the *paitza*."

"I've been concentrating on other matters, but my principal is still interested."

"Could you stop by today? Joseph did want to speak with you."

"My day is pretty well booked."

"How about this evening?"

"I'm not sure just what I'll be doing. Maybe we could meet somewhere for a drink? Say eight o'clock?"

"Where did you have in mind?"

"How about the Officers' club at Fort Mason? Do you know where that is?"

It might have been my imagination, but I thought I heard a sharp intake of breath.

"No, but I'm sure we can find it. Until then, sir."

CHAPTER 14

Rickard was standing in the parking lot outside his office, which was located in an adobe building less than two hundred yards from where Thomas Dashuk's body had been found. He watched me roll into the lot. It had had a view out to the Bay, taking in everything from the Golden Gate Bridge to Alcatraz.

The weather had turned warm for this time of the year in San Francisco, pushing above seventy degrees. The sky was powder blue, with just a few scratches of clouds. A large clipped-grass meadow rolled down to Laguna Street and the Marina Green. The Bay waters were a dark blue, with flecks of white sailboats tacking slowly in the salt-scented breeze. Postcard weather, the old-timers called it. The kind of day when the natives say "Ah" and the tourists say "Ooooh."

Rickard said something quite different when I popped the trunk and handed him the brown paper bag.

"Dashuk's gun," I explained.

Rickard snatched the bag from my hand. "Maybe if you hadn't taken it away from him, he'd be alive now."

That very thought had been floating around my little gray cells.

"Get that in here."

The command came from Col. Jack Colby. He was standing in the doorway, holding on to the frame leading to Rickard's office, as if for balance. The dress code for the day was dark brown slacks, a yellow tennis shirt with the collar turned up, and a olive green nylon flight jacket.

"Good morning, Colonel." I saluted him. "I hear you've got some dirty videos worth watching."

The colonel didn't have a sense of humor. Now that I thought of it, I'd never met one who did. He gave me a withering look, then turned around and disappeared inside the building.

I knew the government was downsizing, but they might have gone just a tad too far with Rickard's office. The floor was covered by faded green linoleum squares, the cracks of which were black with dirt. I looked around at the yellowing knotty pine walls. The top of a large coffin-shaped table was graffitied by knife blades and cigarette butts.

A half a dozen cardboard boxes and a plastic-cased small-screen TV and matching VCR were spread across the table. Several metal folding chairs were scattered about the room.

I peered into one of the cardboard boxes, which was jammed with a video camera, a very expensive Leica and an assortment of spare lenses. There was nothing resembling a laser transmitter and receiver.

Colby stood with his feet slightly apart, his hands clamped behind his back. He was too short and too narrow in the shoulders and chest to get away with the pose. He needed a swagger stick or some other prop.

"You should have told us about the gun last night, Polo," he scolded.

Most people are confused as to just what you are required to tell a law officer in the course of his investigation. Actually, not a hell of a lot most times. Of course, if you're not involved in the crime, you want to help the good guys catch the bad guy. I certainly wanted to see whoever had murdered Thomas Dashuk caught and punished. I just didn't have much faith that this pushy member of military intelligence who was in love with his own commanding voice could accomplish that goal.

"Be nice, Colby, or I'll waltz out of here without telling you what else I know."

His face remained frozen in a scowl, but some of the starch went out of his back. "There's been a murder, mister. It would be to your benefit to cooperate."

I ignored him and looked at Rickard. "Detective, we had a deal."

Rickard placed the brown paper bag with Dashuk's gun on the table and then lifted out six cassette tapes from one of the boxes.

"There were a dozen or more on the shelves in Dashuk's spy hole," I said.

Colby responded, "And a few in his apartment, Polo. We haven't had time to review them all yet. When we do, and if you cooperate, you may get to see them."

Rickard reluctantly shoved the videos across the table, like a croupier awarding a big winner his chips.

I took off my sport coat and draped it over one of the metal chairs. While I slotted a cassette into the VCR, Colby peered into the bag with the gun, nestled it under his arm, and advised Rickard to follow him to the next room.

It took me a few minutes to get the TV and recorder working. When the tape started rolling, I knew why Colby and Rickard had seemed anxious to leave the room.

The scene was of a narrow bed, shot from above. The fish-eye lens had distorted the image, but it wasn't hard to pick up the drift of the script.

There was one episode on each tape. I was wondering if there'd be another tape, one of me taking photographs of Anna and Flaxen Hair at Golden Gate Park, but all the videos had the same setting: a small room with a bed. The cast of characters included one woman—a pretty Asian girl who looked very much like the one who had tried to lure me into Lickie's Tanning Salon the night before. The rest of the cast, appearing one at time, were men, all white, all middle-aged or older, all with sad, lonely faces before, during, and after the girl had satisfied their wishes.

One thing you could say for Lily, she wasn't playing favorites. Each guy came into the room, undressed, lay down on his stomach, received about a fifteen-second pawing of his back, and then was asked the same question by the girl. "Hi, I'm Lily. You want to pay for some real fun?"

Lily's prices were inflexible. "Hundred dollars for French, a hundred and fifty for half-and-half."

There were no half-and-half buyers in this particular crowd. I zipped through the action as fast as possible. There didn't seem to be much originality in her technique, and each episode ended, appropriately enough, in a climax.

Then Lily left the room and the customer jumped into his clothes as quickly as possible.

Colby came and stood beside me.

"Makes sex rather unappetizing, doesn't it?" he said, smiling as if he was talking to a fellow colonel rather than to an irritating private investigator.

"Are the rest all like this?"

"So far."

"The same girl in all of them?"

"Yes. Sweet Lily. I could have used her in Berlin."

"Did you work with Dashuk there? In Berlin?"

Colby shrugged off his flight jacket and dropped it over the back of a chair. A black nylon Velcro-strapped holster rode his right hip. The butt of the gun looked exactly like Dashuk's.

"Berlin, Vienna, Moscow. He was one of mine. I don't like seeing him end up like this."

"Do you think that someone or something from his army background could be responsible for his death?"

Colby gave me a patronizing smile. "No way." He picked up one of the videotapes, then dropped it, as if it had burned his fingers. "He must have tried to blackmail one of Lily's conquests."

"Was there any backup material in Dashuk's office to ID the customers? Any notes? Addresses? License plate numbers?"

"No. Whoever killed him took his keys and went back to his office and apartment and cleaned them out."

"Except for the tapes, Colonel."

"Yes. Yes, he missed those."

"He missed the ones in Dashuk's spy room, but you told me there were also some tapes in his apartment. Why would the killer leave those?"

Colby's pale eyes caught mine for a second, then drifted off.

"Maybe he found the one he was looking for, Polo. I ran a rather thorough check on you. You were with military intelligence for a short time."

"I never volunteered, Colonel. I did my time and got out. Did you ever see Dashuk after he was discharged? At his office? Or his apartment?"

Colby settled his haunches down gently on the edge of the desk. "Yes. We met for lunch. We had a drink once or twice. Always at a restaurant or bar. Not at the office. Not his apartment. We weren't really friends, Polo. He was an enlisted man."

Affirmative action never had a chance in the military. Even if race didn't matter, rank certainly did.

I said, "That's an interesting gun Dashuk had. No manufacturer's name. Was it one of the trophies that he took with him when he left your outfit?"

Colby gave me an enigmatic smile; then his hand moved swiftly. Almost magically, his gun was out of its holster and in his hand. "I helped design this baby. A Walther PPKS frame, but I had the hammer spur removed, the grips changed. Every piece of this baby is Teflon-coated. It'll never jam." He pressed the button releasing the gun's clip, then racked the chamber. A bullet jumped free, landing on the table with a clatter. Colby's hand disappeared behind his back, coming out with a black cylinder the size of a garlic sausage. He spiraled the cylinder onto the gun's barrel. "I wanted to make it a forty-five or a ten millimeter, but that big a slug's too hard on a silencer, so we had to settle on a nine-millimeter subsonic whisper load."

He bent his knee, hoisted his leg to the table, and raised his pant leg. A piece of flat black metal ran from his ankle to his knee. He pulled it free from its Velcro straps and jammed it into the pistol's grip. "Thirty rounds," he said, as if this information would impress me. "It's as good as having an Uzi."

The extended clip of bullets hung from the bottom of the gun like an obscene appendage.

"I thought the Cold War was over, Colonel. Is all that really necessary to survive in Oakland?"

He went through the procedure of removing the clip, silencer, and reloading the weapon, then asked, "What kind of armament do you carry?"

I held my hands up in mock surrender. "Nothing, Colonel. I'm afraid of guns." I removed the cassette from the VCR. "Have you talked to Lily?"

"No. Not yet. I went over there last night, but it was closed. Rickard called Lickie's but Lily wasn't there. At least that's what they told him. Tell me about you and Dashuk. How did you meet him?"

Rickard was nowhere in sight. I handed Colby the cassette. "It's stuffy in here. Let's go outside."

Colby's head retracted between his shoulders. "I hope you don't think our conversation is being recorded."

"The thought never entered my mind, Colonel."

Colby picked up his jacket and draped it over his shoulders like a cape. "It is a little stuffy, now that you mention it."

We strolled slowly over to my car. Colby was whistling a tune I didn't recognize.

"Al Rickard's a babe in the woods, Polo," he said when we reached the car.

"You think this investigation might be a little too much for him?"

Colby took a handkerchief from his pant pocket and wiped the Ford's fender before leaning against it. "That's why I'm here. You might be of help, too, Polo."

"I usually get paid for my help, Colonel."

"I think I might be able to accommodate you there. You'll have to submit a bill, in triplicate. Direct it to me and I'll see that it's approved."

A low-flying squadron of seagulls glided by, their shadows dappling the asphalt parking lot. "What is it you think I can do for you, Colonel?"

"For one thing, tell me what you know about Tom Dashuk. How you met up with him. I know I came on a little hard with you. Rickard is getting frustrated. He's really pissed about the gun.

He's threatening to go to the U.S. attorney or the FBI if you don't cooperate."

Wow. The good guy/bad guy routine. Colby didn't want to cooperate with a pro like Bob Tehaney, but he wanted me to go to work for him.

"I told you I'd run a thorough check on you, Polo. For a man with your background, you come on a little high-and-mighty. How long were you in prison? Six months?"

"Dashuk knew about that, too," I said, unlocking the car door.

After I was behind the wheel, I lowered the window. Colby put his hands on the roof and leaned down so his face was level with mine. "How did you meet Dashuk?"

"He called me and said he wanted to get together. He needed help in an investigation."

"Why did he pick on you?"

"I don't know, Colonel. Maybe he learned about my short stint with the army." I let a few seconds tick away. "From someone."

"What was the investigation Tommy was working on?"

"Something about a rare Mongol coin. He thought a young woman had it. He showed me a photograph of her."

Colby straightened up and rubbed the small of his back. "Then what?"

"I told him I wasn't interested and he got mad."

"Mad enough to come after you in some restaurant with a gun?" Colby scoffed. "What happened to the picture of the girl?"

"The last time I saw it, Dashuk had it in his office."

Colby bent down again and got close enough so I could smell his aftershave lotion. "We didn't find anything like that."

"Maybe the killer took it, Colonel."

"Maybe. What did the girl look like?"

"It was a lousy photograph. You couldn't see her face. Young. Dark hair. That's about all I could make out."

"Did Dashuk give you her name?"

"Just the first name. Tanya."

"Nothing else?"

"No."

Colby pinched his nose a couple of times. "Okay, this Lily, the whore in the videos. I haven't got time to run her down. Why don't you take a crack at it."

"All right. I'd like to look at Dashuk's office. And his apartment."

"For what reason?"

"Maybe the woman's picture—the woman with the coin—is there."

"I told you, I looked and didn't find anything like that."

"Right. But you didn't find Dashuk's spy room, either."

Colby finessed a smile, then pulled out his wallet and extracted a key and a business card. He handed me the key first. "This works on Dashuk's apartment and his office. By the way, what are your fees, Polo?"

"Seventy-five an hour and expenses, Colonel."

He let the card flutter down to my lap. "I'll authorize up to a thousand dollars. Check out the whore. Let me know where she is. I want to talk to her."

CHAPTER 15

I stopped by to see Alex Rostov. His shop was closed. I knew he lived in the apartment above the store, but there was no response to that door, either.

I made a quick stop at my flat, where I disconnected the fax machine from the phone line and stuffed it and the operation manual in a canvas backpack. Then I drove back to Dashuk's place, wondering all the way about the generous Colonel Colby. Colonel. The highest rank I had attained in the army was corporal, and quite often I was addressed simply as "Hey, you."

Colby was willing to spend up to one thousand taxpayers' dollars to have me dig into a homicide because the victim was "one of mine."

I didn't believe it. Dashuk told me that someone in MI told him that they were smuggling everything out of Russia except Lenin's body. I'd bet my Shirley Temple pitcher that that someone was Col. Jack Colby.

I parked a block from Dashuk's office, fingering the key Colby had given me and trying to figure out the colonel's angle.

My stomach alerted me to the fact that it was past lunchtime. I bought a newspaper from a vending machine, then went to the coffee shop on the corner. There was one open booth. Judy, the same waitress who had served me breakfast a few mornings ago, was on duty. She gave me a tired smile. "Back again, huh? Dashuk wasn't in this morning."

"He won't be in anymore. He died last night."

She used the back of her hand to wipe her ringlet of bangs from her forehead. "Are you kidding me?"

"No. He was murdered."

She stepped backward, holding up her pencil and order pad as if they were a shield and sword. "I don't believe you."

"I'm sorry, Judy, but it's true. I identified the body."

She started to say something, then decided against it. She ran behind the counter and got into a heated discussion with the cook.

He stopped flipping burgers long enough to give me a suspicious look.

The waitress kept squinting at me as she carried orders to the customers at the counter and the other booths. She finally returned, carrying a cup of coffee.

"I'm sorry," she apologized, setting the cup down in front of me. "You kind of shocked me. I didn't know much about him, but it's still a shock."

"Do you know anyone who did know Dashuk well? Any particular friends, buddies, anything like that?"

"No. He just came in for breakfast. Lunch once in a while." Her eyes started to tear. "He was kinda cute, really." Her mourning didn't last long. "You want something to eat?"

I ordered a club sandwich and went through the paper, looking for Jane Tobin's column first out of habit. There was no column. There was no Jane. She was still somewhere in Miami, as far as I knew. There was nothing about Dashuk's murder, either.

Judy stopped by every few minutes, asking questions. One was, "Are you a cop?"

"No, I'm private. Like Dashuk. But I'm looking into the murder at the request of the investigating officer. Do you know a girl named Lily who works at Lickie's Tanning Salon?"

Her nose wrinkled. "I don't know any of those people. They come in for coffee and stuff, but I don't know 'em." She twisted her head around to look toward the cook. "Hey, Harry," she called out. "You know someone name of Lily works at Lickie's?"

Harry wiped his hands across his apron and grinned. "I think they're all named Lily."

★ ★ ★

Dashuk's office lock was a double-cylinder dead bolt. Not an easy lock to turn, even with a set of burglar keys like Colonel Colby had jiggled at me the night before. The room was a bigger mess than when I'd last seen it. Apparently, Colby and Rickard had given it a good going-over.

I poked around amid the rubble, finding nothing of interest— no mailing list, no billing files, no accounts receivable, nothing.

I crawled back into Dashuk's little spy room. The shelves were empty; even the ladder was gone.

I hooked up my fax machine to Dashuk's phone line, check-ing with the manual to make sure everything was right, then di-aled the phone company's business office.

This gag didn't work every time, maybe once out of four tries. But what the hell, they were paying .250 hitters millions of dol-lars to play baseball.

"Hello, this is Hazel. How can I help you?" good old Pac Bell's service representative asked me.

"Hazel, this is Tom Dashuk. I've been away a week and I just got back to my office and found that I've been burglarized. I'm afraid someone has used the phone. Probably run up some long-distance bills. It happened to me once before. Someone had called one of those nine hundred sex numbers and ran up a huge bill." Then I gave her Dashuk's number and asked her to check if there had been any toll calls charged to it.

Now Hazel was sitting in her cubicle and Dashuk's number was blinking on her computer, so she knew that was the num-ber I was calling from. She would push a few buttons and check the billing, which would show Dashuk's name and address.

Now it all depended on Hazel. If she was too busy, or too much a stickler for company rules, or if there was a notation that the United States Park Police had requested the information, I was out of luck.

Usually, the phone company wouldn't release billing informa-tion to a law-enforcement agency unless they subpoenaed it. I had to hope that Rickard was a little behind the curve.

"Yes, there have been a few calls," Hazel informed me. "Very few, though, Mr. Dashuk."

"Could you possibly fax the information to me, Hazel?"

"Well . . ."

"My fax number is the same number I'm calling from. I'd really appreciate it, Hazel. You should see this place. It was probably kids. They broke up everything and spray-painted the walls. I'm lucky they left the phone and the fax."

"All right, Mr. Dashuk. I hope the police catch whoever did it."

"Me, too, Hazel. But I don't have a lot of faith in them."

That drew a light laugh. "I know what you mean, sir. Have a good day."

I hung up and waited. Hazel was a hard worker. Within three minutes, the phone rang and the fax chirped on.

Pacific Bell wasn't making much money off of The Thinner Man. There were just four toll calls made on Dashuk's line over the past seven days. One to area code 212, one to the 310 area code, the others to a Bay Area number. The last call Dashuk made from the office was to the local number, at 7:00 P.M., the night before he died.

I dialed the long-distance numbers first. They turned out to belong to the New York City and Los Angeles branches of the Rare Coin Network.

I called the operator and asked where the local exchange was. She said it was for Marin County.

I disconnected my fax machine, then tried the Marin number, hooking up with a recorded message from Joseph Vallin. It advised the caller that he was not at home and could be reached at his office in San Francisco.

I trooped around the corner to Dashuk's apartment. Dashuk's living quarters weren't much bigger than the room Anna the Mysterious had rented on Cole Street. In the small living room, the furniture consisted of a slope-back floral-patterned couch and a large screen TV. There was a VCR atop the TV.

A narrow bookcase held a wide-ranging paperback collection:

Louis L'Amour, a half a dozen of Parker's private eye books, Ludlum thrillers, and Clancy technothrillers. The one nonfiction work was entitled *San Francisco at Night*. I skimmed through the index. Lickie's Tanning Salon wasn't mentioned.

The bedroom was a shambles: bureau drawers hanging out, the contents cascading onto the floor. The closet was in the same condition. The bathroom medicine cabinet was bare; bottles of aspirin, mouthwash, a package of disposable razors, shaving cream, and dental floss now rested in the sink.

The toilet tank's top was akimbo. I slid it free. The ball-shaped metal gadget that rides up with the water flow after flushing had been pulled loose and split in half.

Colby was the type to make a mess and expect his underlings to clean up after him.

For all of Dashuk's black-bag skills, there was no photo-development equipment in either his office or apartment. There was no need to develop the videos, but Dashuk had had a lot of money tied up in the Leica and all those lenses in the box in Rickard's office.

I found a phone book on the bedroom floor and sifted through the Yellow Pages. There were seven photo-development possibilities within a two-block walk from Dashuk's office.

I lugged the fax back to my car, dug a roll of undeveloped film from the trunk, then extracted from my wallet the business card Dashuk had given me in the coffee shop. I printed the name Al Harris neatly on the corner of the card, then started the hunt, using the same line at each stop along the way.

"Hi, I'm Tom Dashuk's new partner." I then dropped the roll of raw film on the counter. "I need a rush on these, and I think we've got something ready for pickup."

The clerks at the first two stores checked their files and informed me that they did not have an account under the name Dashuk or The Thinner Man Investigations.

The scholarly-looking man with rimless glasses behind the counter at Flash Photos on Golden Gate Avenue gave me a sour look. "I told Mr. Dashuk, cash only from now on."

"That's not a problem. Tom said he had something to pick up."
I began pulling twenties from my money clip.

"When did you hook up with Dashuk?" he asked skeptically.

"Last week." I handed him the business card. "I haven't had time to get my own printed up yet."

He chewed the inside of his cheek a moment, then stooped down and began shuffling through a stack of envelopes. "I'm going to have to keep it on a cash basis," he said, sliding a green pocketbook-sized envelope across the counter. "Twenty-eight dollars and fifty-seven cents."

I waited until I got back to the car to examine the photos. The army had indeed turned Dashuk into a professional. A professional photographer, anyway. The photos were crisp, clear, and nicely composed.

There were twenty-four prints. The first four showed a steel-ribbed metal gate set in a white stucco wall. There were two pictures taken at an elevation of twelve feet or so, showing the top portion of the stucco wall and a curving road and tree-thick area just on the other side of the gate. I wondered if Dashuk had climbed a tree to take the snaps or if he had just stood on the roof of his van.

The next photo was of an apartment building—eight stories, gray stone with bowed-out balconies. There was nothing to indicate the street, and no property number visible on the building. It looked like San Francisco real estate, but it could have been almost anywhere in town.

Dashuk had indeed been a busy boy. The next six pictures showed the building housing WLFR on California and Van Ness. Dashuk had been using a telephoto lens—the building's front entrance increasing in size in each photo, the last showing the stoic features of Anna/Tanya/Irina as she exited.

The final series showed a little old lady in black sweeping the sidewalk: Mrs. Damonte. My flats.

CHAPTER 16

◀▶

I arrived at the Bank of America ten minutes before closing time and transferred over to the business account all but five dollars of the $1,143 that were taking temporary refuge in my personal account. Then I put a stop order on a thousand-dollar check made out to WLFR.

Finally, I made out the check to WLFR and slipped it in my coat pocket.

When I got home, the garage door to the flats was wide-open and Mrs. Damonte was squeegeeing off the just-hosed-down floor.

"*Macchia di petrolio.*" She greeted me with a scowl.

Oil drippings from my car. She griped about the few drops of oil as if they were comparable to the spill from the Exxon *Valdez*. In Mrs. D's world, a basement was not a place for parking a car. It was sort of an indoor urban piazza—clean, freshly scrubbed cement bordered by neatly stacked bundles of newspapers and sealed cartons containing her old crockery, pots, pans, and other treasures.

"Where's Carla?" I asked, trying to be pleasant as she splashed Pine Sol on the cement, coming very close to my tasseled loafers.

She lectured me about my not paying enough attention to Carla, then gave me a flicker of a smile. She informed me that Carla was with my uncle.

Carla had been asking me about Uncle Dominic. I flicked a smile right back at Mrs. D. If there was anyone she would have liked to see one of her nieces hook, it was my uncle. His mansion made the flats look like small potatoes.

I went up the front steps and into my place. The answering machine had one message—from Alexander Rostov.

I called him. He sounded tired, half-asleep.

"I was by to see you, but the shop was closed," I told him.

"Doctor's appointment. What news do you have?"

"Are you feeling all right?"

"Yes, sure. A new doctor today. Young. He thinks he knows everything." He gave a dry laugh that turned into a hacking cough.

"I've got some bad news." I told Rostov all about Tom Dashuk's death.

He didn't show much sympathy for the dead private investigator. "These policemen. They know of the *paitza*?"

"Not from me, Alexander. And they're not really policemen. One is a young man with no experience; the other is an army colonel who knew Dashuk personally. I tried to get them to turn the case over to the San Francisco Homicide cops. They may eventually, but right now they're digging into Dashuk's murder on their own. Whoever killed Dashuk removed all the files from his office."

"Then they may never know," he said.

"The killer knows," I reminded him. "Dashuk had Anna's photograph, the one taken from Joseph Vallin's office. Dashuk was working for Vallin. There had to be something there with Vallin's name on it."

I told Alexander of the photos I'd picked up just hours ago. "Dashuk knew where Anna worked, and where I live. I don't know what relevance the other sets of photos have, but they may be where Anna lives."

"Who do you think killed this man, Nick?"

"I don't know. He may have been murdered because of the coin or the *paitza,* or it could have something to do with him filming the people in the tanning salon."

"It was Vallin," Rostov declared with certainty. "He's a crook, Nick. He's always been a crook."

"Vallin wants to meet with me. Tonight."

Rostov no longer sounded tired. "Why? What does he want?"

"I won't know, unless I meet with him. I didn't talk to Vallin directly. I spoke with the man who works in his shop, Nathan Felder. Do you know him?"

"No, but if he works for Joseph, he's a crook, too," Rostov warned.

"I scheduled the meeting for eight o'clock, which won't give me much time, Alexander. I'm supposed to go see your girlfriend Anna at five."

"Anna? You're going to see Anna?"

"You're the client," I advised him. "If you want me to forget about it, that's fine with me."

"But I paid you," he protested. "In cash."

"You didn't pay me enough to deal with murderers, my friend."

The hacking cough came back. "Please, Nick," he said in a strained, hoarse voice. "Twenty-five thousand dollars. Find me the *paitza* and it is yours. I've got to have it. If only for a little while. I've got to have it."

"All you saw were pictures of the *paitza*," I reminded him.

"Why do you think she took the pictures?" Rostov challenged. "Why do you think Anna showed them to me? She has it, and she wants to sell it, Nick. And I want to be the buyer. Me. Not Vallin. Not anyone else. You find it for me. And you will be rewarded."

"I'm not Vallin. I'm not a crook, Alexander."

"I didn't mean for you to steal it," he admonished. "Just find it. Maybe this man, Jonathan, the one in the park, has something to do with the *paitza*."

Rostov went into a long, painful coughing episode.

"Alexander. What did the doctor say about your cough?"

"He told me to stop smoking, what else? The last three doctors I've seen told me the same thing. And I've outlived them all. See Anna, Nick."

I put the computer to work, running With Love from Russia through a series of data checks: fictitious names, California corporations and limited partnership records, bankruptcy, liens, and judgments. All negative.

I then checked both superior and municipal court filings for all the Bay Area counties. Nothing on file. At least none of WLFR's clients had sued them.

The only hit was San Francisco business license records, and that didn't tell me much. S. Bakarich had paid the annual sixty-five-dollar license fee eleven months ago.

Svetlana the Red. No other names. No Jonathan.

I put the computer to sleep and got ready for my date with Anna/Tanya/Irina.

The older I got, the smaller my gun got. In the police department, I had started out carrying a bulky four-inch barrel revolver. When I made inspector, I dropped down to a two-inch .38 snub-nosed revolver. When I left the department, I scaled down to a .32 "belly gun." Now it was a .25 Beretta semiautomatic that was smaller than the palm of my hand.

I found even this weapon too cumbersome and bulky and I seldom carried it, but the sight of Thomas Dashuk's slit neck made it seem essential. I slipped the Beretta in the inside pocket of my sport coat and headed for Van Ness Avenue.

I drove around looking for the maroon Volvo, finally spotting it parked in front of Lafayette Park, a four-block hike from the offices of WLFR. I circled the block twice, once again ending up in front of a fire hydrant, a half a block from the Volvo.

Svetlana was waiting for me at her desk, radiating love and happiness.

"Ah, Nick. You are punctual. Such a wonderful American trait." She smoothed out the desk blotter with her hands. "First the paperwork, then Irina, no?"

"Yes." I gave her the check and she examined the figures. If Svetlana was sharp, and I had little doubt she was, the first thing she would do after I left her office was run asset and credit checks on me. She'd find that I owned the flats; then she'd call the bank branch to see if I had enough money in the account to cover the check.

Since almost anyone can get a peek at your credit records nowadays, a friendly tip. Contact all three of the major credit agencies and review their copies of your file. It's the law now— they *have* to let you examine it. Make sure everything checks out on your loans and commercial accounts; then order them—don't ask; order them—to remove items such as your spouse's name, your date of birth, your occupation, and your telephone number, especially if your number is an unlisted one. It's amazing how many people will go to the extra expense of having an unlisted telephone number, then let it circulate through credit bureaus and voting and tax records. Why make a fuss about having these details eliminated? Because those four items will let someone—like me, for instance—trigger other databases that will have additional information on you.

"Aren't you a little worried, a beautiful woman like you here by yourself so late? Shouldn't you have a security guard working for you, just in case one of your customers gets a little excited or something?"

"I have never found the need," she said, sliding the check in a desk drawer and killing any other questions I might ask about the possibility of Flaxen Hair being part of her operation. She stood up, smoothing her skirt. "And now, Irina."

She crossed to the door leading to the room where I had viewed the videos, and she opened it with a flourish. "Irina," she cooed, "it's your Nick."

Anna/Tanya/Irina was good, no doubt about it. She acted like a nervous little maiden, jittery and afraid. She was bundled up to her chin in a black woolen coat.

Her hair was brushed straight back from her forehead, her cheeks lightly rouged, her lipstick a pale pink.

She walked with her shoulders hunched up a bit, as if she was afraid I might strike her.

"How do you do?" she asked in heavily accented English.

Svetlana dragged the other woman's seemingly reluctant hand over to mine. Her skin was warm and dry.

Svetlana had a suggestion. "Why don't you two go out? Have a drink. Get acquainted."

Anna—let's keep calling her that for now—bowed her head shyly.

"If you want to," she said softly.

She lit a cigarette up as soon as we were in the hallway, making small talk about the weather and the supposed flight from Seattle.

She kept the act going while she sipped champagne and ate dinner. A broiled steak at Ruth's Chris, which was just across the block from WLFR.

The coat came off after the first glass of the bubbly. The dress got my attention, as well as that of the busboy, waiter, sommelier, and the maitre d', who had shown almost no interest in us at all when we'd arrived without reservations.

The dress was a curve-hugging black knit, the kind with scoops of bare shoulders visible beneath a high-neck collar.

I listened to her sad story of how difficult life was in Russia, "not as bad as before, with the Communists, but it is still so hard."

I did what I do best—acted dumb.

Memorizing all her lines must have been hard work, because she knifed and forked her way though a Caesar salad, a twelve-ounce filet, a baked potato, asparagus, and then a hunk of apple pie.

"The perfect American meal," she said, dabbing her patrician chin with a napkin when the last of the pie was gone. "So, what do you think, Nick?" (This came out *Neeeek*) "Do you want to see me again? Do you think we are . . . compatible?"

"Definitely. Why don't we go somewhere and listen to music and dance? Or over to my place."

She glanced at her watch, her lips forming a pout. "Oh, Svetlana told me I could not do that." She slithered her hand across the table and squeezed my fingers lightly. "Not on the first date. How about tomorrow? Would you like to take me to lunch?"

A $1,000 check, a $136 dinner bill, and so far all the sucker had gotten was his fingers stroked. "I'd love to. Come on. Let's go somewhere. I'll call for a cab."

"You don't have a car?"

"Yes, but once you get to know this town, you'll find that you can never find a parking space."

"Oh, I better not. Svetlana is waiting for me." She dipped her chin and lowered her voice. "She is very strict."

Wait until you see her when the check bounces, I thought. "All right. I'll walk you back to Svetlana."

I had to decide whether to keep the appointment with Joseph Vallin, or stick with Anna. It wasn't a difficult decision. Anna and Svetlana exited the building twenty-five minutes later, arm in arm, chatting merrily, Svetlana's head wheeling back and forth several times, causing me to sink deeper into the darkened doorway. She gave Anna/Tanya/Irina a hug and a kiss on the cheek, then scurried east on California Street.

Anna lit a cigarette, then took off in that long-strided athletic gait of hers and headed back in the direction of the Volvo. I was congratulating myself on my stealthy surveillance techniques when she sailed right by the Volvo and slipped between the twin palm trees at the entrance to Lafayette Park.

Lafayette Park was a four-block square of urban greenery that during the daylight hours offered a haven and nice views of the city. After dark, it offered what all city parks did: the chance of being raped, robbed, or mugged.

At that time of night, most sane people wouldn't have dared enter the park without a pair of drooling Dobermans or an Uzi.

I jogged down Sacramento, took a right on Clay Street, and caught her exiting the park. She seemed none the worse for wear.

She turned into the lobby of an eight-story gray stone apartment house with bowed-out balconies—the building in Dashuk's photographs.

I caught a glimpse of her through the ornate iron-grilled door as she entered the elevator. The bell plate showed twenty units. All had a name neatly typed next to the bell, with the exception of number seventeen.

I scrolled down the names, none of which were vowel-bloated Russian ones.

CHAPTER 17

The girl who opened the door to Lickie's Tanning Salon wasn't the same one who had tried to coax me inside the night before. Chinese or Vietnamese was my guess. Her silky black hair hung down to her jawline. Her bangs were cut razor-straight across her forehead. A small pearl was pinned in the flare of her left nostril. Not more than five feet tall, she was wearing a short pleated plaid skirt, a white shirt and striped tie, white ankle socks, and Mary Janes. She could easily have passed for sixteen or seventeen.

"Hi, do you want a treatment?" she said in a purring, statutory-rape voice.

"Is Lily in?"

She smiled widely. "You like Lily? She not in. Back later. But I can help you. Just like Lily. My name is Kim."

"No. It has to be Lily. I'll just wait for her."

"She not back till tomorrow." Her tongue slipped out and took a slow, wet tour around her lips. "You don't want to have to wait until then."

"Maybe I better speak to the manager."

Her hands started floating around like butterflies. "Why you want the manager. I can take—"

"It's about the man next door. Mr. Dashuk. He was killed. Murdered."

"Dashuk? I do not know him."

"Call the manager. I'm from the police."

Her face aged about ten years, and her voice lost its schoolgirl lisp. "You wait here."

She slipped through a doorless archway curtained with strings of red glass beads. The room I was standing in was painted ketchup red. There were three mismatched overstuffed chairs, a bare-topped desk, and a table littered with magazines, the covers displaying Asian girls with enormous breasts spilling out of microbikinis.

I pushed through the beads into a coco-matted hallway. The walls were more of the ketchup color. There were ten white doors, five on each side of the corridor, and one black door at the far end.

Kim looked over her shoulder at me, stopped, and shouted, "You wait!" Then she jerked open the black door, went in, and slammed it after her.

I tried to get my bearings in relationship to Dashuk's office, where the *Sports Illustrated* calendar and the secret spy room were situated. His south wall was Lickie's north wall. I knocked softly on the nearest white door.

"Anybody home?" When no one responded, I eased the door open. It was more of a cubicle than a room. A narrow mattress sat on a wood frame; it was covered by a clean white sheet. A small table held an assortment of clear plastic bottles, cans of talcum powder and neatly folded hospital-fresh white towels.

A strip of scroll-saw gingerbread molding rimmed the wall, some six inches from the ceiling.

I climbed up on the bed and ran my fingers over the molding. The small hole was nicely hidden in the curling grooves of the wood.

I could hear a door smack open, then the thudding of footsteps. A clean-shaven man in his forties with a weight lifter's build burst into the room.

He looked up at me and his mouth made a big circle, as if waiting for a dentist.

"Are you the manager?" I asked as I jumped down from the bed.

He looked even bigger at floor level—a couple of inches over my six feet. His face was pear-shaped, with wide-set eyes. A line of diamond earrings rimmed one ear. He was wearing tan shorts, a sweat-stained T-shirt, and leather gloves, the fingers cut off at midknuckle on each hand.

"Who the hell are you?" he challenged.

I showed him my badge.

It produced a different reaction than what I was expecting. His features relaxed. "Have you checked in with the district captain? We're good friends."

"Good enough to overlook a homicide next door?" I reached over and tapped on the Sheetrock. "Tom Dashuk—the private eye. He was murdered."

He gave an unconcerned shrug of his muscular shoulders. "I don't know nothing about the man."

"All you need to know is that he's dead. His throat was slit." I gestured up to the ceiling. "And that he's been filming your action in here through a peephole."

Now I got the reaction I was looking for—another circle with the mouth and a nervous twitch of the eye.

"Maybe we better talk about this," he conceded.

The room behind the black door smelled of sweat and unwashed clothes. The floor was covered with a gym mat. The walls were floor-to-ceiling mirrors. A collection of exercise equipment took up most of the space: punching bag, rowing machine, workout benches, and a half a dozen or more barbells loaded down with cast-iron weights.

A small desk and two folding chairs looked out of place in one corner of the room. The desktop was littered with magazines, pencils, and a flip-page calendar.

"My name's Kevin," the big man volunteered, peeling off his weight-lifting gloves. "I don't know anything about the dick next door. That's the truth. What are you talking about? This peephole thing?"

"Dashuk was filming your little parties in here through the wall. All those soothing tanning sessions that Lily was providing."

He looked longingly at the telephone.

"You can call the captain, or the lieutenant, or the sergeant you're doing business with, but it won't help you, Kevin. Where's Lily?"

He balled one glove in his hand and flung it toward a mirrored wall. "Lily. That bitch. She didn't show up today."

"Surprise, surprise."

Kevin straddled a workout bench. "I'm just the manager here. Not the owner. The owner is Jack—"

"I know all about the owner. And his connections, Kevin," I lied. "What I don't know about is Lily." I made a beckoning gesture with my fingers. "Give."

He took a deep breath, then pushed himself to his feet, rocking back and forth on his heels for a few moments, as if debating with himself. "Okay," he finally said, going to the desk drawer and pawing through a bunch of folders before finding what he was looking for.

"This is a legitimate operation," he protested, then handed me the file. "If Lily was doing something, she was doing it on her own."

"She was doing a lot of it, Kevin." I skimmed the file. A photograph of Lily in her nurse's uniform, a bored expression on her face, was stapled to a single page that listed her full name—Lila "Lily" Wong—and her address—742 Redwood Street—as well as her phone number, Social Security number, and date of birth.

The loose-leaf desk calendar was a collection of Far Side cartoons. I tore a page off. The cartoon showed a goofy-eyed cowboy on top of the roof of a log cabin, pounding nails with the butt end of his revolver. Another cowboy was standing below, his hands perched over his holsters. The caption read: "I hear you're pretty handy with a gun, mister."

I began scribbling Lily's particulars under the caption.

Kevin started to protest.

"Relax," I advised him, dropping the folder back on the desk. "I know the captain, too."

CHAPTER 18

Breakfast was a pleasant surprise. The aroma of fresh coffee and baked goods brought me out of a dream—a nightmare really. In it, Jane Tobin had been lying on a white sandy beach surrounded by muscle-bound, golden-tanned Greek godlike figures. I kept trying to make my way through their baby-oiled bodies to Jane, but every time I got by one, another would take his place.

"Good morning!"

I pried an eye open and saw Carla Borelli with a breakfast tray in hand. The tray had fold-out legs, so once I had struggled into a sitting position, Carla set it gently over my lap.

She was dressed to kill again—or underdressed to kill: a cherry blossom pink long-sleeved top, scooped low and laced together at what I believe the fashion magazines call the décolletage.

"Angelica made the *uova da monacella* this morning," she said cheerfully, bending down to pour me a steaming cup of coffee from the espresso pot.

My hands were above the blankets, but if she kept bending down like that, the breakfast tray was going to appear to levitate on its own.

Uova da monacella—nun's eggs. Mrs. D boils the eggs until they're barely hard, then peels them, cuts them in half, mixes the yolks with bread crumbs, herbs, and a little of whatever sausage she has in the refrigerator, stuffs all that back into the whites, dips them into beaten egg whites, and fries them lightly in olive oil.

Carla poured herself a cup of coffee, then told me, "Angelica let me into your flat. I hope you don't mind."

I stuffed my face with one of the eggs and mumbled an undecipherable response.

Carla smoothed the bedspread with one hand while her eyes roamed around the room. "I am free today. I thought maybe you could show me your city, Nick."

"I'd love to, Carla, but I have to work. How did you and Uncle get along?"

She walked her fingertips across the spread, found the outline of my foot, and began stroking it as if it were a cat. "Dominic is wonderful. He knows some people in Hollywood who are going to help me."

"Help you do what?"

She hunched her shoulders, adding to the pressure against her blouse laces. "The movies, of course. I did some modeling at home. I think I could be a good actress. Your lady friend—have you heard from her?"

"Jane Tobin? No. She's still in Miami."

"Oh." She clamped her fingers on my big toe and pinched it lightly. "What if we—"

The phone rang as the breakfast tray started moving skyward. It was Joseph Vallin. "Mr. Polo, I'm sorry about last night."

"What happened last night?" I asked, watching Carla spring to her feet and wander over to my closet.

"I wasn't able to make our meeting. I hope you didn't waste too much of your time. I know I should have called, but it was just one of those things. I apologize."

"Apology accepted," I responded graciously. Since I hadn't shown up either, there was no sense making an issue of it. "What kept you away? Did you find the *paitza*?"

"No. Although I may have a lead. Why don't you come to my place for lunch?"

"Your office?"

Carla was sliding her hands over my suits and sports coats. She slipped a terry-cloth robe that Jane had given me last Christmas from its hanger and inspected the label.

"No," Vallin said. "I'm at home today. In Nicasio. Near the reservoir. Fourteen twelve Halleck Creek Road. I know it's a long drive, but I'm sure I can make it worth your while. Say noon? We can lunch here."

"I think I can make that."

"Good. Halleck Creek is off Nicasio Valley Road. Turn right and go for a mile and a half, then take another right onto a dirt road. It's the only one for miles, so I'm sure you'll spot it. Did you see the morning newspaper?"

"Not yet."

"There's a story about a man who was found dead in his car at Fort Mason. A private investigator named Thomas Dashuk. Did you know him?"

"Should I know him?"

"It's curious. Him being killed in Fort Mason and you suggesting we meet there. I'll see you at noon."

Vallin rang off. Carla draped the robe over her arm and came back to the bed.

"It has to be this morning? Right away?" I said into the droning receiver.

Carla's lips pouted as I made a helpless gesture with my free hand.

"Okay, I'll be there," I promised, then settled the phone back on its cradle.

"Business," I explained. "I have to go out right away. Maybe later I can show you around town."

She laid the robe gently at the foot of the bed, put her fingers to those gorgeous lips, and blew me a kiss. "Enjoy your breakfast."

I did just that, but it took a good five minutes for the breakfast tray to settle back down on its legs.

I showered, shaved, and dressed: blue blazer, gray slacks, blue cotton sport shirt. Vallin didn't rate a tie. What he did rate was a gun, so I clipped the Beretta's holster on my belt, added a pocketknife, then called Alexander Rostov and told him about my luncheon date with Joseph Vallin.

"Why does he want to talk to you?" He hacked into the receiver.

"He's probably fishing. But so am I, Alexander."

"Be careful," Rostov warned. "He's a snake, Nick. A real snake. What about Anna? Did you see Anna?"

"Yes. We had dinner together. I played dumb, but I followed her to her home. She's living in an apartment building at Twenty-one fifteen Clay Street. I'm not sure which apartment, but number seventeen is the only one without a name. That could be hers."

"She doesn't know who you are? Or your interest in the *paitza*?"

"No. But this is one of the buildings that the dead private investigator took pictures of, Alexander. He knew where Anna lives. What do you want me to do about her?"

"Nothing. I'll talk to her. Go and see Vallin. And be careful."

"You, too, old friend. Anna won't be very happy to see you pop up at her front door."

"She's Russian," he said, as if this explained everything.

I had one stop to make before visiting Joseph Vallin, and I didn't want to depend on Patel giving me a key or on bribing little Maya. I rummaged through my kitchen drawers and picked up one of the world's best burglar tools—at least an Italian burglar's tool—a spatula. I put the spatula into a Ziplock bag, dousing the blade liberally with olive oil before sealing the bag. Then it was off to Anna's safe house on Cole Street. There had to be some type of tripping device in the apartment. Dashuk seemed to have had access to all sorts of Uncle Sam's latest exotic spy gadgets, so even if it was still there, I might not find it.

Still, it was puzzling. Dashuk had somehow known that I had entered the apartment, and that Anna went in a while later. He could have put a bug in the phone or answering machine and then he would have had access to all of the telephone calls.

But a telephone bug was a pain, even when set up with a voice-activated tape recorder. Someone had to sit around and monitor the damn thing. A simple trip alarm of some type, one that went off as soon as the door was opened, would have been better. Dashuk's office and apartment were at least two miles from Anna's place. That would have been putting a strain on even the best electronic motion traps, and if he had been at his apartment or office, anyone entering the apartment would probably have been gone by the time he got there.

A pile of bicycles was blocking the front entrance to the building again. The door to the Mercury Messenger Service was open halfway, and I could make out the hands and arms of the man I'd seen behind the desk on my first visit.

Anna's door was still locked. Someone had been there since my last trip, though. There were fresh gouge marks around the frame, both above and below the lock. I worked the blade of the pocketknife into the gouge marks above the lock, unwrapped the spatula, slipped the slick edge into the crack, then kept the pressure on with the knife while forcing the spatula down, disengaging the lock from the faceplate.

The door swung open. I knelt down and examined the door frame. There it was for all to see—if you got down on your knees and looked closely. A thumbnail-sized anodized metal contact plate on one side of the jamb, a smaller, dime-shaped nickel-cadmium battery set in under the lock's faceplate. A *honey tap* was the generic term. Every time the door was opened, the contact was broken and a signal was sent—somewhere—alerting someone that Anna was home or having visitors.

My neck began tingling the way it always did when I took it into places it didn't want to go. I surveyed the room before making a move, half-expecting to find something unpleasant, like maybe Anna, or her remains, waiting for me. She wasn't there. Neither was the telephone or the answering machine.

The bedsheets and blanket were jumbled on the floor. The mattress had been cut into shreds, clumps of packing oozing out of the wounds like biscuit dough rising over a cookie mold.

The kitchen cupboard doors and drawers were open. There was an overturned aluminum ice tray in the sink. I touched the rust-colored porcelain. It was dry. The ice tray was room temperature.

The vodka bottle and the two shot glasses were still nestled in the freezer compartment. I checked the bottle. Someone had been partaking. The level was well below the label now.

The top of the toilet tank was lying on the bathroom floor. That hollow, globe-shaped metal gadget that rides up and down with the water flow was broken in half and lay on the bottom of the empty tank—just like the one in Dashuk's apartment.

I picked the two pieces up, fitting them together. It would be a great place to hide something, I conceded. Something the size of a coin. Or the *paitza,* maybe.

I heard footsteps in the hallway. I dropped the two metal pieces to the floor, my hand groping for the Beretta. By the time I got to the stairway, the footsteps were two flights down. I paused at the rail, listening for the sound of the front door opening and closing.

It never happened. I went back to Anna's apartment, dug the honey trap from the door with my knife, then went downstairs.

Leo, the manager of the Mercury Messenger Service, was ensconced behind his desk, a phone tucked under his chin.

He gave me a defiant look, then swiveled his chair around so that his back was to me.

I shoved my thumb on the phone's disconnect button, and he swiveled back.

"What the hell do you think you're doing?" he said, throwing the receiver at my hand.

For a man who worked behind a desk, he had a weather-creased face. Broken blood vessels spiderwebbed his cheeks. His nose was a little out of true. His shirtsleeves were rolled up to his elbows. His forearms were thick with the same curly black hair that crowned his head.

He was breathing heavily through his nose.

"You didn't have to run away, Leo. I won't bite you."

"Listen, buster, I don't know what the—"

"How much was Dashuk paying you?" I began flipping through the folders and papers on his desk. The walls behind the desk were lined with bookcases that were stuffed with old telephone directories.

Leo stuck that hatchet chin of his out at me as if it were a weapon. "You better get your ass out of here, buster, because I'm going to kick the living shit out of you if you don't."

The opposite wall, which was hidden from the hallway, held two poster-sized maps, both of Vietnam, with the insignias of the American ground combat units that had served there during the war. A Lucite-encased certificate was centered between the maps. The engraved document proclaimed that Sgt. Leonard S. Dupree had been a member of the United States Army Airborne Division, 5th Special Forces "A" Team, Republic of Vietnam, from 1970 to 1972.

"Is that how Dashuk enlisted you? The old army spirit?"

Leo suggested I perform an unnatural act upon myself. In fact, his exact description would have made it an unnatural act even for a double-jointed circus acrobat.

I stabbed at the map with my index finger. "Not an easy spot to forget, is it?"

He stared hard at me, like a dog getting ready to lunge. "You were there?"

"Yep. For sixteen months."

"What outfit?

"Eighty-second Division."

"What'd you do?"

"Wet my pants morning, noon, and night."

Leo climbed laboriously to his feet and smiled ruefully. "Yeah. We all did that."

"He's dead, Leo. Tom Dashuk's dead. You know that, don't you?"

He opened his mouth, no doubt ready to give me some more

explicit sexual advice, but then the wind seemed to go out of him. He flopped back into his chair. "No. I didn't know that. You're not kidding me?"

"No." I gave him one of my cards, a real business card this time.

"Another private eye, huh?" He flipped the card in the wastebasket. "What's all the fuss about, anyway?"

"You tell me your deal with Dashuk and I'll tell you about the fuss."

Leo made it short and sweet. Dashuk had approached him. Seeing the Vietnam memorabilia on Leo's wall must have given Dashuk the hook he needed. He made army talk, then gave Leo a cigarette pack–sized battery-operated receiver. Every time the door to Anna's apartment opened up, it would buzz, and then Leo was to call Dashuk.

"It only happened that one day. Right after you showed up. I called Dashuk as soon as you stuck your nose in here asking about unit six upstairs. Then the good-looking woman came by. I watched her go up the stairs."

"Just that one day?"

"Yeah. It wasn't worth all the effort. I was going to get a hundred bucks a call. I never did get my money."

"What about at night?" I asked him. "When you went home."

"Dashuk bunked here. In the office. Twenty-five bucks a night." He jutted his jaw to the floor. "A sleeping bag, right there. I think sometimes he slept in one of the empty units upstairs." Leo shook his head sadly. "I never got that money, either." He leaned back in his chair, folding his arm behind his head.

I could see a tattoo—a dagger dripping blood—on the milk white skin on the underside of his forearm.

"Did you ever see Dashuk with anybody?"

"No, I . . . well, yeah. He went by one day with a guy. I really didn't get a look at him."

"You know he was a man, so you must have seen something."

"I saw Dashuk. He had somebody with him. They went up the stairs. All I saw was a suit or a coat."

"Age? Color of hair? Height?"

Dupree tugged at an earlobe. "I don't know. I was here at the desk. Dashuk stuck his head in the door to let me know he was going upstairs. I barely saw the other guy. How'd Dashuk get it?"

I ran my thumb under my neck. "A knife. Ear to ear. By someone who was strong. Someone who knew what he was doing."

Leo Dupree's gaze turned toward his trophy wall. "Where at?"

"Fort Mason. Quite a coincidence, don't you think?"

Dupree never answered my question. He just kept staring at that wall.

CHAPTER 19

If you had to commute to and from the city, there were worse journeys than the Marin County one.

The sky was a bright blue, with just a few gauzelike clouds hanging over the East Bay.

The bay waters gleamed like dark jade. Paper-hat sailboats bobbed in the wake of block-long tankers and freighters.

A seal black United States Navy submarine glided under the Golden Gate Bridge. I mentally pictured the captain on deck, pulling rank so he'd be the last one on board to take a final look at the San Francisco skyline before ordering his crew to "dive, dive, dive."

Traffic on the bridge was its usual bumper-to-bumper mess. The pedestrian lane was just as crowded: walkers, joggers, bicyclists, women pushing baby carriages, elderly couples holding hands as they cautiously peered over the railing.

The bridge was our number-one tourist attraction. It was also the number-one suicide attraction.

Once, during those long-ago high school summer vacations when I worked on a fishing boat, we were coming back with a full load of crabs and rock fish. The water was glassy smooth, more like a lake than the merging of the Pacific Ocean and the Bay. We were just coming out of the shadow of the South Tower when something flashed down alongside us.

The body hit the water with a loud splat, landing not ten feet from the bow of the boat. It was a woman, a redhead. She was floating facedown, dressed in just panties and a bra, her hair splayed out, arms akimbo, her back and shoulders sprinkled with freckles. I learned later that her dress had been torn off by the force of air during her fall—a final indignity.

There were air bubbles around her mouth, and for a moment I thought she was still alive. A few lucky souls had jumped and survived. Not this one. We pulled the body on board. It was my first up-close and personal look at a dead human being. A small article in the newspaper the next day said she was twenty-two years old and had been despondent over a broken marriage.

Once over the bridge, I went through the Waldo Tunnel and down into flatlands and the beginning of a string of bedroom communities.

The tang of exhaust dissipated once I was off the freeway and on Nicasio Valley Road. The surrounding hills were wearing their green spring coats.

I followed Joseph Vallin's directions, turning north on Halleck Creek Road. I set the odometer, and after a mile and a half of two-lane asphalt, I turned onto a bumpy dirt road bordered on both sides by strings of pine and eucalyptus trees. The road ended in front of massive steel-ribbed gate. A white stucco wall pushed out from both sides of the gate, disappearing into thickets of oaks and more of the pine and eucalyptus. It was the gate in Tom Dashuk's photographs.

I got out and stretched. My extended hands stopped at least two feet short of the top of the fence and gate. Three chicken hawks wheeled in lazy circles in the distance.

"Hello, Mr. Polo."

I jerked my neck around. "Hello."

"Get back in your car. I'll open the gates."

Joseph Vallin's voice was coming from a mesh-covered microphone in the brick wall. There had to be a TV monitor somewhere, but I couldn't spot it.

The gates swung inward without so much as a creak. I followed a serpentine gravel lane for a hundred yards or so, past a small lake, complete with a lattice-roofed gazebo and a pier hosting an aluminum rowboat, before the house came into view.

It wasn't the kind of house for people who like to throw

rocks, but it was an exhibitionist's dream come true: all concrete, glass, and steel, with an emphasis on the glass. Fully three-quarters of the place was taken up by large steel-framed windows sans curtains or blinds.

Joseph Vallin was waiting for me under a huge oak that flung its branches all the way across the road and a good twenty feet beyond it.

"Welcome, welcome," he boomed as I climbed out of my car.

Vallin was dressed in white slacks, a white tennis shirt, and white suede shoes. A red-and-navy ascot at his throat provided the only splash of color. Round-lensed mirror-fronted sunglasses concealed his eyes. The lenses shone like silver dollars. His beard was glossy black, looking as if he had just oiled it.

"Come over by the pool. I've prepared lunch," Vallin said. "I hope you didn't have any trouble finding the place."

The outdoor table was an oversized flower box, the center filled with flaming scarlet geraniums. The rough log-hewn chairs at each end of the table were half-covered by climbing English ivy. A man-made waterfall plunged over a stone wall into a rectangular-shaped swimming pool that ran right up and into the house. The decking on each side of the pool was glazed ceramic tile, in a blue that matched the water perfectly.

"Nothing too fancy, I'm afraid," Vallin apologized. "Sandwiches, quiche, and wine or beer. Help yourself," he offered.

Plates of food, napkins, and knives and forks were laid out in tidy alignment. I pulled a bottle of Anchor beer from a hammered-brass ice bucket, twisted off the cap, and took a long sip before following the swimming pool up to the house. The water lapped right up a window. There was a low arch in the center, so that a swimmer wouldn't have to dip his head under the water to get inside the house. All I could see of the interior were white walls and elaborately framed paintings.

"Do you do it much?" I called over my shoulder.

Vallin was stooped over, loading up two plates with food. "Do what?"

"Swim from inside the house to outside. Or vice versa."

"I'm not a swimmer, I'm afraid. Nathan is the athlete. Come. Eat. The quiche is excellent. Crab and lobster."

"Just the beer, thanks."

Vallin set the plate he'd prepared for me down on the table. He plopped into one of the chairs and picked up something I hadn't noticed before: a rifle.

"Relax," he said when he saw my nervousness. "It's a BB gun. The birds. Poor old Tiara is just too lazy to do anything about them, and they do make a terrible clatter in the mornings."

The Siamese peered out from under the table, gave me an indifferent look, then retreated.

Vallin pumped the BB gun's stock several times. The more pumps, the more air in the chamber, the more velocity on the BB. He took aim into a cluster of red-and-white-flowered oleanders on the opposite side of the pool.

"So, have you had any luck in your hunt for the *paitza*, Mr. Polo?"

"I'm still looking."

The rifle belched. There was a cracking sound and a black-crested blue jay exploded out of the oleanders. Vallin jumped to his feet, cocking the rifle, drawing it to his shoulder, and getting off another shot as the bird flapped toward the woods.

The jay cartwheeled to the ground. Vallin grinned widely, stooped down, picked up the cat, and tossed her in the direction of his kill. "I wish I could teach her to fetch like a dog," Vallin said, settling back into his chair.

"I'm still looking, too," Vallin said. "For that *paitza*. You stirred my interest, Mr. Polo. I've made some inquiries. The last anyone can recall actually seeing such an item was in Russia."

"Maybe it's still there. Do you know anybody in Russia?"

"I know people everywhere," he boasted. "I made some inquires about you, too, Mr. Polo. You're a private investigator. You didn't mention that when you came to my shop."

"I locate people. And things."

Vallin sampled one of the one-bite-sized sandwiches. "Ummm. Fresh salmon and dill. You really should try one."

"Maybe you should hire a private investigator," I suggested. "To help you find the *paitza*. Or maybe you already did."

Vallin licked his fingers, then began pumping the air rifle's stock again. "You think that might help? I thought that we might work together. Pool our resources."

"How much are you thinking of putting in the pool?"

"That depends on just how much help you'd be to me."

"If I'm no help to you, you can get rid of me. But not like Tom Dashuk."

"Ah, Mr. Dashuk. The unfortunate gentleman mentioned in the newspaper article."

"That's the one. I'm working with the United States Park Police on the homicide investigation."

"Really? How interesting. I didn't know that the police hired private investigators in matters like this."

I took a swig of the beer. "Where's good old reliable Nathan. Did you give him the day off?"

"He's out playing golf. It's a passion of his. What are your passions, Mr. Polo?"

The Siamese was back, rubbing her side against my leg. "The usual. Right now, it's the *paitza*."

"Your principal is still interested?"

"Very. Can we do business? Or is this just a social chat?"

"Oh, I want to do business. Very much so. I will pay you a fee, a very substantial finder's fee, if you can put me in contact with the present . . . holder of the *paitza*."

"I've already got a client."

Vallin started pumping the BB gun again. "So you say. But is your client willing to pay you a hundred thousand dollars? Let's stop all this game playing. You lead me to that item and the money is yours. No questions asked."

"But I'm a man who asks a lot of questions. Tom Dashuk. I talked to him before he was killed. He knew about the *paitza*. He wanted me to help him find it, too. Look what happened to him."

"He was a man in a dangerous profession. Like you are."

"Dashuk looked and acted like a sap, but he wasn't. He was an electronics expert. Whoever went through his office and his apartment wasn't very professional. They missed a lot. A whole room, in fact. In back of his file cabinet. You have to pull away the Sheetrock, then get down on the floor and crawl in."

"God, but you're melodramatic," he scoffed, bringing the BB gun to his shoulder. He swung it in a lazy arc, until it was pointing at my head. I could feel the BB whiz by my ear.

"Sorry. There was a jay in the bushes behind you. I missed it."

"You missed a lot, Vallin. Dashuk had some film out being developed. I picked up the pictures yesterday. They show this little spread of yours."

He twisted his head to look up at me. I stared back at my twin images in his mirrored glasses.

"You're not very good at bluffing, Mr. Polo. I would advise you to avoid playing poker. If I had hired this Mr. Dashuk, I would have done it in order to have him help me with my quest. Killing him certainly wouldn't put me any closer to the *paitza*. It simply would have been counterproductive. My offer still stands. A hundred thousand dollars. Surely that's more than your principal is prepared to pay." He dropped the rifle to the ground and pulled a roll of bills from his pants pocket.

"A thousand dollars. Consider it a retainer. Give me the name of your principal and I'll triple it. Right here. Right now."

I slipped the packet of photographs from my coat, thumbed through them, and handed Vallin the set showing his front gate.

He pushed the glasses up onto his bald dome and stroked his beard as he examined the photos, then said, "Anyone could have taken these. You included."

"Dashuk took them," I insisted.

Now it was Vallin's turn. He pulled a single photograph from his back pants pocket and handed it to me. "I want to find this woman."

It was a duplicate of the photo that Dashuk had shown me. Anna Tanya on Post Street, just below Vallin's office.

"It's not much good, is it? You can't really see her face. Who took it? Felder?"

"No. I did. Unfortunately, Nathan was out on an errand at the time. I thought you might have come across this woman in your . . . pursuit of the *paitza*."

"What makes you think she knows where it is?"

Vallin's eyes hardened in anger. He dropped the glasses back on his nose.

A voice called from behind me. "Hello, everyone. How's lunch?"

I turned, to see Nathan Felder. He was dressed in a suit and tie.

"How was the golf game?" I asked him.

"Not bad." He helped himself to a slice of the quiche, gulping it down and licking the crust crumbs from his fingers.

"Mr. Polo is being difficult," Vallin explained to his hired hand.

Felder slipped off his coat, loosened his tie, and rolled up his shirtsleeves. "Really? Why ever for? I thought we were all after the same thing."

Vallin sighed theatrically. "Mr. Polo has the strange idea that we are responsible for his fellow private investigator's death, Nathan. I'm afraid he's under the impression we actually killed the poor man."

"Under the impression," I agreed. "But not sure. I know you hired him."

Felder picked up a handful of the finger sandwiches. "And just what makes you think we hired this man?"

"He told me you did. He told me he traced a telephone number for you. He also told me that you didn't trust him. Maybe that's why he bugged your office."

Vallin and Felder stared at each other for several seconds. Vallin broke the silence. "Even if you are right and we did hire this man, there's no crime in that, Mr. Polo. Did he tell you that he . . . bugged my office?"

"He hinted at it. Then when you served me that cup of tea, I spotted the bug."

"He's lying," Felder snarled. "He never—"

"Never had time to plant a bug? I told you Dashuk was no sap. Uncle Sam taught him all kinds of electronic tricks. That's how he learned about the *paitza,* and the coin."

"I still don't believe him," Felder protested.

Vallin did. He went to his pants pocket again. "A thousand dollars if you can tell me just where this supposed bug is, Mr. Polo."

Felder acted as if it was his money. "Joseph. If what he says is true, I can find the damn thing."

Vallin ignored him. "A thousand dollars, plus another two thousand if you can identify the woman in the photograph."

I stooped down and picked up the BB gun. "Her name is Tanya. She had an apartment on Cole Street. I don't think she uses it anymore."

"Don't you have anything else on her? A last name? A new address?"

"That's all I've found out so far."

Vallin shoved the money back in his pants. "It seems I was wrong about you, Mr. Polo. I don't think we can work together."

"I have a hunch you killed Dashuk—you and your athletic friend Nathan, who plays golf in a business suit. After you killed him, you raided his office, but it didn't do you any good, did it? You still don't have Tanya."

Vallin grunted an obscenity, then added, "You are a major disappointment. Get him out of here, Nathan. Now!"

Felder dropped the sandwiches. His hands were at his sides, cupped, as if to scoop water. Or throw a karate punch.

"Do me a favor, Polo, and try to put up a fight," he taunted.

"You made a mistake, Nathan. You were seen on Cole Street. The guy on the ground floor spotted you and Dashuk going up to check out Tanya's flat."

The two of them locked eyes again. Vallin semaphored some kind of a signal with a head nod and Felder went into a crouch and came after me.

I cocked the rifle once, pointed the barrel at Felder's groin, and pulled the trigger.

Felder swore, bending over at the waist, his hands grasping at his crotch. The cat woke up and streaked toward the house.

While Felder was still stooped over, I put my foot on his butt and pushed hard. He wobbled unsteadily for a few feet, then went headfirst into the pool.

Joseph Vallin clucked his tongue against the roof of his mouth.

"That wasn't very smart. I imagine that hurt poor Nathan. He's the type who has to get even."

I swung the rifle over my head and heaved it toward the house. The sound of breaking glass made Vallin wince.

"Me, too," I said, then hurried to the car.

CHAPTER 20

Vallin and Felder's game playing had me confused. Denying that they had hired Dashuk. They might have given Dashuk cash, not a check. They might have figured that once they cleared out his office, there'd be no connection to them. And if it hadn't been for Dashuk's toll calls to Vallin's house, they might have gotten away with it. Inspector Tehaney wouldn't have waited for a subpoena for those phone records. He'd already be on top of Vallin. But not Rickard and Colby—at least not yet.

If Vallin and Felder were the ones who had killed Dashuk and burgled his office, what had they found? Obviously not enough to lead them to Anna, or Flaxen Hair. Or the *paitza*.

And Felder. Playing golf in his Brooks Brother's best.

The car phone buzzed me back to the present. Only a handful of people knew the number for my cell phone, the number-one finger on that hand belonging to Jane Tobin.

I snatched it up eagerly.

"Have you found that whore yet?" Col. Jack Colby demanded in a cold, officious tone.

I didn't want to give him the satisfaction of asking how he'd gotten the unlisted number.

"I'm working on it, Colonel. Anything new on your end?"

"Just a fresh pair of shorts. I reviewed all of Tommy's tapes. It's the same whore every time. She could be the key here, Polo. Get her for me."

"I'll do my best. Did you check Tom Dashuk's toll calls with the phone company, Colonel?"

"Sure, sure," he said hurriedly. Too hurriedly. "Rickard's working on that. Get that whore. Call me later today and report your findings."

Since I had the phone in hand, I touch-toned the number for my answering machine. I was very popular all of a sudden.

The first call was from Svetlana at WLFR, politely asking me to call her as soon as possible.

A call from Alexander Rostov, who sounded bright and cheerful, despite the ever-present wheezing sounds. "Anna came to see me, Nick! She wants to make a deal. Call me right away."

Inspector Bob Tehaney's gruff voice came on next: "Colby is forty-four years of age. Born in Bayonne, New Jersey, on April fourteenth. He's been in the same job for twenty-two years. He's been at his present rank for six years. Nothing naughty on his record, Polo, so let him handle the investigation."

Six years in his present rank. Colby's burred head had hit the brass ceiling. The next step up was a brigadier general. The army wasn't handing out many of those stars nowadays. Colby was stuck in place. He didn't seem like the type who would adapt to civilian life easily.

There was another message from Svetlana, her tone a little less polite this time. "Call me right away, please. It's urgent."

A call from Detective Rickard, advising me that he was going to have to insist that I provide a written statement relating to my personal contacts with Thomas Dashuk.

I phoned Alexander while traffic ground to a slow crawl as I approached the bridge.

He was so happy, he was giggling.

"You got my message?"

"Yep."

"This morning, Anna just walked into my shop. She's still interested in selling the *paitza* and the coin! I convinced her that I was the one to handle the deal. I'm sure of it."

"Then she definitely has the *paitza.*"

"She didn't have it or the coin with her," he said clarified. "But she says she will soon have them both. Isn't it wonderful?"

"I'm not so sure, Alexander. Remember, someone's been murdered. And Anna is involved in a phony love-match operation. Keep in mind that she's not the most trustworthy person in the world. Did she give you a specific time or date as to when she'd have the merchandise?"

"Possibly by tonight." He went into one of his coughing spasms, then said in a strained voice, "I know I told you that I would pay you twenty-five thousand dollars for getting me to the *paitza,* Nick, but I—"

"Joseph Vallin just offered me a hundred thousand bucks if I could drop it in his lap."

"A hundred thousand!"

"Yes, and three thousand in cash if I could identify a lady in a photograph—your Anna—and tell him the name of my client."

"You didn't tell him," Rostov said, his voice sounding as if his tongue were stuck to the roof of his mouth.

"No, Alexander, I didn't. But Vallin is determined to get the *paitza.* Be careful."

"I will," he assured me. "And your fee, the one we agreed on. The twenty-five thousand. It's still yours, Nick. You know that."

I knew that if I hadn't mentioned Vallin's offer of a hundred grand, I would have been lucky to end up with another Shirley Temple pitcher or Errol Flynn's cuff links. "What do you want me to do now?" I asked.

"Nothing," he said hurriedly. "I hope to hear from Anna this afternoon. Don't do anything until I hear from her, Nick. I don't want to frighten her away."

I didn't think there was much in this world that could frighten Anna, but Alexander was the client. "Don't meet with her unless I'm with you," I advised him.

"But she will recognize you," he protested. "She will—"

"I won't let her see me," I said soothingly. "Do you have enough money to cover what she wants?"

"Yes, yes. The money isn't a problem. But Joseph Vallin may be. I don't want to lose this to him, Nick."

"My meeting with Vallin took place at his house over in Marin County. His right-hand man came in late, Alexander. He was out somewhere, digging around." I described Nathan Felder. "Look out for him."

"How could he know of me? You didn't—"

"No. Vallin didn't get your name from me. But he knows the business, Alexander. He knows Anna is shopping the *paitza* around. He knows the competition. That means he knows you're a possibility."

"All right, all right," he agreed hastily. "I'll be careful. But don't do anything until I call you, Nick. Please."

I couldn't remember ever having had a client who used the word *please*.

Colonel Colby had probably never uttered the word in his entire adult life. Still, he, or the United States Army, was a client. While I waited in line to pay the three-dollar bridge toll, I thought about my next move. Lily of Lickie's seemed the logical choice.

I reluctantly handed the toll taker three one-dollar bills. I mean, it's a great bridge, but three bucks? If some of that money went into a suicide barrier, maybe it wouldn't rankle so much.

I was willing to bet that there had never been a redwood tree within fifty miles of Redwood Street. The 700 block was a narrow dead-end alley crowded with wood-framed buildings that appeared to lean on one another for support. Not a tree of any kind in sight. Rusting old junkyard-reject cars and trucks lined both sides of the street, most of them parked halfway on the sidewalk.

Number 742 was the basement unit of a ramshackle three-story building that had been remodeled so many times, it was impossible to image what its original construction had been. The entrance to Lily's place was painted, appropriately, a bright red.

The door knocker was a tarnished brass lion's head. I rapped out an SOS.

The door swung open immediately, as if she'd been expecting someone. Lily had forsaken the twin ponytails. Her hair fanned straight down to her shoulders. She was wearing a chain-metal bustier and shiny chili pepper red vinyl pants with a zipper that ran all the way down until it disappeared between her legs. A gold snake bracelet was curled around her right forearm. Her lipstick was so thick, it looked in danger of sliding off.

"Hi, honey, sorry—"

"Don't you remember me, Lily?"

"Sure I do, honey, but I've got someone coming and—"

"The other night. In front of Lickie's. You tried to lure me inside. A girl in your profession should be better at spotting cops. Bad timing on your part. I had just ID'd Tom Dashuk's body. He was murdered in his van, at Fort Mason."

Her lips peeled back from her teeth and she yelled, "Shit," then tried to slam the door shut.

I bumped my way into the apartment, kicking the door closed with my heel.

She put her hands on her hips and yelled, "Get out of my house."

"Lily, if this is a house, there's a five-letter word that goes in front of it."

She threw her hands up in the air, pivoted around sharply, and started shouting in Chinese.

I watched her move away with great interest. The pants zipper, which had disappeared between her legs in front, now reappeared and went all the way up to the waistband in back. The damn pants zipped in half.

I was afraid she'd try and run out the back, so I followed her down a dimly lighted hallway and into a jasmine-scented room. The rug was a beige woolen shag, the pile so long that it looked like spaghetti. A white bed with a cloudlike canopy dominated the room. A pyramid of mahogany boxes with highly polished brass locks and hinges climbed up one wall. Gridded shoji doors screened off three-quarters of an archway leading to a small kitchen area.

The doorbell rang.

Lily flopped onto the bed. There was a black leather purse on the nightstand. She clutched it to her breasts. "Come on," she pleaded. "Give me a break. I'm keeping a friend waiting."

I made a gimme gesture with my fingers. "Let's see the purse."

She took a deep breath, then bundled up the purse and threw it at me in disgust.

I caught it in both hands. It must have weighed fifteen pounds. I undid the snaps. The first thing that caught my eye was the money: stacks of bills, neatly bundled and held together by rubber bands.

I riffled the edges of one pack, a mixture of fifty- and twenty-dollar bills.

Her john was now banging on the front door.

Lily got to her feet. "Let me tell him I'll be a little late."

"He'll figure it out, 'cause you're going to be real late." I dumped the contents of the purse on the bed. There were six bundles of bills—each and inch or so thick—a coin purse, a makeup bag, a hairbrush, a key ring, a pack of smokes, a disposable lighter, and a cylinder of papers ringed by a rubber band.

Lily sat there fuming as I rolled the band off the papers, four sheets of plain white bond. They held a list of names arranged in alphabetical order, starting with a James P. Andow. After Andow's name came an address, a telephone number, his driver's license number, then a license plate number, and a notation: "Wife, Jane. Owns house since August 1968."

The next in line was William Cleek. The same type information was neatly recorded after his name.

I skimmed through the rest, turning to the fourth page and checking the last entry: Alvin Westberg.

There were penciled notations alongside almost two-thirds of the names—an *X* and a dollar amount that ranged from $1,000 to $2,500.

"What happened to the ones with no *X* alongside their names?" I asked Lily. "You and Dashuk didn't get around to them? Or were they smart enough to tell you to buzz off?"

She went to work, leaning back, her hands behind her, rolling her shoulders, causing her silicone breasts to jut out, her nipples poking through the weave in the bustier.

"Listen," she said in a husky B-movie voice. "Let's talk about this. There's a lot of money there. What say we split it. Right down the middle. And honey, I'll give you the ride of your life." She sat up, her hands going to her pants now, sliding the zipper up and down. "I'll do things to you that no one has ever done before. I'll—"

"Forget it, kid."

Her hand moved faster, the zipper making raspy noises.

"Why not? Who's to know?"

"I would."

The smile slowly slipped from her face. "You're not a fag, are you, Officer?"

"Zip up and tell me about Tom Dashuk. Did you kill him?"

She jumped to her feet. "Me? Are you crazy? You're not going to hit me with that. I didn't know he was dead until I read it in the newspaper."

"Oh, no?" I began shoveling everything except the money and the client list back into her purse. "This sucker list was missing from Dashuk's office. So were his files. Your fingerprints are all over his place."

She involuntarily glanced at her hands, then folded them under her arms. "I knew him. He was an all right guy. But I didn't kill him." Her face melted; tears formed at the corners of her eyes. "Honest. I didn't. Please. Give me a break. Please."

"That night, after we found Dashuk's body. Did you see anyone go in or out of his office before I got there?"

"No," she answered promptly. "I told you, I didn't know he was dead until I read it in the paper, Officer."

"If you're lying, you're going to be in deep trouble, Lily."

"No. Swear to God. I didn't see anyone. I was busy that night. Come on, Officer. Give me a break."

I tossed the purse to her. "Have you had lunch?"

CHAPTER 21

Isn't it strange how things run in streaks? You can go for the longest time without hearing a word or phrase and then all of a sudden it pops up all over the place.

Alexander Rostov asked me *please* not to screw up his deal from Anna. Svetlana asked me to *please* call her right away. And then Lily Wong begged me *please* not to throw her in jail.

I couldn't remember ever having been questioned as to whether or not I was of the homosexual persuasion. Then that came up twice: first from luscious Carla Borelli, next from Lily Wong. And all because I wouldn't drop my drawers when asked. Maybe I was getting old. There was a time when I'd have willingly done so without being asked.

Lily got domestic, brewing up a pot of coffee and making a grilled cheese sandwich, all the while telling me about her partnership in crime with Thomas Dashuk.

Of course, her version made Dashuk the villain. She had been doing nothing worse than "choking the sheriff" at Lickie's before meeting The Thinner Man.

"Choking the sheriff" was a new one on me. When I asked for an explanation, she pumped one hand up and down rapidly. "Whacking them off."

"How did you hook up with Dashuk?"

She refilled my coffee cup, then sat down in the chair across from me. "In front of the shop. I was having a smoke. You can't smoke in there."

Of course not. Oral sex, straight sex, half-and-half sex, sheriff choking, but heaven forbid—no smoking.

"We got to talking, you know, kidding around. He showed me his office."

"And you suggested that the two of you go into business together?"

"No. It was Dash's idea."

"Dash?"

"Yeah, he liked me to call him Dash. I think there was some writer by that name who was a private eye, and he liked the connection, I guess."

"Dashiell Hammett. He created The Thin Man," I informed her, mad at myself for not picking up the connection before. Dashuk—Dashiell. The Thin Man to The Thinner Man.

"Oh," she said, totally unimpressed. She nudged an unfiltered cigarette from its pack, tapped one end against the table, then fired it with her lighter.

"I saw Dash a couple of times before he hit on me with the video idea. Dash was a watcher." She grazed her tongue over her lips to pick up a strand of tobacco. "He liked to watch. Even when I was doing him, he'd have a video on the TV of me doing a guy at Lickie's."

She closed her eyes and smiled. "He sure loved to watch."

"Was he filming the action before you two decided to go into the movie business?"

"No. At least I don't think so. I let him into Lickie's one night when Kevin, the manager, was out having dinner. It was slow. I was the only girl working. He had a small drill." She held her hands a few inches apart. "It ran on batteries. He put holes in two of the A rooms."

"A rooms?"

She tilted her head back and watched the cigarette smoke drift up toward the ceiling. "Yeah. Automatics. When you know the customer is going to want some real action, you take them in one of those rooms. They're bigger; the walls between the cubicles are insulated, so you don't have to worry about making a little noise."

"How do you know the customer is going to want some real action?"

Lily's eyes twinkled knowingly. "I can tell within thirty seconds just by looking at them," she boasted.

"Then what?"

"Now what?" she countered. "I'm doing a lot of talking; all you're doing is listening and eating my food."

I slammed my fist on the table hard enough to rattle the dishes. "I'm not interested in the games that were going on in Lickie's. All I want is Dashuk's killer. You come clean with me and I'm out of your hair."

"What . . . what about the money?"

"Tell me about Dashuk; then we'll talk about the money. Who contacted the sucker? Who picked up the money?"

She inhaled deeply, holding the smoke in her lungs for a long time, then releasing it in a long, narrow stream. "Dash handled all of that. I'd call him when I knew I had an automatic. He'd film us, then follow the guy back to his car. Then somehow Dash would find out where the guy lived." She aimed the tip of her cigarette toward the list lying alongside my coffee cup. "He'd get all that information; then he'd call the guy and tell him to go look in the front seat of his car. Dash was good with cars. He had some tool, a long metal thing. He'd slip it in a car window, jockey it around, and unlock the door. He was good. I watched him do it a couple of times." She snapped her finger rapidly several times. "Quick. Like that. He'd leave the tape and a note on the front seat. Depending on what he found out about the guy, he'd mention a price. I thought he was being too cheap. I mean, he asked some guys for only a thousand bucks, another maybe two thousand. The most was twenty-five hundred."

She stood up, walked to the sink, dropped her cigarette into the disposal, then turned to face me, her arms folded across her chain-linked chest. "I tried to tell him we should ask for more money, but he told me that if you ask for too much, the sucker balks. 'Hit him soft, so they can get the cash without wifey finding out,' he said. So that's what we did. The sucker had one day to get the money. Dash had them drop it off in a paper bag in a gas station men's room. In the wastebasket."

"So the suckers never saw Dashuk?"

"No. He'd tell them he had a duplicate of the tape and that if they tried any tricks, the tape would go right to the wife, or their kids." She hugged herself. "He'd mention the wife's name, or the kid's name. It scared the hell out of them."

"Didn't any of the customers go back to Lickie's and complain?"

"Not a one," she said. "Of course, I never had Dash film any of my regular customers. Just drop-ins," she added with an air of confession.

"How long had this business partnership of yours been going on?"

"Oh, not long. A month. Maybe a little longer. Then he got busy. He said we had to lay off for a while."

"When was this?"

She languidly held up one finger. "A week ago. Something like that."

"Did Dashuk tell you what it was he was working on?"

She wagged her head, her hair swishing around her shoulders like curtains in the wind. "No. He was excited, though. And he was gone all night. I stayed over at his apartment sometimes." She placed her palm on the table as though she was taking an oath. "But I haven't seen Dash in a week. I swear it."

I took a sip of the lukewarm coffee, staring at her over the rim of the cup. "He must have told you something, Lily. Did he tell you about the coin?"

Her eyes widened. "Coin? What coin?"

I stood up, the chair's leg making scratchy sounds on the linoleum. Lily jumped back as if she feared I was going to hit her.

"I'm going to go through this place, and if I find something you haven't told me about, you're going into a cell. Right now."

Her hand went to her face and she nibbled on a nail for a few moments. "I've got some of Dash's tapes. Under the bed. That's all. Honest, that's all." She reached for the cigarettes. Her hand was shaking. "Dash gave me a copy of the client list a week ago. I haven't been in his office since. Really. Give me a break. I've always gotten along with you guys. At Lickie's. On my own. I always—"

"This isn't about turning a few tricks, Lily. It's murder. Do you understand that? Murder."

"I know, I know. I've got to get out of here. Whoever killed Dash might try to kill me, too." She went to work with her eyes. Tears started streaming down her pale gold cheeks. "Please? Can't you help me? I want to get out of here for a while."

There wasn't much I could do to stop her, really. Colonel Colby and Detective Rickard might want to run Lily through the wringer, but I didn't think they'd get much more than I already had.

As a conscientious, upstanding civilian, I could turn her over to the San Francisco cops on the prostitution angle, which would make me about as popular as a rabbi in Baghdad. She'd just deny everything, and if the manager at Lickie's was right about having connections with the district captain, it would all be swept under the rug. There might even be enough room under that rug for me.

"Where are you planning to go?" I asked her.

"I've got some friends in San Jose." She blotted her eyes with the back of her hand. "I need a vacation. I really do."

"All right. Where's the bathroom?"

"Down the hall." Her hand crawled down to the zipper on her pants. "You sure you don't want me to do you?"

"Positive. I'm going to use the facilities. It'll take me a few minutes."

She tilted her head to one side. She wasn't sure. Not yet.

"A long few minutes."

She got the message finally, snatching up her purse and staring lovingly at the stacks of bills.

There wasn't much I could do about the money, either. The

men on the sucker list would most likely deny knowledge of it even if I dropped it in their laps.

The bathroom was a shambles: soiled clothing on the tile floor, the basin cabinet jammed with cosmetics, perfumes, used tissues, and cigarette butts.

I waited until I heard Lily slam the front door before venturing back to the bedroom. The videocassettes were just where she said they'd be—under the bed. Eleven of them.

I gave the room a quick toss before leaving. There was nothing of interest except a stash of marijuana, some strap-on sex aids in one of the mahogany boxes in the bedroom, and another pair of those pants, this one an oily purple-black eggplant color, with the zipper running from stem to stern. I tried to think of what possible advantage there was to such a garment. Even to someone in Lily's chosen profession.

CHAPTER 22

I could see right away that Mrs. Damonte wasn't in a good mood. Knowing her, there could be a variety of reasons: The price of olive oil had gone up a few cents; the price of semolina flour had gone up a few cents; the price of anything had gone up a few cents. Or, worse than that, there had been no wake to go to today. A day without a wake was like a day without sunshine to Mrs. D.

Whatever it was, I was going to find out pronto.

She stood there statue-still, her eyes narrowed to hawklike slits, waiting for me as I started up the steps to my flat.

"Buon giorno," I greeted her, knowing that whatever she was about to lay on me was going to make the rest of the afternoon not so good.

She started with, *"Cos-hano miei nipoye che na va?"* Then she rambled on in rapid Italian, her arms slicing the air as if she were a conductor waving a baton.

I understood about half of her symphony. She wanted to know why was I upset with her nephew. Mrs. D had three nephews that I knew of, but the only one I did any business with was Vincenzo, the one who was an insurance broker. The one who Mrs. D insisted I use, no doubt because she got a percentage of his commission.

Sure enough *di assicurzaioni,* "insurance agent," was one of her high notes.

"I'm not upset with Vincenzo," I assured her.

It took me awhile to calm her down and get the rest of the story. A man—a *naso puntina,* "needle nose," was her unkind description—had come by claiming he was my new insurance agent and wanting to see the flats.

Mrs. D had caught him at my front door. He had tried to con his way inside, but of course Mrs. D was having none of that. He was lucky to have gotten away alive. Other than the needle nose, her description of the invader was that he was in his thirties and had brown hair.

I asked if his forehead was *scottato.*

Indeed it was. Nathan Felder, sunburned forehead, needle nose, and all.

I asked her what time the man had come to the door. She said 9:30. Shortly after I had left. Felder had probably been waiting out on the street and had seen me take off.

I assured Mrs. D that the man was a *ladro,* "a thief," and not an insurance agent. While you might argue that there's not a lot of difference between the two, it was good news to Mrs. D. Her lips twitched for a minisecond, meaning I was off the hook with her—for the moment.

Now I was almost as angry as Mrs. D. Joseph Vallin had fiddled me over to his place just so Felder could try to get into my flat.

There was yet another message from Svetlana the Red waiting for me. "Call me." And no *please* this time. That bounced check of mine was driving her up the wall.

I ran the first few moments on each of the videotapes I'd retrieved from under Lily Wong's bed through the VCR. More of the same head-bobbing sexual aerobics. Lily was bound to encounter some health problems along the way, but she'd never have to worry about a double chin.

The phone rang. I let the recorded message do the answering, fearing that it was Svetlana again. I had my hand on the receiver in case it was Jane Tobin calling.

No such luck. Col. Jack Colby's snarly pipes were commanding me to report my findings as soon as possible.

I picked up the receiver just before he hung up.

"Colonel. I just got in the door. I found Lily Wong."

"Good. Bring her in. I'm at Rickard's office."

"I said I found her; I didn't say I had her tied up in the trunk of my car."

"Did you talk to the whore?"

"Yes, and—"

"And you let her get away?" he admonished.

"I couldn't arrest her, Colonel. I'm not a cop. And neither are you."

Colby's response was something between a laugh and a cough. "I want to see you and I want a written report on everything she told you. Where's she living?"

I gave him Lily's address. "She had some more videos. I just looked at them. They're just like the others. I did pick up something interesting. A list of the men Dashuk videoed with Lily."

"Great. Get it over here right now."

"I can't, I have—"

"Then fax the damn thing, Polo." He recited Rickard's fax number. "I want to see that list pronto. And your report."

"Do you want the bill in triplicate, or just the report?"

"I don't give a damn, Polo. I just want it right away."

I checked my watch. "I won't be able to deliver it to you until six or seven, Colonel."

"Eighteen hundred. Dinnertime. Is there a decent restaurant close to Rickard's office?"

"Good food or just a pizza joint?" I asked, only *pizza* came out more like *paitza*.

"Good chow," Colby responded without missing a beat.

"The Buchanan Grill is just two blocks away, at Buchanan Street and North Point."

"Good. Make the reservations. I'll see you there. And Polo, add an hour to your bill to pay for dinner."

I went through the tedious chore of reattaching the fax machine to my phone line, sent Dashuk's sucker list over to Colby, then cobbled together a report and a bill. I added more than an hour to cover dinner. Colby had authorized up to a thousand dollars. I used all of my creative-writing talents to doodle the bill up to $976.

Col. Jack Colby was wearing a heavily starched tan shirt, tan slacks with a saber-sharp crease, and a saddle brown leather bomber jacket.

He had commandeered two stools at the far end of the bar. "This isn't a bad place," he said, as if he was disappointed that I hadn't suggested a dump for our rendezvous.

The Buchanan was one of the city's better sports bars. The ceiling was rimmed with skis and hockey sticks. The walls were covered with football, baseball, and basketball memorabilia.

My favorite was an old black-and-white photograph of the young Joe Lewis and an equally young Joe DiMaggio, sitting at a bar, dressed in street clothes. The great boxer and the immortal baseball star were born the same year, 1914. DiMaggio was a revered local legend. If certain parts of that legend were true, then Lewis undoubtedly was buying the drinks in the photograph. *Tascas stretto,* "tight pockets," was one North Beach description of Mr. DiMaggio's spending habits.

There was a photo of Richard Nixon swinging a golf club, fierce scowl in place. Even in golf togs, Nixon looked as if he was dressed for a congressional hearing.

Colby patted the stool next to him. "Sit down." He pointed to an empty cocktail glass. "You're late. I ordered you a martini."

"I'm glad it didn't go to waste, Colonel."

He drained the remains of his drink, then gestured with his glass to the bartender. "Do it again. For both of us. Stoli Crystal up, with a twist."

He watched the bartender with rapt attention while the drink was being made, nodding his satisfaction when the ice in the cocktail shaker made popping sounds as the Russian vodka dribbled over it.

Colby sipped his drink carefully. "Good booze," he said approvingly.

Since this was his third drink, I thought he should have already figured that out by now.

"I was in Russia for almost two solid years. I got to the point where I could handle vodka like some people drink coffee. There's a private label that only the big muck-a-mucks in the Kremlin can get there hands on. It puts this stuff to shame. Let's sit down and eat."

We were escorted to a corner table. After the waiter, a smooth-faced young man, informed us his name was Denny and explained the specials on the menu, I handed Colby my two-page report.

He read, sipped, and hummed to himself for a couple of minutes, then looked at the bill and snorted. "Nine hundred and seventy-six bucks to find one whore?"

"The lady didn't want to be found, Colonel. I had to use several confidential informants to get her actual name."

Colby grunted and picked up the menu. "I might as well get a decent meal out of this." He lowered the menu to glare at me. "You are planning to pay for dinner, aren't you?"

"The United States Army is," I confirmed.

He buried his head back in the menu, then dropped the menu to his lap. "Where's the whore now?"

"Lily Wong could be anywhere. She knows the heat is on."

"And just how does she know this, Polo?"

"She can read, Colonel. Dashuk's murder made the papers. I'm disappointed in you. I thought you'd keep his murder strictly in-house."

"Some reporter got wind of it, probably from someone at the morgue, and called Rickard," he responded gloomily. "He should have referred the bastard to me." He fished the lemon twist from the martini and popped it into his mouth.

"What's your read on the whore? Did she kill Tommy?"

"Dash. She called him Dash. After Dashiel Hammett."

"Dash. How cute. Did she kill him?"

"No. I don't think so."

"But you're not sure, Polo."

"I'm not sure about anything in this case."

Colby took a swallow of his martini. "I looked that sucker list over. A bunch of losers."

"Did you talk to any of them?"

"Nah. Not yet. I'll let Rickard handle them."

"According to Lily, no one on that list ever saw Dashuk. They never knew who they were dealing with. He'd break into their cars, leave the video, then call them. The money drops took place in a gas station rest room. The customer would drop the money into the waste can and take off."

"Did the whore see anyone going in or out of Tommy's office the day he was murdered?"

"Just me. She was at the door when I got there ahead of you and Rickard."

Colby smiled. The lemon peel was pasted neatly across his upper teeth. "I think she could have done it. She had a reason to."

The waiter returned, and Colby quickly sent him away with an order for another round of drinks. "The whore was in business with Tommy. There's no telling how many old goats they fleeced. They probably had a fight over money. He wasn't giving her enough, so she killed him."

"Soaking wet, Lily Wong would weigh less than a hundred pounds. Whoever sliced Dashuk's neck had to be strong."

"Not necessarily," Colby answered almost dreamily. "I had a girl working for me in Berlin. About the same size as this whore. She was undercover, spiking in with the Red Brigade. She cut up a guy bigger than Dashuk. Quartered him like a pig." He went into the gory details of the man's death while the waiter served our drinks.

"Lily didn't kill Dashuk. She would have taken off right away if she had."

"What kept her around? Love of mankind?" he asked sarcastically.

"I think she was going to try to bilk some of the men they had filmed for a little more money, then take off."

Colby picked up my report. "Yes. That's what it says here."

"Lily told me that Dashuk was a watcher. He watched those videos while they had sex together."

Colby dipped into his drink, then gave me a crafty smile. "Yeah. To be any good at black-bag jobs, you've got to have a kinky streak, Polo. I had a setup on a Frenchy one time, some NATO flunky who was dumping everything that came across his desk to the Russkies. He's in Paris. He's got money to burn. We've got cameras all over his pied-à-terre. First thing he does when he comes back from dinner is look at some soft-core porn on the TV. Then he gets all gussied up, fancy pajamas and a silk bathrobe. He had a date with a whore. One of our whores. A big-knockered French dancer. The dork wanders over to the window while he's waiting. He stares through the curtains. He gets all excited. Starts falling in love with his own body. Our whore comes to the door. He sends her away! Then he goes back to the window. We finally spotted the competition. This is one of those Paris streets that are about an arm's-length wide. A young couple is in the apartment across the street. They're going at it hot and heavy. Frenchy would rather play Peeping Tom than jump on our girl's bones."

He did that act with the lemon twist again. "Polo, I've got a hunch. My hunch tells me that sweet Lily told you a lot more than you put in this report."

"Why would I hold out on you, Colonel?"

"Style. That's why, Polo. Everyone has there own certain style."

"And what's mine?"

"You're a do-gooder. A one-man crusade. One of those guys who thinks he can make a difference. A frustrated Lone Ranger type. Champion of the underdog. All that hokey bullshit. The whore probably cried on your shoulder and you let her go. You say she didn't kill Tommy. But if it wasn't her, then who?"

"Whoever took his keys and cleaned out his office and apartment."

Colby stuffed my report and bill in his jacket. "I've got another hunch, Polo. All this video stuff was just tree dressing. Mickey Mouse stuff. Nothing to do with his murder. There's got to be something else. Something bigger."

"Like what?"

"Like what Tommy wanted your help with, Polo. What was that? You never really told me much about your meetings with him."

"Once he asked me to work with him; the next time he shoved a gun in my back."

Colby went through a pantomime of acting confused. "Yeah. Sure. Let's see. He calls you, out of all the private investigators in town, and asks you pretty please to help him find some mysterious woman. You say no and then he comes after you in a crowded restaurant with a gun. Gee, why is it I just can't swallow that?"

"Speaking of swallowing, I'm getting hungry."

Colby reached angrily for his menu. "Yeah. Let's eat. I might as well get something for my nine-hundred and seventy-six bucks."

CHAPTER 23

◀▶

It was too bad that Anna the Mysterious couldn't have joined Colby and me for dinner. It would have been fun watching them fight over the French bread and the butter.

Whether it was just that Colby wanted to eat a big chunk out of my profit or that he was starving, I wasn't sure, but he went through the menu like Sherman went through Georgia, destroying everything in sight. Crab cakes, salad, soup, "the biggest steak you've got, blood-rare," and a bottle of the most expensive red wine.

I had my share of the wine, a salmon fettuccine, and an after-dinner Amaretto over ice.

Colby amused himself while boring me with war stories of his career in military intelligence, including one highly improbable episode of inserting a transmission bug in the hump of a camel known to be a favorite of Muammar Qaddafi. He passed up dessert and ordered another vodka. He swirled the clear liquid in his glass, then let out a loud burp.

"So what now, Polo? Are you going to try to screw good old Uncle Sam out of another thousand dollars before you tell me something useful?"

"I found Lily Wong for you, Colonel."

"Sure," he said disgustedly. "Found her and lost her. Or shooed her away. By the time she shows herself again, it'll be too late."

"Too late for what?"

"For helping me find Dashuk's killer. You know the drill, Polo. Or at least you should. If you don't turn up anything in the first forty-eight hours of an investigation, the odds are you're never going to solve it."

"That's why I think you and Rickard should call in the local police."

"Why? Would you cooperate with *them*? Because you're holding out on me. I know that. What I don't know is why."

"It's a two-way street, Colonel. Why did you leave the honey trap on the door of the Cole Street apartment?"

He tilted his head to one side and squinted at me. "You lost me there, Corporal."

"I don't think so. Dashuk set up a honey trap in unit six at Three-oh-four Cole Street. A woman used the place as what I'm sure you'd call a safe house." I dug out the photo of Anna the Mysterious leaning against a cypress tree in Golden Gate Park. "This woman."

Colby casually studied the photograph, then slipped it into his pocket. "I figured I paid for this. Pretty lady. What's her name?"

"Didn't Dashuk tell you?"

"No. Why the hell would he?"

I was getting tired of Colby's act. "Because he needed your help. He needed your help to check me out. Needed your help to walk away from the army with that storeroom supply of electronic wonders and the exotic gun I took away from him, Colonel. Whatever happened to the laser transmitter? I didn't see it at Rickard's office. Was it in Dashuk's truck, or did he give it back to you once he'd gotten what he needed?"

Colby's face registered confusion. "You're not making any sense, Polo."

"Dashuk might have been an expert with a black bag, but he was in over his head with the coin and the *paitza*."

"The what?"

"Don't act dumb, Colby. Dashuk told me that he was getting information from a source in MI. The source told him all about the goodies that were being smuggled out of Russia."

"You're hallucinating. If you can't handle your liquor, then you shouldn't drink."

"You made another mistake, Colby. At Dashuk's apartment—in the bathroom. Ripping apart the plumbing. You did the same thing at the Cole Street safe house."

He brought the vodka up to his nose and inhaled sharply, as if it were a respirator to clean his sinuses. His eyes were watering, his speech starting to slide into a slur now and then. "I found a cache of secret documents in a toilet tank in Budapest once." He made a gesture with his hand, as if pushing the memory away. "You were a waste of time, and money. I do believe I'm going to suggest that your bill not be paid."

"You are clever, I'll give you that. Your set of master keys came in handy for slipping the lock on Cole Street. The gouges in the wood and leaving the honey trap behind were nice touches."

"I don't have a clue as to what you're talking about, Polo."

"Leo Dupree, the Vietnam vet on the first floor at Cole Street. Did Dashuk manage to con Dupree by himself, or did he call you in to wave the flag?"

"You're not making any sense, Polo."

"That's too bad, Colonel. From what Dashuk told me, he was onto something. Something worth a lot of money. A hell of a lot of money."

"I'm not adverse to a lot of money, Polo." He nursed a pause, then said, "The coin and this other thing, what did you call it?"

"The same thing Dashuk did."

We stared at each other for a long moment. Colby was dry-eyed again. It was shop-or-drop time. Either Colby was going to throw my report and bill in my face and try dragging me over to Detective Rickard—which meant that Dashuk hadn't told him anything—or he was going to try to make nice-nice with me. To make it work, he had to think I was as greedy as he was. I must be a wonderful actor.

Colby rubbed his chin thoughtfully. "Tommy did mention something about a coin awhile back. Some Mongol coin."

"Did he now?"

"Yes. But he didn't go into specifics." He shook his head as if it hurt. "If I knew just what was going on, maybe I could help."

"Help who, Colonel?"

"The living, Polo. Even if I find his killer, it won't do Tommy any good now."

"I'm among the living," I reminded him.

"True. So true. Why don't we stop horseshitting each other around and help each other?"

I leaned forward, my elbows on the table. "Good idea. You first, Colonel."

Colby rotated his head slowly, examining our fellow diners as if they were possible enemy agents. "Dashuk would call me now and then. For help."

"And you certainly helped him, didn't you?"

"I gave Tommy the gun. It was a gift, Polo. I gave a gun to all my boys. And you're right. I did lend him a laser transmitter and scanner." He pinched the bridge of his nose as if a headache was coming on. "I shouldn't have, but I did. He brought the laser back. I don't know what the hell he was using it for. I didn't ask."

"What about all the electronic equipment in his truck and his spy room, Colonel? Did you loan that to him, too?"

"No. I don't know where he got all that gear."

"What else did Dashuk get from you? The DMV information for the men on his sucker list?"

"No. He must have gotten that from another private eye, Polo. Or some crooked cop. He did call me for some advice. He told me that he might be onto something. Artifacts smuggled in from Russia, or Germany."

"Dashuk was sure that's where they were coming from?"

"That's what he said. He wanted to know how the action was over there—what was coming in, from whom, from where, that kind of thing."

"And you told him what?"

"That it's like water over a dam. The customs people can't stop the flow, no matter what it is—weapons, drugs, artwork, you name it."

"But he was specific about the coin?"

"Yeah. That's what he wanted to know about all right. He said it dated back to around A.D. 1200. He knew it was valuable, and he thought that there might be a lot of them."

"So what did you do for Dashuk?"

Colby took a small draft of the vodka and swished it around in his mouth. "I made some inquiries. There was a rumor. Some Asian art stuff had been ripped off from a high-ranking Russian banker. This was several years ago. Among the items were some rare Mongol coins. Genghis Khan time crap."

"Chingis Khan," I corrected him, as Alexander Rostov had done to me. "What were the other items?"

"A tablet—a kind of ID tag. A *paitza.* Solid gold. Supposedly, it belonged to one of the Great Khan's kids."

"Dashuk hadn't heard of this before?"

"If he had, he didn't tell me."

I stirred the melting ice in my drink with a finger. "What does Rickard say about all this?"

"Rickard," he mocked, loudly enough to draw a curious glance from a couple of gray-haired, gray-suited businessmen at the nearest table. "I wouldn't trust him to gas up my Jeep."

"Your sources in Europe, Colonel. What did they say about the *paitza* and the coin. What are they worth?"

"The coin's no big deal, but the *paitza* thing will bring in enough to buy an M sixty tank, if that's what you wanted for some crazy reason. For me, even if I split the profits with you, I'd say I'd end up with half a million dollars."

"You already have a buyer?"

"No, but I'm sure I wouldn't have any difficulty in locating one, should we get lucky. What do you think, Polo? Are we going to get lucky?"

I handed the waiter my credit card.

"What about the woman in the picture, Polo? Who is she? Where is she?"

"Dashuk told me her name was Tanya."

"What else did he say?"

"He said he had a client who wanted her found. Dashuk found her, but I don't think he'd gotten around to telling his client."

"Because he figured she had the coin and the *paitza*?"

"That's the impression he gave me," I confirmed.

"Who's the client?"

"He never told me."

Colby leaned forward and cupped his chin in his hand. "Polo, give me a break. Why did Tommy contact you? Because you've got a pretty face? Because you send Christmas cards to all your friends every year? He called you because he knew you had an interest in Tanya, or the Russian loot." He leaned over the table, lowering his voice. "Tommy was a loner. He liked working alone. I could put him on a job by himself for days at a time. A sleeping bag, a portable john, some tinned food, some crackers, that's all he needed. He wouldn't hit on you unless you had something he wanted. Like more info on this Tanya lady. So what is it, Polo? What have you got?"

"A client."

"The same client? Tommy's client?"

"No."

Colby's eyebrows rose in comprehension. "Yes, yes," he said, taking a deep breath and expelling air as if it were cigarette smoke. "So Tommy found out you and he were after the same thing. He called you to pump you, to find out what you had."

"Something like that could have happened."

"Could have indeed. Tommy was great with gear, but not too swift between the ears. You would have run him all around the flagpole. Let me take a wild guess. He didn't learn diddly from you, but you picked his pockets."

"I never touched his pockets, Colonel. I advised him to come clean with his client."

"Who's the client?" he pressed.

"Mine or Dashuk's?"

"All of the above."

"Mine's none of your business. Dashuk never told me who he was working for."

Colby grimaced. "It's too bad you bailed out of the service, Polo. You'd have gone far. 'Dashuk never told me who he was working for.' Tommy may not have *told* you, but somehow you found out, didn't you? His client is a definite suspect. I want to know who he is."

"How do you know it's a he?" I pointed out.

"He, she, it. I don't care. I want to know who."

"He never told me," I repeated. "Were you able to pull any fingerprints from Dashuk's van?"

"Other than Tommy's, there're a dozen or more that don't ring any bells on the fingerprint computer. Could be anyone's. Garage mechanic, gas station jockey, anyone's. We didn't find yours, if that's what you're worried about, Polo."

That wasn't a worry. If Rickard and Colby had been thorough, Lily Wong's prints should have been there. I told Colby so.

He shrugged the information off lightly. "Maybe the whore wore gloves. Maybe what she had her hands on doesn't take prints," he added with a leer.

CHAPTER 24

Things were coming at me in streaks again. This time, it was clients. Alexander Rostov was willing, rather reluctantly of course, to pay me $25,000 for helping him acquire the *paitza*. Joseph Vallin pushed the marker up to a hundred thousand. And now Col. Jack Colby was willing to split a million dollars with me, which meant Ögödie Khan's neckwear was worth a lot more than that to someone. Quite possibly the someone who murdered Dashuk.

Colby gave me a little officer-to-enlisted-man pep talk as we walked to his car, a silver BMW coupe that was parked in a red zone just fifty feet from the restaurant's entrance.

A strong breeze was flapping a parking ticket tucked under the BMW's windshield wiper.

Colby slipped the ticket free and tossed it up in the air. It rode the wind like a crippled bird for a while before dive-bombing into the gutter.

"You think about it, Polo. Think about it hard." Those were Colby's final words of advice. Then he got behind the wheel. In seconds, the motor growled nastily, and he was at freeway speed before he got to the corner.

Dramatic little bastard.

My car was two blocks away, hugging a fire hydrant, as usual. Ticket-free.

By the time I reached the Richmond district, the wind was really gusting. The streetlights were pale white smudges. Leaves and discarded food wrappers rattled along the sidewalk, skidding by my feet, ending their journey in closed up storefronts.

I could see Alexander Rostov peeking out the window of his store, his nervous fingers scissoring the slats of the venetian blinds.

"You're early," he chided me as he jerked open the door.

"Those were the very first words my mother ever said to me," I informed him, hoping to draw a smile. No sale. I checked my watch. It was 10:22. I had told Alex I'd be there at 10:30. "Have you heard from Anna?"

"No, no." He poked his neck out, surveying the street in both directions before closing the door.

Rostov's face was flushed and he was rising and falling on the balls of his feet. "I don't know if this is such a good idea, Nick. What if she sees you?"

"She won't," I guaranteed him. "Let's take a look at the lay of the land."

The land lay pretty good. There was a back door in Alexander's private office that lead to a bathroom; another door connected to a small back alley, where outside stairs lead up to his residence on the second floor.

The bathroom door had an old-fashioned barrel-bolt lock. I squatted down and peered through the skeleton head–shaped keyhole. It provided a narrow view of Rostov's office. As I straightened up, the realization of what was about to happen made me grin. One of the great private eye clichés of all time. I was about to become a keyhole peeper.

"Does Anna know what room this door leads to?"

"No," Rostov said, going through the ritual of lighting a cigarette.

"Okay, I can watch and listen from here. If she asks, tell her it's a storeroom and you keep it locked. Let's take a look upstairs."

Alexander's living quarters were more cluttered than his shop. I followed his stooped-over figure though a maze of cardboard boxes, life-sized statues of Greco-Roman-figures and mismatched pieces of furniture, all old and musty-smelling.

The windows in the front room windows were covered by

heavy baize curtains as thick as carpet. I unslung the binoculars from around my neck, brought them up to my eyes, and took a slow tour of the street.

"I'll camp out here until they show up," I told Rostov, who was leaning over my shoulder, blowing cigarette smoke onto the opaque window glass.

"Anna won't be here for over an hour," he protested. "Do you want something to drink?"

"Just coffee, Alexander."

He returned twenty-minutes later with a Turkish *ibrik*—a tall, long-handled copper coffeepot that has no cover and tapers toward the top.

The coffee grounds were boiled with sugar—boiled as many as three times before being removed from the fire.

"Are you prepared to give Anna what she wants for the *paitza*?" I asked him.

He poured the syrupy coffee into fragile espresso-size cups.

"I'm not crazy," he assured me. "I have cash, enough cash for the coin. Enough to assure her that I'm serious. I have arranged the financing for the *paitza*. That is not a major concern."

I took a sip of the coffee. It was close to scalding and the strongest brew I had ever tasted. "How much is she asking?"

"A hundred percent arabica beans," he said when he saw my face pucker.

"How much?" I repeated.

"It is not of your concern, Nick."

"Over a million dollars was a price I heard bantered about."

His eyes racheted onto mine. "Where did you hear such a figure?"

I told him about my conversation with Colby. "He was willing to split it with me, Alexander."

"The man is crazy."

"No. A thief, perhaps, maybe even a murderer, but not crazy."

Rostov brought his cup to his lips. His hands were visibly shaking. "You never would have known of the *paitza* if it was not for me."

I gently placed my hand on his bony shoulders. "Relax, Alexander. I have no intention of taking Colby up on his offer. Or Joseph Vallin on his. They're both dishonorable men. I don't believe a thing they say about the money, while you, my friend, have been showering me with priceless articles: a Shirley Temple cocktail shaker and Errol Flynn's cigarette case."

Rostov nodded his head slowly, then refilled my cup. "And you will have your twenty-five-thousand-dollar fee, Nick. You have earned it. As soon as I have the *paitza*. I have sixty thousand dollars in cash. For the coin, Nick. I'll go downstairs and wait for Anna."

"A man has been murdered, Alexander. I have to believe his death had something to do with your treasure hunt. Be careful."

He elbowed his cardigan sweater open and patted the pearl-handled revolver holstered at his hip.

"I will be," he confirmed.

It was ten after twelve when the light-colored sedan cruised by the front of Rostov's shop for the third time. I focused the binoculars on the car. It backed into an open parking spot in front of a Vietnamese restaurant that had shut its doors for the night.

There was a time when I could have told you the make and model of just about any car on the road. That's when they all looked different—fins, fenders, distinctive grilles. Now all I could tell was that it was big, boxy, and American-looking.

Both front doors opened at the same instant. The car's interior lights puddled the darkness. I zoomed in on the occupants. Anna was climbing out from the passenger's side. The driver was Jonathan, Flaxen Hair, from the garden at Golden Gate Park.

Flaxen Hair stood in place, waiting for Anna to come to him. They had a brief discussion; then she linked her arm in his and they started walking toward Rostov's shop.

I swept the binoculars up and down Clement Street, looking for uninvited guests. Several cars cruised by, but they showed no special interest in the handsome couple crossing the street.

I gave them a couple of minutes, then slipped out Rostov's front door, dragging a knee-high statue of a nymph strumming a harp to the jamb to keep the door from closing. Then I hustled down the steps and over to their car.

It was a Buick—a shiny tan color that probably had some exotic name like desert frost. The color of the car was of no interest to me, but the license plate was red, white, and blue and issued by the United States of America. It was a diplomatic plate.

Alexander Rostov had trouble keeping his slippers on the ground after Anna and Flaxen Hair left.

They should have been pretty happy, too, being sixty thousand dollars richer.

"He had it, Nick," Rostov exclaimed excitedly. "Did you see it? Did you see it?"

All I was able to see through the keyhole were Anna's lovely legs, an occasional glimpse of Flaxen Hair's as he wore a path in Rostov's carpet, and the crossing jet streams of Anna's and Rostov's cigarette smoke.

I could hear what they were saying, but since it was all in Russian, it did me no good.

"By 'it,' I guess you mean the *paitza*," I told Rostov.

"Yes, yes." He joined his hands in a prayerlike gesture. "Unbelievable, Nick. Unbelievable."

"Did Jonathan tell you who he was? Or how he came into possession of the *paitza*?"

"No, no." Rostov got yet another cigarette going, coughing harshly at the first inhale. "It doesn't matter where, or how. He's got the *paitza,* and a provenance." He pointed to his rolltop desk. "He gave me a copy of the provenance. It traces the *paitza* from the museum in the Kremlin to Germany and a dealer in Switzerland."

"What about the banker in St. Petersburg? The one whose family was burned to death?" I asked. "The last person that you know of who had possession of the *paitza*?"

Alexander pretended he hadn't heard me. "Perhaps you should have followed them, Nick. Found out where they went."

"I imagine that a man with sixty thousand dollars in cash and an invaluable trinket in his pocket would be pretty careful about the possibility of being followed."

Rostov clicked his tongue against his teeth. "Yes, yes. You are right. I don't want to frighten him."

"Is Jonathan Russian?"

"No. German."

"You're sure?"

"Positive. He speaks Russian fluently, but he has a German accent."

"Did he tell you anything? His name?"

"No. Anna introduced him as a *freundin*—a friend. No names were mentioned."

I told Rostov about the diplomatic license plate on the Buick.

"Ah," Rostov murmured, settling down slowly in his chair, like a man lowering himself into a hot bath. "Yes, that makes sense, doesn't it? He can bring things into the country as a diplomat. The customs people wouldn't check his luggage, right?"

Right, as far as I knew. "When are you going to make the deal for the *paitza*?"

"He will call me. Tomorrow perhaps."

Rostov plucked a small packet from the pocket of his cardigan and passed it to me.

The Mongol coin was encased in a thick plastic holder. It looked as if it might have been minted yesterday.

"History, Nick. You are holding ancient history in your hands."

"Thomas Dashuk's murder isn't ancient history, Alexander," I reminded him. "You paid Jonathan cash for this. How are you going to pay him for the *paitza*?"

"A money transfer—to the numbered account in his bank in Switzerland. It is complicated, but it will work. The procedures have already been put in motion. We can complete the transaction by phone from this office."

I handed the coin back to Alexander. "I'll find out which consulate he's with, and his full name. It may help."

"Yes," he said, staring dreamily at his treasure. "Eight hundred years old. Think how many people handled it, bartered with it, hoarded it."

I was thinking of something else: how many people had died for it and the *paitza,* and if Tom Dashuk was the latest person on that list.

CHAPTER 25

The lines of attorneys, bail bondsmen, cocky criminals, nervous witnesses, and irate citizens protesting traffic tickets were nowhere to be seen on Sunday morning at the Hall of Justice.

The only people milling about were there to visit the inmates on the sixth and seventh floors.

The detective bureaus were abandoned—no secretaries, no brass, no clumps of plainclothes detectives at coffee cup–littered desks, just the unhappy inspector whose turn it was to pull weekend duty.

Paul Paulsen was slumped in a chair, his feet up on the desk, semidozing, when I walked into the General Works detail.

Paul was a tall, good-looking man with ginger-colored hair frosted with gray at the temples. He was wearing a golf shirt, and the arms that filled the shirtsleeves were dusted with freckles.

"Nick, what brings you down to this dump on a Sunday?" He yawned widely, then added, "As if I didn't know."

You're talking to someone about a recent trip or vacation. You ask them how it went; their responses tell you a lot about their real interests and personality:

The weather was great.

The girls on the beaches were fantastic.

The boys on the beaches were fantastic.

The golf courses were breathtaking.

The fishing was unbelievable.

The shopping was spectacular.

When I asked Paul about his recent trip to New Orleans, I got nothing about the weather, the women, or any cop talk about the prisoner he'd gone there to pick up. Paul's response was pretty predictable. He was a man who went to bed at night reading cookbooks.

"Deep-fried turkey," he told me enthusiastically. "They get this big, big pot, fill it with peanut oil—that's the only oil you can use, 'cause it doesn't burn. They heat it up to five hundred and fifty degrees, then drop a turkey into the pot. The whole bird cooks in about thirty minutes. Fantastic."

I murmured, "Sounds good," then listened for about five minutes to his adventures with mussels, crawfish, and gumbo.

"Sounds great, Paul. Listen, have you got time to check out a few things for me?"

"You don't want to hear about the redfish pie?"

I didn't, but I pretended I did, then gave him Svetlana Bakarich's name and the license plate number for the Buick that Flaxen Hair had driven.

"Let's go see what Big Brother has to say."

I followed Paul into the cubicle that housed the detail's main computer.

Paul two-fingered his way into the proper databases, and in seconds, the printer spit out the results.

Svetlana Bakarich's driver's license showed her to be thirty-eight years of age. The only address listed was on Van Ness Avenue, the offices of With Love from Russia.

The plate was registered to the U.S. Consulate Office, which I already knew, but it confirmed that the car was detailed to the German embassy, which was on Jackson Street.

"How about lunch?" Paul asked after he had given me the information.

"How about a couple more checks? Addresses. Three-oh-four Cole Street and Twenty-one fifteen Clay."

The computer stored police responses to a street address for one year. I was pleasantly surprised that the definitions for the police response codes had remained in my watery memory bank. The flats on Cole Street had several reports for 448—petty theft—all to unit one, the Mercury Messenger Services, and a 595—

malicious mischief, graffiti in this case. Nothing for unit six. "The petty thefts were probably stolen. bicycles," I told Paul. "Don't bother pulling up the reports."

He clicked in the Clay Street address.

The list was a little more varied: a 408—ambulance response—809—missing person—an 851—stolen vehicle—and the final entry, 459—burglary—four days ago. The day before Dashuk had been murdered.

"Run the four fifty-nine, please, Paul."

Paulsen pushed the proper buttons and the three-page report flowed out of the printer.

Anna Romanoski. I finally had a last name for the mysterious Anna. A resident of apartment seventeen had reported a burglary, sometime between 9:00 A.M. and 7:00 P.M. The items reported as missing were all jewelry: a silver necklace, gold earrings, and a gold bracelet in the shape of a snake.

Well, well. Lily had lied to me. She said she hadn't seen Dashuk in a week. He must have given her the snake bracelet right after he burgled Anna's apartment.

The report listed Anna as twenty-six years of age and gave the apartment telephone number and her work number. The work number was certainly familiar: With Love from Russia.

"You look like you found something good," Paul observed.

"Very good," I agreed. The reporting officer had indicated that there were no signs of a forced entry. The apartment was described as "ransacked."

Ransacked. As if someone had been looking for something special. Someone like Thomas Dashuk. He no doubt had taken the jewelry to make it look like a professional burglary.

"Well, then, how about that lunch?" Paulsen prodded.

"Next week," I suggested. "You'll probably be hungrier by then."

"I'm hungry now, Nick. That airplane food. Yuuuck."

I parked on the corner of Jackson and Octavia Streets, in the Pacific Heights section of the city, where, when the upper class give dinner parties, the elite meet to eat.

If I craned my neck and looked up a block or two, I could see the looming mansion of one of the world's best-selling authors, but you'd never Steel her name away from me.

You could search through the entire city and not find a more suitable building to house the embassy of the Federal Republic of Germany than that on Jackson Street. It was a magnificent three-story reddish brick structure, with a balustrade-lined roof, elaborate windows set on a 150-foot frontage, enough space for six houses in San Francisco's residential areas. The front garden was laid out with foot-high box hedges protecting perfect squares of lawn. All it lacked was a moat.

In lieu of the moat, it had an eight-foot wrought-iron fence, in the middle of which stood a lacy iron gate. Behind the gate was a member of America's number-one growth industry at the moment: a security guard. He was a private security guard, who, like most engaged in his profession, looked bored out of his skull.

His main responsibility seemed to be to open the gate for pedestrians wandering in and out of the compound. No one he had spoken to in the last hour had been asked to show any iden- tification. Maybe he knew them by sight, or maybe he was lazy. I was about to find out.

I trailed a group of two men and a woman, middle-aged, dressed in casual clothes and walking shoes. They were chatting away in a harsh, guttural language that all my hard-earned de- tective training made me think was German.

I waited while the security guard opened the gate for them. The woman smiled and said in heavily accented English, "Thank you, Donny."

Donny was still young enough to have acne on his cheeks. The emblem on his dark blue uniform jacket read RAPID SECURITY.

I had a pretext ready for him, but he beat me to the punch.

"I saw you parked up the corner. You with the feds?"

"No. Local."

His eyes brightened. "Local. You mean the San Francisco Po- lice Department?"

"Right."

"Hey. I'm on the waiting list for the job." His eyes dimmed a bit. "Number a hundred sixty-two, but they say I've got a chance. What do you think?"

"I hope you make it. We can always use good men. Especially ones with a little experience. How do you like this job?"

"Ah . . . the pits." He shoved a hand through the iron gate. "Don Devaney. Pleased to meet you."

I shook his hand. "Inspector Harris. I've a . . . a rather delicate situation. There's a possibility that one of the members of the consulate was involved in a . . . shall we say encounter with a lady. One minute, she wants to file charges; the next, she says forget about it."

Donny rubbed his hands like someone moving closer to a fire. "Yeah, I get you. One of the guys here, huh? Which one?"

"I believe his first name is Jonathan."

"Hey, Inspector. You don't have to give me a con. I already talked to the army guy about Moss."

Army guy. The Thinner Man strikes again? "Ah, army guy. You mean the tall young fellow? Wears his hair like Elvis?" I snapped my fingers impatiently. "What the hell's his name?"

"Lieutenant Andrews," Devaney disclosed. "He was over here a few days ago. Only he told me that Moss was, like, maybe involved in a hit-and-run accident."

"He knew Moss's name?"

"Just the first name. Like you."

I shrugged my shoulders. "I'll have to talk to Andrews. The lady involved is a civilian employee of the government. What were you able to tell Andrews?"

Devaney was starting to worry. "Ah, listen, Inspector, I was just—"

I put some authority in my voice. "I'm not very happy about all of this, Devaney. Andrews should have kept his big nose out of it. Now, exactly what did you tell him?"

He was back on the hook. "Inspector, all I told him was Moss's name, and that he comes and goes a lot." He jerked a thumb over his shoulder. "I don't get in there, except for a piss break. I have to stand out here even in the rain, so I don't know what the hell is going on. Moss is some kind of cultural attaché, that's all I know. I see him for a few days; then he's gone and I don't see him for a few weeks."

"Have you seen Jonathan Moss today?"

"Yeah, Inspector. He took off about ten this morning." He turned his head to scan the street. "Hey, Inspector, anything you can do to push me up on that list would be appreciated."

I spread my hands in a helpless gesture. "I really wish I could."

I walked back to my car. I had Moss's name now, but Dashuk had beat me to the punch again. Dashuk must have run the Volvo's plate, just like I had, so he would have had With Love from Russia's address. He followed Anna/Tanya right to Moss. Or he picked up some information on Moss when he burgled Anna's apartment. All the while I was belittling his investigative skills, he had been running circles around me.

I was still in a sour mood when I got back to my flat.

Mrs. D's door was ajar as I was trudging up the steps.

Her sour mood made me look like Mary Poppins. Orders from headquarters. I was to take Carla out to dinner. No excuses.

Even if I'd had an excuse, it wouldn't have done me much good. She slammed the door before I could respond.

CHAPTER 26

I called Alexander Rostov. His voice had that distant, bottom-of-the-barrel sound that indicated he was talking to me on a speaker phone.

Before I could tell him the news about Jonathan Moss, and Anna Romanoski, he cackled a warning. "Nick, he was here. He left just minutes ago."

"Who?"

"Joseph Vallin. He questioned me about the *paitza,* and the coin. And you, Nick. He asked me if a Nick Polo had been by asking about the *paitza.*"

"What did you tell him?"

"That I never heard of you. Why is he—"

"I went to Vallin's shop," I reminded Alexander. "At your request. Asking about the *paitza.* And to his house. He's no doubt checking with everyone he can think of to see if I've been around. Alexander. Your buyer—would Vallin be able to figure out who he is?"

"Well, it's possible, I guess. He's a well-known collector, so—"

"So if Vallin makes some inquiries, he'll know what's happening."

"My buyer would never give out my name," he said confidently.

"What if Vallin could promise him the same merchandise at a cheaper price?"

"No. No, I don't think so," he said with much less confidence.

"Well, there is some good news. I traced the car with the diplomatic plates. The German embassy. Jonathan's last name is Moss. Jonathan Moss. He's a cultural attaché."

"I've got some more news. Anna does live on Clay Street. She goes by the name Anna Romanoski."

"How did you find this out?"

"Her place was burgled a few days ago, Alexander. Someone turned her apartment over. He left with some jewelry, but I think what he was looking for was your coin, or the *paitza*."

Rostov took a few seconds to respond. "God, who . . . You think it was this Dashuk? The man who was killed?"

"I think that's a good bet. Have you any word from Moss, or Anna?"

"No. I—hold on, a customer."

I could hear Alexander ask someone if he could be of help.

The deep baritone of Col. Jack Colby responded. "Yes. I want to know about the man who left a few minutes ago."

"Man? What man?"

Colby's voice got louder. "Joseph Vallin. I'm with military intelligence." There was a pause. "I'm investigating a murder that took place on military property three days ago."

"You're with the police? And you think Joseph Vallin is involved?" Rostov queried.

"I didn't say that, Mr. . . ."

"Alexander Rostov. I know nothing about any murder, I'm just a shopkeeper. I—"

"Rostov. You're Russian?"

"Da."

Da. Yes. That was the last of what I understood for a minute or two while they growled Russian at each other.

Alexander brought the conversation back to English by asking, "The man that was killed—he was a friend of Joseph's?"

"Maybe. What did Vallin want?"

"He was looking for an item. A coin."

"What type of coin?"

"Old. Too old for me. Look, I'll show you what I've got. Some nice American eagles, some silver dollars, and some Indian-head pennies that—"

"Exactly what was Vallin interested in?"

"A thirteenth-century Asian coin. I have nothing like that, believe me."

I could imagine Colby looking around at all the junk in that store and then believing Alexander.

"Why would Vallin come here?"

"I'm a dealer. Sometimes I come across something that interests him. But nothing so grand as what he was looking for today."

Colby pressed. "Did he mention anything else? A tablet. A *paitza*?"

"A what?"

"Never mind," Colby instructed. "Listen good. My work is confidential. I wouldn't want you calling Mr. Vallin and telling him I was asking questions."

"A dead man, I don't want any connections to, believe me."

I could hear Colby's footsteps, then his voice barely audible when he said, "What about a man named Polo? Nick Polo. Do you know him?"

"Polo? Like Marco Polo, you mean?"

"That's right."

"No. He's not a collector, or a dealer, Mr. Policeman. I don't know of him."

The footsteps sounded again. Colby's voice came back at full strength. "Take a look at this picture, Mr. Rostov. The woman— do you recognize her?"

A minute, maybe more, then Rostov said, "No. She's very beautiful. Is she Russian?"

"You've never seen her?"

"To my regret, no. Is she involved with this murder?"

"That's what I'm trying to find out. Here's my card. If you hear anything more from Vallin, let me know."

"Joseph Vallin deals in different circles than I do, Mr. Policeman. I don't see him very often."

"Well, in case—"

My other phone rang. I hung up on Alexander and grabbed the ringing line.

"Polo, here."

"Nick, Dick Ferge at the *Bulletin*. Have you heard anything from Jane?"

Ferge was Jane Tobin's editor. "Not for a couple of days, Dick. How about you?"

"No, not directly. But a buddy from the *Herald* down in Miami called me. He said he saw Jane and some guy doing the town. He said they were engaged. I figured if anyone had the scoop, it was you."

"Haven't heard a word, Dick," I said in a voice that sounded more like a croak.

"Well, keep me posted, Nick. I don't want to lose Jane."

I sat there for a while listening to the soft burr of the phone line. Ferge didn't want to lose her. Jesus Christ! What the hell did he think that I—

The phone rang again.

"What?" I shouted.

"Nick, Nick. What's the matter? Are you all right?"

"Yes, Alexander. I'm fine," I lied. "Did he leave? Do you know who that was?"

"He did. His name was on his card. Colonel Colby. He's the one you told me about, isn't he?"

"Yes. He's supposed to be helping in the investigation of Dashuk, the dead private investigator."

"How did he come to me? What brought him to me?"

"I don't know," I confessed. "He didn't get to you through me. It had to be Vallin. He must be following Vallin, Alexander. You handled him well."

"Perhaps, Nick. He was not happy when the phone rang. He saw my speaker was on. He knows that someone was listening to us."

"What did you tell him?"

"Just that there was a customer on the line and that I had for-gotten about him."

"Why don't you lock up the store, Alexander? Lock up and wait for Anna or Moss to get in touch with you."

I could tell the suggestion didn't appeal to him. The next person in the door could be carrying another long-lost treasure.

"You think this Colby can ruin things, Nick? I'm so close. I don't want to lose the *paitza* now."

"Lock up. As soon as you hear from Moss or Anna, call me." I gave him the number for the cellular phone. "Call me right away."

"What are you going to do?" he asked.

Getting blind drunk was the first option I had in mind, but I didn't tell Alexander that.

CHAPTER 27

◀▶

It's juvenile, senseless, harmful to your health. You get a little bad news and try to drown yourself in booze. It never works. But I tried it anyway. Just yesterday, if I'd had four shots of Jack Daniel's, I would have been stumbling around on my heels. But that was yesterday. Today, the liquor had no effect, and I was stone-cold sober. Stone-cold sorry for myself. So sorry that I hadn't given much thought about how Col. Jack Colby had gotten to Alexander Rostov. I'd been careful in my driving, sure I wasn't followed when I'd gone to Alexander's shop, or to Joseph Vallin's house in Marin County. How had Colby picked up on both of them? It might have been my using the cellular phone. Using a cell phone was about as secure as broadcasting on C-Span. That could have been it, or he could have hooked onto Vallin and followed him to Alexander's place.

But Colby wasn't what was causing me to put on the gloves with old John Barleycorn. It was Jane Tobin. Miami. Engaged. It had to be a joke. It had to be—

The phone again. Jane calling to explain the hoax. She had set me up with her editor. It was all just one of her jokes.

I grabbed for the receiver, ready to accept her apology.

No Jane. What I heard were the acid tones of Detective Al Rickard telling me, "I have a federal subpoena ready to forward to the United States attorney's office. If you aren't in my office in an hour, I will have the subpoena served on you this afternoon!"

Rickard broke the connection without waiting for my response.

I considered my options while I eyed the Jack Daniel's bottle. I could either run down to Rickard's office or sit in the kitchen getting plastered and wait for him to come after me with the federal subpoena.

I decided on a compromise. I'd go to see Rickard, but I'd take the bottle with me.

Rickard greeted me in a voice that throbbed with resentment. "Well, well, so nice of you to decide to show up."

"Detective, I'm in a bad mood. Don't make it any worse. Ask your questions politely or I'm out of here."

He cocked his head and eyed me suspiciously. "Have you been—never mind. Come into the office.

"Sit down," Rickard ordered as he settled himself in the chair behind his desk. "I'm going to record this conversation, Mr. Polo. Do you object?"

"Probably, but let's try it anyway. Where's your boss?"

Rickard shot his cuff and consulted his watch. "If you mean Colonel Colby, I expect him shortly."

"Before you turn on the tape recorder, let's get some ground rules straight, Rickard. Do you trust Colby?"

The question seemed to surprise him. "Trust him? In what way?"

"In every way. He pushed his way into your investigation. He's been telling you—"

"Colonel Colby has been very helpful, I think."

"Are you sure he was in Oakland when you called him the night you found Dashuk's body?"

"Yes, of course I'm sure."

"You're sure you called an Oakland number, but it could have been rerouted. Forwarded to another location. Like here in San Francisco."

"What's your point, Polo? Are you trying to suggest that Colonel Colby could be a suspect in Dashuk's murder? That's ridiculous. He's been very—"

"Colby says he wouldn't trust you to gas up his Jeep."

Rickard's face went through a color chart, from light pink to rare roast beef red.

"I don't think we'll get anywhere if you—"

"Did Colby show you my report regarding Lily Wong?"

"No. But he told me the details. Where's this Wong woman now?"

"Good question. Your guess is as good as mine. Dashuk's murder has her terrified. She admitted that she was working with him. She'd let him know when she had a customer and Dashuk would video them. Then Dashuk would run a background check on the guy to see if he had any money, if he owned his house. Then they'd set him up for a payoff."

"Blackmail," Rickard said. "I know. Colonel Colby gave me the list you faxed him."

"Dashuk didn't do any filming the entire week before he died. Lily said Dashuk was working on something else. It had to do with a rare coin and something called a *paitza,* a very old artifact from the days of the Mongols. Dashuk's client hired him to locate a woman who had been shopping the merchandise around. The woman had an apartment on Cole Street. She didn't live there; she just used it to pick up messages, maybe meet her boyfriend."

"How do you know all this?" Rickard demanded.

"That's why Dashuk called me. He wanted my help in finding the woman. Colby also knows all about the Cole Street address."

"Why the hell didn't you tell me this in the beginning?" Rickard demanded.

The door opened with a thwacking sound and Col. Jack Colby himself barged in.

"Because Polo thinks he can get his hands on the items himself," Colby said with a wide smile. "Hello, Polo. What the hell are you doing here?"

"Detective Rickard invited me down for a chat."

Rickard rose slowly to his feet. "I'm going to get a taped statement. A complete taped statement," he threatened. "Have you got his report?"

"Yeah, yeah." Colby unzipped a black nylon briefcase, dug out my report, and dropped it on Rickard's desk blotter. "I don't know if she's going to be of much help, Al, but maybe you should pick up the whore for questioning."

Rickard sank back down in his chair and read the document. His eyebrows rose when he came to the bill. "Nine hundred and seventy-six dollars?"

"I'm in the private sector, Detective, not civil service."

I looked up at Colby. He had a self-satisfied grin on his face. "Have you submitted my bill to the proper authorities, Colonel?"

"The U.S. Army is a good as gold. Don't worry about it." He rapped on the desk to get Rickard's attention.

"Forget Polo's report, Al. I've got something more important to discuss with you."

Rickard slipped the report in his desk drawer before asking, "What?"

"I'll fill you in later," Colby said casually. "Are you finished with Polo?"

"I haven't even started," Rickard protested heatedly. "What have you got?"

Colby eyed me for a long moment before responding. "I've got Dashuk's phone records—from his office and his apartment. He made only a few toll calls in the week before his death. A couple to an outfit called the Rare Coin Network in New York City and Los Angeles, and the others to a man I think is his client."

"Joseph Vallin," I piped in, wondering if perhaps I shouldn't have had that last swig from Jack Daniel's neck.

"How did you come up with that?" Colby demanded.

"A lucky guess, Colonel. Have you spoken to Vallin?"

Rickard threw his arms in the air in frustration. "Who is Vallin? Will somebody tell me what the hell is going on here?"

Colby pounded his right fist into the palm of his left hand, his angry expression making it crystal clear that he'd rather be whacking away at my face.

"Vallin is an antique dealer," he said in a voice that would have frosted a beer mug. "He specializes in rare coins and weapons."

I saw no reason not to push the envelope a little further. "Colonel, didn't you tell me that Dashuk had called you, asking about a rare coin?"

"Dashuk called you, Colonel?" Rickard challenged.

"I told you he called me from time to time, damn it. A lot of my men do. I help them when I can."

"Someone helped Dashuk into an early grave," I pointed out.

Colby was close to foaming at the mouth. "How did you come up with Vallin's name? You had to get it out of Dashuk."

"No. I got it the same way you did, Colonel. His phone records."

"We had to subpoena those records from the phone company," Rickard protested.

"That's the hard way. I just called them from Dashuk's office, said that the place had been broken into and that I wanted to know if the thief had run up a phone bill."

Colby kept staring daggers at me. He was weighing it in his mind. He didn't believe me, but he had to admit it was possible.

"Have you spoken to Vallin?" the colonel asked, biting off the words, making each one sharp and emphatic.

"Yes. I've been to his house in Marin County. So had Dashuk."

Colby dropped down to one knee, like a football player on the sidelines, and glared at me. "He told you that?"

"No. Dashuk took photographs of Vallin's place."

"Where did you find the photos?"

"At Flash Photos on Golden Gate Avenue. Dashuk had an account there."

Rickard decided to join the inquisition. "Who told you that?"

"I'm an investigator, Detective. It's my job. I'm good at it. Dashuk had a trunkful of cameras. He didn't have any developing equipment—ergo, he had the work done professionally. I checked with the photo processors in the area. It wasn't hard."

Rickard had the decency to look embarrassed. "Why didn't you turn those photographs over to us?"

"I was going to include them in my next report. That is, as soon as I get paid for my first report."

Colby put a hand on the edge of the desk and leveraged himself to his feet. "I had you pegged all along, Polo. A do-gooder, a crusader. The Lone Ranger. What other little treats have you got in store for us?"

"I'm all out of treats, gentlemen. And tricks. How about you, Colonel? Did you talk to Joseph Vallin?"

Colby's response was to stand by the doorway and jerk his thumb over his shoulder. "Al, I think we're finished with Mr. Polo, don't you?"

Rickard looked bewildered.

"Yes," he finally muttered. "I think we're finished for now."

"Let me ask just one question before you kick me out, Detective. Do you know how to cook a frog?"

Rickard screwed up his face and looked to Colby.

"If you boil a pot of water and then throw a frog in, he'll jump right out. But if you put him in there when the water's cool, then turn the heat up, he'll just wait, until the water's too hot, until he can't move; then he's cooked. The water's getting warm, Detective. Call in the real cops."

CHAPTER 28

I don't know if my little fable got through to Detective Rickard, but the thought of boiling a frog in water left a bad taste in my mouth. I rinsed it out with a swig of Jack Daniel's before heading for home.

A car was parked in my driveway, a car very similar to the one I was driving—a nondescript four-door sedan, whip antenna, and spotlight. Only this one was a real police car.

Inspector Bob Tehaney was standing by the front steps, talking to Mrs. D. She was gesturing to him with the tip of her broomstick. Mrs. D spent more time with a broom than the Wicked Witch of the West did.

I parked in the neighboring driveway. Tehaney saw me and gave a grateful wave.

"I thought I'd let you know I got a courtesy call from the Dixon PD this morning."

"What were they courteous about?"

Tehaney took a toothpick from his lips and flipped it toward the street. Mrs. D was on it with her broom and dustpan like a linebacker going after a fumble in the end zone.

Tehaney slipped another toothpick in his mouth, then said, "They found a body, Nick. An Asian female. They ran her prints. Lila Wong. Her DMV record had a San Francisco address on Polk Street. Guess where? Lickie's Tanning Salon. Her CI and I sheet showed a yardstick of hooker busts. Do you know her?"

"Yes. I know her. She goes by the name of Lily. I was at her apartment yesterday. Seven forty-two Redwood Street."

"You think her death has something to do with the murdered PI?"

"Yes, I do. How did she die?"

Tehaney twisted his hand as if turning an invisible doorknob. "Broken neck."

Dixon is located some seventy miles northeast of San Francisco. Farm and cattle country. "Do they think she was killed in Dixon?"

"They don't know. Her body was discovered in a refrigerated poultry truck. In back of a pile of frozen chicken. The truck was loaded at the produce market off Bayshore, here, then made stops in Oakland, El Cerrito, Richmond, and Vallejo before getting to Dixon."

"So she was probably killed here," I ventured.

"I don't know. I'm waiting to hear from the Dixon investigator before I open a file."

"Jesus, Bob. She had to have been killed here!"

"I can't take their case away from them," Tehaney said defensively, tossing his toothpick to the sidewalk.

Mrs. D scooted over. This time, the bristles on her broom scratched across Tehaney's shoes.

"Fa schifo!" she hissed.

Tehaney backtracked for his car. "What the hell's the matter with the old lady? What'd she say?"

She said he was disgusting. If I didn't get Tehaney and his toothpicks out of there, he'd be getting a shot from the water pistol Mrs. D kept loaded with roach killer.

"She's my downstairs tenant and she's a little touchy about litter," I advised Tehaney.

He opened his car door, got in the front seat, rolled down the window, then said, "I'll keep in contact with Dixon, but it's their baby for the moment."

"Did Rickard call you yet?"

"The U.S. Park Police guy? No. And I hope he don't." He squinted through the windshield at Mrs. D. "Is that a gun the old woman's holding?"

"It's just a water pistol, Bob. Tell the Dixon cops I'll be happy to talk to them about Lila Wong. Do you know anything about the people at Lickie's being connected to the district captain?"

Tehaney made a face, as if he'd bitten into a rotten apple. "Christ, Polo. What is it with you? Every time you come to see me, it's grief. Pure grief. I don't know anything about any connections." He switched on the ignition, punched the accelerator, and, over the growl of the engine, shouted, "And I damn well don't want to know."

The car took off in a clamor of clanging iron. Mrs. D hurried over to inspect the driveway. Luckily, there wasn't a drop of oil visible on her precious cement.

"He's a policeman," I told her.

"Proprio uno stronzo," was the description she attributed to Inspector Tehaney. Delicately put, it narrowed in on a certain portion of his anatomy, and he was perfect.

Now she went after me, reminding me that I had a date with Carla and that I was to take her to someplace *meraviglioso. Romantico.* Wonderful. Romantic. And expensive. She wrapped her gnarled little fingers around my jacket lapel and imparted a final piece of criticism. *"Ma che cosa ti se messo?"*

"I'll wear my best suit," I promised her.

I called Detective Rickard and gave him everything that Inspector Tehaney had told me.

"Dixon? Where's that?" he wanted to know.

"About twenty miles south of Sacramento, Detective."

"It . . . it has to tie in with Dashuk and the tanning salon. One of the customers must have killed them both."

"That would be convenient, wouldn't it?"

"It's the only thing that makes sense. I'm going to call the Dixon Police Department. Who's handling the case?"

"You'll have to find that out for yourself. Good luck. Is the colonel around?"

"No. Not at the moment."

"Make sure he hears about Lily Wong. It will probably make his day."

My orders had been to take Carla somewhere romantic and wonderful, but when I arrived at Mrs. D's doorstep, Carla quickly informed me that she wanted to go where the action was.

Carla was certainly dressed for action. She wore a low-cut sequined silver sheath that stretched all the way down to midthigh.

I decided to compromise. We started with martinis at Butler's, a transplanted New York saloon on Union Street, then walked a half a block to Luisa's, one of the most romantic restaurants in the city.

You entered through a small cobbled alleyway bordered by bamboo and ivy. The interior had soft lights, dark wood, crisp white napery, and low-volume music. The entire ceiling was covered with empty Chianti bottles in their straw baskets. Each bottle was marked with the name of a couple and the event: an anniversary, a birthday, a first date. There were three bottles dangling above us with Jane's and my name: two birthdays and one for the day she was promoted to columnist.

We ordered a bottle of the Chianti, along with homemade Sorrentina gnocchi, and chicken puttanesca, sautéed with black olives, tomato sauce, and capers.

Carla inscribed our names and a heart pierced by an arrow on the basketed bottle of wine.

Then it was off for the action, which meant a trip around the corner to Fillmore Street and the Annex.

It was always a pleasure to be in the company of a beautiful woman, and not just for the obvious reasons. The side show was a trip: grown men, some overgrown, no doubt prosperous captains of industry, hardworking, no-nonsense construction workers, titanium-hearted bankers. Gents that could and would fire an underling with the flick of an eyelid suddenly turned googoo, ga-ga when a gorgeous woman showed up. Eyes rolled, mouths gaped, tongues dangled, lips drooled, and necks made cracking noises. Their eyes glided slowly over the beautiful woman and then moved to her companion. Disgust, anger, "you lucky bastard" looks.

The Annex had a dance floor, which suited Carla fine. The table we shared suited me. I watched her wear out the legs of a half a dozen men who had come over to the table and stammered out, "Ya wanna dance?"

Carla always wanted to dance. And she always cut them off at the knees after that one dance.

This didn't hinder the would-be Romeos who kept sending drinks over to our table. I suggested that we move on, but Carla wouldn't hear of it. Not until she had her turn on the karaoke.

Carla picked a number entitled "Whole Lotta Love." At least I think that was the name of the song, because she repeated that line over and over, interspersed between some growls, grunts, shakes, shimmies, and raspy Italian patter.

Her neck, shoulders, and the vee of her dress were sweat-sheened when she hoofed it back to our table.

She placed both hands on my shoulders and leaned over to blow me a kiss. "You like?"

The applause and catcalls were still ringing in my ears.

"I like very much, Carla."

"Good. Let's go home to bed now."

CHAPTER 29

I had had way too much to drink, Carla was nibbling on my ear, and I was trying to think of a way to put her to bed—her own bed in Mrs. D's flat, not mine. Still, that was no excuse. I never should have let it happen.

I pulled in the driveway and Carla opened the passenger-side door. A dark figure emerged from the shadows and forced his way into the car.

"Back up," Nathan Felder ordered.

"Hey, what the—"

"Back up!" He waved a gun at me.

"No BB gun this time, asshole. Back up!"

Carla started to speak and Felder jammed the gun into her breasts.

"Shut up, bitch. And start driving, Polo, or I'm going to blow away your friend's assets."

I edged out into the street. "Where to, Nathan?"

"Joseph wants to see you."

"All he had to do was call and I—"

"Shut up! Drive!"

Carla turned her saucer-sized eyes on me. "Nick, I—"

"Tell Tanya I'm not fooling, Polo. If the both of you don't shut up, I'm going to do something nasty."

"Felder, this isn't—"

"Shut up!" The gun was a long-barrel revolver. He rolled the barrel over Carla's forehead, down her nose, then back to her breasts.

"Okay, okay." I reached over to pat Carla's knees.

"Both hands on the wheel," Felder ordered. There was a loud double click as the gun's hammer snapped into the firing position.

I drove in silence for several blocks, then tried to start a conversation. "Listen, Felder, if you'd only let me—"

"Quiet!" His voice had an edge of panic. "Just drive!"

I just drove. There was a .38 snub nose in the hollowed-out headrest where Felder's oily head now rested. The little Beretta was holstered on my right hip. Both were useless at the moment.

Traffic was light. Coils of fog obscured the towers on the Golden Gate bridge. At one point, a California Highway Patrol car had drawn up alongside us.

"Don't be a hero," Felder cautioned ominously, jamming his gun back into Carla's anatomy.

I sneaked a glance at Carla now and then. She was sitting stiff-backed, her neck muscles taut, her hands joined in a prayerlike clasp.

I thought of a half a dozen possible things to try: Drive too slow and attract the cops. Drive too fast and attract the cops. Speed up and ram the car in front of me. Jam on the brakes and let the car behind crash into us. Swerve off the side of the road. Make a move for the Beretta.

I just drove. Felder spoke only to give directions—left here; right there. Even that was unnecessary. I knew how to get to where we were going.

I flicked on the high beams when we came to the dirt road leading to Joseph Vallin's house.

When we approached the metal gate, Felder took a small plastic contraption from his pocket. The gates swung open.

"I'm back," Felder said into the contraption. "I've got Polo, and the girl."

"Don't try anything cute," Felder cautioned as I got out of the car. "Keep your hands away from your body. We'll have a nice strip search with both of you once we're inside."

Joseph Vallin was waiting for us at the front door. He was

dressed in a burgundy brocaded robe. The triumphant look on his face melted away when he spotted Carla.

"Who is this?" he demanded.

"Tanya. She was with Polo, so I—"

Vallin banged the heels of his hands against his head. "This is not Tanya, you bloody fool!"

"But I thought she was—"

" 'I thought she was,' " Vallin mimicked in a squeaky voice. He reached out to Carla. "My dear woman, I'm so sorry. Let me apologize for this . . . this imbecile. Believe me, I had no intention—"

"Do you think you could get your imbecile to put away his gun?" I suggested.

Vallin turned his bushy eyebrows back to Felder. "Put that ridiculous gun away. Now."

"But you said—"

"Now!"

Felder gave me a blistering look; then his shoulders sagged and he slipped the revolver into his waistband.

Once it was safely tucked away, I pulled out the Beretta.

"Everyone stand perfectly still."

Vallin began spreading oil over the troubled waters.

"Please, Mr. Polo. A tragic mistake has been made. Nathan acted like a fool, and I intend to make amends—to both you and your charming companion." He spread his arms wide. "Please. Come inside. Let's all have a drink."

I pocketed the Beretta, then crossed over to Felder and yanked his gun free, flipped it over, held it by the barrel, and drove the grip into his face in a hammerlike blow.

Felder's nose burst open, sending a mist of blood into the air. When his hands went to his face, I clubbed him over the head. Blood was squirting through his clasped fingers. He sank to one knee and I slammed a sideways shot with the gun grip against his left ear. He tottered for a moment, then fell forward, his head making a sound like ice cracking when it impacted the tiled floor.

Joseph Vallin's ruddy features had turned chalk white. "Please, please, there's no need for this. It was a mistake. I'm sorry for—"

I jabbed the gun into his stomach. "I'm calling the cops, you son of a bitch. Kidnapping and sexual assault. Who the hell do you think you are?"

"Listen," he pleaded. "It was a mistake. Nathan's mistake. I told him I wanted to see you. I didn't order anything like this. Please. Please come in and let me make it up to you."

Carla spoke for the first time since Felder had jumped into the car.

"I need a drink," she said in an quavering voice.

"Yes, yes," Vallin agreed readily. "We all do." He looked down at Felder. "What about Nathan?"

I bent over and worked my fingers around his neck until I found his carotid artery. "He'll be all right."

Vallin cupped Carla's elbow in his hands. "Please, this way, my dear."

Vallin lead us down a long paneled hallway and into a spacious room. The floors were off-white marble that took on a lavender tone from the overhead lighting bouncing off the burgundy leather sofa, chair, and ottoman. The velvet wallpaper was a shade darker than the furniture.

The ceiling had masterfully done rococo plaster images of cherubs cavorting around garlands of flowers. On one wall, there was a gilded plaster scene of a robed gentleman in a toga sticking a lance at a creature with human legs and the wings and head of a goose.

Vallin hurried over to a drink cart and began rattling through the liquor bottles.

"Is cognac all right?" he asked nervously.

I draped an arm around Carla's shoulders. "Are you okay? Do you want to leave now?"

She shook her head determinedly. Her eyes were glossy. "I will do what you want to do." She raised up on her toes and whispered, *"Sie molto bene caccia."* Carla was impressed with the way I handled Felder.

"Here, here," Vallin chirped, holding out two balloon snifters. His eyes dropped to my right hand, which was still clutching Nathan Felder's revolver.

"Is that necessary now?" he inquired, moving back to the cart to fix himself a drink.

I sighted in on the creature with the goose head and pulled the trigger. The roar of the gun caused Carla to gasp and Vallin to cry out in pain, or anger, or both.

"Don't! I swear to you that Nathan acted on his own. He's still mad about what happened at the swimming pool, when you shot him with the BB gun. All I asked was that he contact you. I'll do anything to make it up to you."

Vallin tilted his head back and downed most of the drink, then replenished his glass and invited Carla and me to sit on the sofa.

"Most regrettable, most regrettable," he recited. "I don't know what got into Nathan. I assure you, I will reprimand him. I really don't think it's necessary to involve the police, do you?"

"It's up to the lady," I advised him.

Carla sighed heavily. "It was quite an ordeal. I thought I was going to be killed. I—"

Vallin flipped open his robe and pulled his wallet out. "I understand. Please. Accept this as a peace offering." He began doling out hundred-dollar bills onto the cushion next to Carla.

"Some new clothes. Some jewelry," he suggested as the stack got higher and higher.

"What was it you wanted to see me about?" I asked when Vallin had emptied his wallet.

He seemed grateful for the change of subject. "To congratulate you, Mr. Polo. I've heard you've been successful in your quest."

"Which quest is that?"

"The *paitza,* of course. I've learned that a certain gentleman in Singapore is purchasing the item." He paused, watching Carla tap the bills on the couch to straighten them out and then begin counting. "I assume that the gentleman in Singapore is your— what did you call him? Principal."

When I didn't respond, Vallin said, "I must admit that I'm disappointed in you, Mr. Polo. Turning me over to the police like that."

"Police?"

"Yes. A Detective Rickard, investigating Mr. Dashuk's unfortunate death. He called. He wants to interview me tomorrow."

"I didn't tip Rickard. Dashuk called you here from his office. It was a toll call. Rickard got the number from Dashuk's phone bills. Did he mention Lily Wong?"

Vallin's eyebrows rose in confusion. "Lily Wong?"

"A prostitute Dashuk knew."

"I have never heard of her."

"Maybe your man Nathan did."

"I doubt that Nathan would associate himself with a female prostitute, Mr. Polo."

Carla joined the conversation. "Twenty-eight hundred dollars," she said, riffling the edge of the bills.

"I hope that's satisfactory." Vallin smiled. He looked at me. "Is it, sir?"

"Maybe." There was a figurine on the coffee table, a thin, naked man, his head titled back, one foot uplifted, resting on a rock, his arms folded across his chest. "Do you like the sculpture, Carla?"

"It is very beautiful," she said, her voice back to full strength, strong, clear, and a little greedy.

Vallin took a handkerchief from his robe pocket and blotted his forehead. "Yes, it is very beautiful, my dear." He put the handkerchief away. "It's yours," he added with a sorrowful look.

I tossed the sculpture onto the couch. "Tell me more about your dealings with Dashuk."

He slowly crossed his right leg over his left, resting his ankle on the kneecap. "I did hire Mr. Dashuk. But only to obtain an address for the woman who had come to my shop with a photograph of the *paitza* and a coin." He gave Carla a quick smile. "The woman whom Nathan unfortunately confused you for, my dear."

"Have you spoken to a man by the name of Colby?"

Vallin shook his head so vigorously that the wattles under his chin began flopping. "No."

"Dashuk checked out the telephone number that Tanya had given you. He told you where the phone was located, right?"

"Correct. A dismal apartment on Cole Street, from what Nathan told me. He'd gone there with Dashuk and searched the place thoroughly, but neither the coin nor the *paitza* was there."

"Then you had Dashuk stake out the apartment."

"Yes," Vallin admitted. "Nathan tried it for a day, but when Tanya didn't appear, we decided to use the investigator."

"And Dashuk told you that Tanya never showed up."

"Correct."

"Didn't you try calling her there?"

"Oh, several times. I left messages on the answering machine, but they were picked up electronically from somewhere else, then erased. She never responded."

Carla was fidgeting, making squishy sounds on the leather sofa. The pile of money was no longer in sight.

I flipped open the revolver's cylinder and emptied the bullets in my hand. "How did you find out about the buyer in Singapore?"

Vallin gave an enigmatic smile. "I have my sources, Mr. Polo."

"What else did you learn from the man in Singapore?"

"That he was willing to pay three million dollars for the *paitza*."

Carla mumbled something in Italian.

"Forget about the *paitza*," I warned him. "It's out of your reach."

"If you say so, sir. However, if it is still in your reach, my offer stands. One hundred thousand dollars."

I tossed the revolver to him. It hit his hands and tumbled to the floor. "It's out of my reach, too."

CHAPTER 30

The girl was sixteen and a half. A full year older than I. A huge difference at the time. Her name was Valerie and she had long legs and a rather prominent overbite.

Her father was a fireman and worked twenty-four-hour shifts at the firehouse. He'd mark the calendar with a big red *X* for each day he'd be away from home for those around-the-clock work-days.

Valerie and her mother would take full advantage of that knowledge. Her mother got loaded and Valerie brought boys home to a small room in the basement.

I remember being dry-mouthed and scared to death by every little noise, like Valerie's moaning and the squeaking of the mattress springs.

I lived in mortal fear of her father coming home with an ax in hand and breaking the door down, or her mother sobering up long enough to spot Valerie leading me through the mysteries of puberty.

I had the same feeling that night with Carla. I imagined that Mrs. D was in her flat below, listening to every footstep, every creak, crack, murmur, and gasp.

I woke warily, edging one eye open. The clock showed it was a little after noon. I got brave and opened eye number two. There was no sign of Carla, no Mrs D hovering over me with a priest at her side and a shotgun in her hand.

One of my last sober reflections from the previous night was Carla saying she was flying to Los Angeles in the afternoon. I had agreed to drive her to the airport, or at least that's what I thought I'd said.

Carla was one tough biscotti. Rather than terrify her as it should have, the episode with Vallin and Nathan Felder had turned her on. She treated the whole thing as if it were the plot for a movie she hoped she would one day appear in. And I was hero in her version of the drama.

The hero felt like the idiot he was. My Sicilian blood is slow to warm, but once it reaches a boiling point, I do stupid things. Like pistol-whipping Felder. Like shooting at Vallin's wall. Like letting Carla waltz out of there with the money and the statue. I had no idea how much the skinny guy with his foot on a rock was worth, but judging from the look on Vallin's face, it was a pretty penny.

Vallin was scheduled to talk to Detective Al Rickard. In fact, they might be together now, as I was recovering from my present hangover.

All Vallin had to tell Rickard was that I'd forced my way into his house, beaten up his manservant, and shot up the place. Rickard would salivate over the chance to throw his legal weight at me.

It would be my word against Vallin's. My word and Carla Borelli's. Carla was the kicker. Vallin had to be worried about her going to the police and filing charges.

So maybe I'd gotten lucky. A standoff. Vallin and Felder would keep their mouths shut. And Carla would be happy with the cash in her purse, and the statue of the naked man.

The statue was on the nightstand. I picked it up. It was bronze. Carla had fondled it in the car on the way back to the flats, and I promised her I'd have it appraised.

I showered, shaved, dressed, bundled up the statue, and managed to get down a piece of toast and a cup of coffee before walking down the flight of stairs to Mrs. D's and confronting Carla.

Mrs. D came to the door. She was smiling. Shit!

The news wasn't good. Carla was still in bed. She had decided to postpone her trip to Los Angeles.

"Buon viaggio," she advised me as she slowly closed the door, this time smiling so wide, I could see the pink of her gums. It had been years before I was even sure she had teeth, and now she was flashing her gums at me.

Have a nice journey. Where the hell did Mrs. D think I was going? And with whom?

I trudged back up to my flat, cursing my stupidity and my hormones.

The safe, cowardly thing to do at the moment was get the hell away from the flats. I had no particular place to go, but anywhere was preferable to hanging around and being leered at by Mrs. Damonte.

Alexander Rostov hadn't taken my advice about closing up his shop. The OPEN sign was hanging in the window and Alexander was showing a middle-aged man a shoe box full of small metal cars.

He threw me a sly wink when he spotted me. The customer settled on a gray finger-sized Tootsietoy vehicle in the shape of an ambulance—$125 purchase.

I was thinking what a sucker the customer was when I remembered that Errol Flynn's cigarette case was resting in my coat pocket.

"Nick, Nick, I'm glad you came. I heard from Jonathan. He is ready to deal. Here. Tonight. Or rather, tomorrow at one o'clock in the morning."

"Why so late?"

"Because it will be ten o'clock in the morning in Zurich. My client is transferring the necessary funds. Moss will call his bank, and when he is satisfied that the money is actually there, he will hand over the *paitza* to me."

"Won't that be a little hard on your client in Singapore, Alexander? What's the time difference between here and Singapore? Fifteen, sixteen hours? It'll be the cocktail hour for him."

Rostov went rubber-legged, staggering backward against the wall.

"How do you know where my client is? How?"

"Joseph Vallin told me. Last night at his house. Vallin's desperate, Alexander. He had his buddy drive me over to his place at gunpoint."

"And he told you about the sale? About—"

"He didn't tell me the buyer's name, but he said he knew the *paitza* was being purchased and that the buyer was from Singapore. He mentioned the price—three million dollars."

"This is terrible," Alexander wailed. "Terrible."

"Maybe not. I don't think Vallin has you pegged as the middleman. He still seems to think that I'm the one handling the deal. How are you going to deliver the *paitza* to your buyer?"

"He will come here from . . . overseas. He's from Singapore. Vallin was right about that. But he's traveling to Switzerland— now, as we speak. Then he will come directly here to San Francisco."

"You won't have the *paitza* for very long, will you?"

Rostov nodded in agreement and nibbled at one end of his reading glasses. "No. But long enough, Nick. Long enough. I will have it all to myself for a day. I'm satisfied." He pinched the bridge of his nose as if a headache was coming on. "And I have the coin. I'll always have the coin."

"You're keeping the coin?"

"Yes, for now." He seemed to be thinking it through as he was talking. "Perhaps in time, I will sell it. Or donate it to a museum." He perched the glasses on the end of his nose and peered at me. "You are concerned about your fee? The twenty-five thousand dollars?"

"No. I'm concerned about you, Alexander. I'd better be here tonight. There's been another murder."

"Who?"

"A young woman. A prostitute by the name of Lily Wong."

Rostov waved a hand vaguely. "I know no prostitutes. What does she have to do with me?"

"She was working with the private investigator who was killed in Fort Mason."

"Prostitutes, investigators—they have nothing to do with this," Rostov protested.

"I'm not so sure. I think both murders are connected to the *paitza,* and the coin. Alex, once you get the *paitza,* where are you going to keep it?"

"My safe in the back. It will be secure there."

"No," I argued. "Someone has already killed two people. They wouldn't stop with a third or a fourth. And for that kind of money, if they couldn't get the combination from you, they would cart off the whole damn safe, Alexander. You better store it in a safe-deposit box at a bank until your buyer arrives."

He clearly didn't like the idea.

"I'll stay with you until the morning. We'll drive to the bank together."

He still didn't like it.

"You can spend all day at the bank playing with the precious thing," I proposed. "But if you keep it here, someone is going to come for it."

"Someone," he scoffed. "Who?"

"I'm not sure—yet."

Rostov began rambling on about how he could take care of himself.

I placed the statue Vallin had reluctantly given to Carla on the counter. "Give me an estimate on this, Alexander."

He picked up the bronze, turning it over to check the base.

"It's a Wilhelm Lehmbruck, Nick. Where did you get this?"

"Joseph Vallin gave it to a friend of mine."

Rostov went into one of his coughing spells. I leaned over and patted him on the back.

"I'll get you some water."

"No, no." He settled the statue on the counter and lit up a cigarette, then spoke through an exhalation of smoke.

"Do you know what this is worth?"

"No. How much?"

He picked up the statue, clutching it gently to his chest, like a mother with her newborn. "If it's authentic, then I would think fifteen thousand dollars would be a reasonable amount. Lehmbruck died in Berlin in 1919. His works are in great demand."

Fifteen grand. No wonder Vallin's eyes had almost popped out of his head when I tossed it on the sofa. That added another charge to the list that Vallin could throw at me. Assault, battery, discharging a firearm, and now grand theft.

"Check it out for me, Alexander."

"Vallin would never give this away without expecting something in return. What was he after?" he asked suspiciously. "Information on the *paitza*?"

I gave Rostov a watered-down version of the visit to Vallin's house.

When I finished the woeful tale, Alexander closed his eyes and massaged his temples with his fingertips.

"I think that perhaps you are right. You had better be here tonight."

CHAPTER 31

My Green Street flats were located on a hill. It wasn't an exceptionally steep hill by San Francisco standards, but if you were out of shape, you might do a little huffing and puffing by the time you got from Powell Street to the front steps.

At the bottom of the hill was a restaurant, Capp's Corner, the best of all the Italian family-style spots in town.

Across the street from Capp's was the Green Street Mortuary. From my stool at Capp's bar, I could see both the mortuary and my flats. My car was parked around the corner on Vallejo Street.

I was nursing a beer, waiting for three o'clock, because that was the time when Mrs. Damonte always ventured out. Her first stop was usually the bank. After assuring herself that her money was safe, she was off for a spot of shopping, which meant terrorizing the greengrocer or shaming the butcher into adding another slice of veal to her order. Then, if the weather was nice, she might sift through the rubbish cans at nearby Washington Square. Unless there was a wake that day—then it was straight to the mortuary.

She liked to arrive before the grieving family, if possible. Then it was home for a quick meal and right back for the services, again arriving early, so that she could say fifty or a hundred Hail Marys before the priest started the rosary.

I was in luck. She had on her little black hat with the veil, which meant a wake.

I waited until she disappeared into the mortuary, then slunk home, tiptoeing up the steps in case Carla was up and about.

I wanted some time to myself, with no interruptions by Mrs. D, Carla, Colonel Colby, or Detective Rickard. I still had a headache. I gulped some aspirin and a bottle of Pepsi, then crashed on the couch in the front room.

The phone rang several times. I could hear my recorded message, then the caller's response: Detective Rickard saying he wanted to see me again. Svetlana the Red giving it one more try on the bounced check. Then the commanding voice of Col. Jack Colby. "Call me, you son of a bitch!"

I dozed on and off, my mind wandering, usually ending up in Miami—chic restaurants, striped umbrellas on white beaches, gaudy neon-tubed nightclubs. Jane Tobin looking suntanned, windblown, and sensational. There was always a man with her— tall, broad-shouldered. I never saw his face, or even his hair. He had a broad-brimmed Panama hat that shielded his features.

Around five, a car pulled up in front and I carefully parted the drapes.

Carla Borelli exited a taxi, her arms full of nicely wrapped packages. The cabbie opened the trunk and carted more packages up the stairs for Carla.

She hadn't wasted any time putting Joseph Vallin's cash into circulation.

Twenty minutes later, there was another car—a white sedan with the blue markings of the United States Park Police on the side door.

Detective Al Rickard looked amazingly like Barry Manilow through the peephole, the distorted lens giving his nose that look you get when you spot your reflection in the bathroom faucet.

Colonel Colby was at his shoulder. Rickard rang the bell for a couple of minutes; then Colby began pounding on the door with his fist.

I could hear them debating. Colby had his ring of keys in hand and wanted to break in, but Rickard was having no part of that.

"It's against the law, Colonel, and besides, Polo probably has a burglar alarm. Why don't we—wait, here comes someone."

I lost sight of the dynamic duo, but I could here Rickard introducing himself, then Mrs. Damonte shouting, *"Andarsene!"* Go away.

Rickard was persistent, I had to give him that. He kept explaining that he was a policeman and had to talk to Nick Polo.

"Allora, vattene." Get lost, or else.

Carla Borelli's voice joined the fray, demanding to know what was going on.

"We're the police," Colby informed her. "We're trying to contact Mr. Polo. He wasn't in. Do you know where he is? Or when he'll be back?"

Carla assured him she did not, Mrs. D got in a few final curses, and Colby and Rickard gave up the hunt. I watched their car drive up the hill and out of sight, then flopped back down on the couch.

The hangover was hanging on. Mrs. D had a surefire cure for this particular malady, a thick shoe polish brown, home-brewed concoction that tasted as if it had been strained through a coal miner's sock. She also claimed that if you rubbed it in your scalp daily, it would prevent baldness. She sold mayonnaise jars full of the stuff to gullible *paesanos* in the neighborhood, who, come to think of it, all had full heads of hair.

I lay back and suffered in silence, trying to make some sense of the last few days.

Thomas Dashuk and Lily Wong. Partners in a sleazy blackmail scheme. I'd bet the value of the bronze statue against a bottle of Mrs. D's home brew that neither Dashuk's nor Lily's death had anything to do with the videos and their blackmail scheme, but it was something that should be looked into. By the police—if they were interested.

Poor Lily. Ending up in a chicken truck. The cops would look at her rap sheet and yawn. A crime wherein the victim is a prostitute, be it assault, rape, or murder, gets kicked down to the bottom of the work basket. That old "She was asking for it" stereotype persists.

Still, whoever had killed Lily was very smart, or lucky. A refrigerated truck—she'd be half-frozen. The coroner would have a hell of a time coming up with an approximate time of death.

Tehaney said the truck took off from San Francisco but made stops in Oakland, El Cerrito, Richmond, and Vallejo before the body was found in Dixon.

The Dixon cops would have to check with all of those departments. And that would take time, and money. And with the squeeze on police budgets, shortcuts would be made: Phone calls would replace personal visits. Possible witnesses who weren't readily available would be forgotten. An Asian whore. Forget about it. There must be more important matters to worry about in Dixon. A dead sheep in the road, a crop duster buzzing the highway, cattle rustlers, the new schoolmarm. A dead whore. Worse, a dead San Francisco whore. Once you got more than a few miles north of the city, San Francisco was known to law-enforcement personnel as "down there" or "the land of fruits and nuts."

A dead whore. Forget her.

A dead private detective. A dead blackmailing private detective who had no knock. No one who'd really care if he lived or died. Forget him. Dashuk and Lily Wong. Their bodies would cool in the morgue for a few weeks; then, with no families to claim them—or, more important to the county, no one to pay for their funerals—they would be shipped off to whichever crematorium had submitted the low bid for services rendered and they'd be disposed of. Ashes to ashes, dust to dust, and if payment wasn't received in thirty days, a late charge of 1.5 percent would be added to the bill. *Hasta la vista,* baby.

A local TV newscast had recently done a series on unsolved Bay Area mysteries. One of those cases involved a long-ago Mafia killing of a local gangster. "A crime that has baffled Bay Area law-enforcement officials for over forty years," was the way the ad read in the *TV Guide.*

I had got news for them. No law-enforcement official had bothered even to look at the file for the last thirty-nine years. Ancient history. In two weeks' time, that was just what Dashuk and

Wong would be. A few pages stapled to a manila folder in the back of a filing cabinet.

A few thousand bytes in a computer base that would be purged in a year or so. Ancient history.

The phone again. Carla this time: "Nick. Where are you? I miss you. I'm meeting Dominic for dinner at Donatello's. Join us. We can go dancing again. Ciao."

The downstairs door opened and closed and I spotted Mrs. Damonte on her way back to the wake. A few minutes later, a car horn beeped—a taxi. Carla off to her dinner with Uncle Dominic.

That meant I was no longer a prisoner in my own home. I brewed a pot of coffee, ate some leftover linguini, showered, changed clothes, and headed off to those oh so mean streets.

"It's only eleven o'clock," Alexander Rostov announced when he unlocked the door to his shop.

"It's your magnetic personality that draws me, old friend. Are you all set for Moss and Anna?"

"Yes, yes," he said, locking the door behind me.

I had spent some time driving between the German embassy and Anna's apartment on Clay Street, but I hadn't spotted either the maroon Volvo or Moss's Buick with the diplomatic plates.

For the last twenty minutes, I'd been hugging the doorway of a used-furniture store down the block form Rostov's shop. No Volvo, no Buick, and no sign of Colonel Colby, Rickard, or Joseph Vallin and Nathan Felder.

Of course, with Colby's black bag of tricks and Vallin's interest in the *paitza,* it didn't mean that there wasn't someone there.

Rostov fumbled around in his cardigan pockets and sleeves for a cigarette, coming up with an empty pack.

I offered him a smoke from Errol Flynn's cigarette case.

"Thank you," he said, coughing at the first inhale.

"You really should give those things up, Alexander."

He gave me a wintery smile. "A man has to have a vice, Nick. At my age, this is all that's left."

I followed him back to his office. His first move was to dig a fresh pack of cigarettes from the rolltop desk.

The Mongol coin was lying on the desktop, alongside the brass Turkish coffeepot and a half-filled cup.

"So, you are going to hide in the bathroom again?" Rostov guessed.

"No. I'll be right here. With you. And try to speak in English as much as possible."

"No, no. Anna will recognize you. She will know that you were working for me when you met her. She will—"

"She will be so happy to get whatever part of that three million dollars you're paying Moss, she won't care about me."

"No," he protested. "She will not like it."

"Who cares what she likes, Alexander? She's in it for the money. You've got Moss hooked."

We argued for a good ten minutes. Rostov wanted me out of sight. I wanted to be close in case Moss decided to get clever and keep the *paitza* once the deal was consummated.

"In a matter like this, you have to show strength. Anna seeing me will give us an edge. Moss probably doesn't know about all the men she meets through With Love from Russia. She may not even acknowledge me."

He agreed—reluctantly.

By the time one o'clock rolled around, Alexander had gone through half a pack of cigarettes and I had downed four cups of his strong Turkish coffee.

Six of his clocks bonged out the hour.

Rostov got to his feet and shrugged in defeat. "They're not coming," he predicted. "They've been scared off."

The doorbell rang and his head twitched toward the door like the needle of a compass tracking north.

"Show time, Alexander. Be careful."

CHAPTER 32

All that worrying about what Anna might say or do when she saw me turned out for naught. Jonathan Moss stood alone at the door to Alexander's shop.

He was dressed in the same green parka I'd seen him wearing at the Queen Wilhemina Tulip Garden.

Moss took one step across the threshold, then froze when he spotted me.

"Wer ist er?"

"A representative of Mr. Gee. Come in, Jonathan; there is nothing to fear," Rostov assured him in English. "Come in."

Moss hesitated and spouted some more German.

"Mr. Gee's representative does not speak German. Or Russian, I'm afraid," Rostov apologized on my behalf. "Where is Anna?"

"She will be here soon," Moss replied, as if it was of no importance.

Now that I knew the name of Alexander's client, I said, "Surely you didn't expect Mr. Gee to let you two transact this without a personal representative?"

"You should have mentioned this before, Rostov," Moss said hotly. He hesitated a moment, took a deep breath, then slipped inside, closing the door after him and leaning back against the frame. "All right. Let's get this over with."

Rostov shepherded us back to his office, once again asking Moss about Anna.

"She's not sick, I hope?"

Moss paused when he entered Rostov's office, his eyes roaming the room. "No more surprises?"

"None. You have the *paitza*?"

Moss pulled a paper-wrapped package from his pocket. "Here it is."

Alexander accepted the package with shaky hands. He placed it on the desk blotter and used a bone-handled letter opener to slice through the string.

"Ahh," he mewed when the *paitza* came into view, cradled in a blanket of cotton. He stared lovingly at it for several moments, then picked it up gently, blowing away the tiny strands of cotton stuck to the gold.

He screwed a jeweler's loupe into his right eye and examined the *paitza* under the gooseneck lamp.

Moss's eyes flicked between Rostov and me.

Alexander was breathing heavily, audibly wheezing. He used a wooden ruler to measure the *paitza,* then placed it on a small electronic scale. The digital numbers on the LED remote display screen read 8.92 ounces.

"Are you satisfied?" Moss asked impatiently.

Rostov said, "I still need the provenance, Jonathan."

Moss retrieved an oilcloth envelope from his pocket and tossed it on the desk blotter.

Alexander went over the documents carefully, using a hand-held magnifying glass to study the seals and watermarks. Finally, he said. "Yes, yes, Jonathan. I am quite satisfied."

Moss slapped his hands together in a loud clap. "Good. Then let's call the bank."

"I'd like to see it first," I said, drawing a sneer from Moss and a confused look from Rostov.

Alexander's reply was slow in coming. "All right," he eventually said, and reluctantly passed the *paitza* to me.

The gold glittered in my hands. A little more than a half pound of gold, the metal alone worth no more than a few thousand dollars. I traced the inscriptions with a finger. The carvings were slightly imperfect, the lettering on one side less clear than on the other.

Alexander seemed to be reading my mind. "Ögödei Khan

wore the *paitza* over his heart all his life as a memento of his father."

"Body acids. That's why one side is different from the other," Moss explained irritably. "Can we make that phone call now?"

I handed the treasure back to Rostov, who lowered it back into its cotton blanket, then picked up the phone, put on his glasses, and read numbers off a small piece of scratch paper as he placed the international call to Switzerland.

He spoke for several minutes in Russian, then handed the phone to Moss.

Moss clasped his hand over the receiver and nodded his head in my direction, then asked Rostov something in German.

"*Nein,* Jonathan. I assure you he does not understand a word. You may speak German, Russian, either one."

Moss gave me a superior look, then got on the phone. It didn't take long. Three minutes at the most, and suddenly Moss was $3 million richer.

He smiled triumphantly when he passed the phone back to Alexander, who thankfully switched back to English.

"This calls for a celebration." He went to an ornately carved walnut chest and withdrew a dusty bottle and a tray with four silver shot glasses.

"Napoléon brandy," he announced proudly as he uncorked the bottle and filled the glasses. "I had hoped—"

The clanging of the front doorbell halted him in midsentence.

"It's probably Anna," Moss volunteered. "The damn woman is always late."

I elbowed my way past Moss. "I'll get the door, Alexander, just in case it's someone else."

It was Anna the Mysterious all right, bundled up in her black woolen coat.

She pursed her lips when I opened the door for her.

"You? What are you doing here? Where is Jonathan?"

"Relax, Anna. I'm here helping Alexander. I—"

"I knew it," she rasped. "I knew it. You were too easy. Too . . . different. Svetlana was afraid you were the police. But you work for him. You've always worked for Rostov. It was a trick."

"That's right, Anna, Tanya, Irina. Come on in. You're just in time for a drink."

She managed to jam her heel on my instep as she scooted by me. As soon as she got to Moss and Rostov, she started spouting Russian. She pecked Rostov on the cheek and gave Moss a big wet kiss.

"*Gertrunken,*" Alexander said. "Join us in a celebration drink, Anna."

Anna took a glass, tilted her head back, and tossed the brandy down her throat. Even before she had swallowed all of it, she started coughing, pounding her chest with her hand. She lurched backward, knocking a brass-cased mantel clock to the floor.

Anna began apologizing, dropping to her knee and picking up the damaged clock.

"I am so sorry. Is it valuable?"

"Yes. Yes, it is. Mid-seventeenth century. The face was engraved by John Gooden Wingham," Rostov said sadly.

Moss decided to be bighearted. "I will be happy to pay for the damages."

Alexander protested that that would not be necessary, but Moss insisted. He took out his checkbook and began scribbling. "Will five thousand dollars handle it?" He paused for effect. "After all, I can now afford to be generous."

Rostov said, "That would be most generous."

Moss ripped the check free, waving it back and forth as if to dry the ink, even though he'd used a ballpoint pen. Then he reached out to Anna. "It's time we were on our way. *Auf Wiedersehen,* Alexander." He gave me a triumphant grin. "And goodbye to you, my friend."

I let them get to the door before calling out, "Wait. Why don't you take this with you?"

Alexander Rostov let out a loud gasp when he saw me holding the *paitza* in one hand, the Beretta in the other.

I tossed the *paitza* to Moss. He let it hit his arm and fall to the carpet.

"Pick it up, Jonathan, but leave the real one—the one you switched while your girlfriend was playing sick."

The left side of his lip lifted like an uneven curtain.

"You are mistaken, *mien Herr.*"

"No. I'm not. Your right coat pocket—that's where you put the real *paitza.* Take it out." I cocked the Beretta's hammer. "Very slowly."

He followed orders, that weird sardonic smile stitched onto his face.

He held the *paitza* in his palm.

Rostov wrested it free. "Why? Why did you do this? We paid you the money? Why?"

"Let me take a wild guess," I volunteered. "You were going to sell it again, weren't you? Maybe to Joseph Vallin. You probably figured Vallin would be a difficult man to fool. But not poor old Alexander here. What about the coin he bought from you? Was it real?"

"Oh, yes," Moss mocked. "Seed money. Isn't that what you Americans call it? You paid too much for the coin, Mr. Rostov. It's not as rare as you think. I have another five, in even better condition."

Rostov was shaking his head mournfully. "A crook. You're nothing but a goddamn crook."

"Me?" Moss laughed bitterly. "Don't act so high-and-mighty, old man. You don't really care where the coin or the *paitza* came from." He bent down and picked up the phony *paitza,* then turned his back to us and kissed Anna on the forehead. "Let's go now, *schatzi.*"

I never did find out whether Anna slipped Moss the knife or if he pulled it out of his coat pocket, but he swiveled in one rapid movement and I saw the briefest glint of metal before the blade entered my shoulder and threw me backward. My legs hit a chair and I tumbled to the floor. I pulled the trigger, sending a bullet on a harmless trip to the ceiling.

Moss came right at me, stomping at the hand holding the Beretta, kicking at my head, then the shoulder with the knife protruding from it. He reached down and snatched up the gun. "You stupid man. You stupid, stupid man. Here, let me help you."

His idea of help was to twist the knife as he wrenched it from my shoulder.

I struggled to a sitting position. I could feel the blood flowing down my arm, see the stream run over my hand and fingers and pool onto Alexander's expensive rug.

Moss was standing over me, like a boxer in the ring taunting his vanquished opponent.

"Is that the knife you used on Tom Dashuk, Jonathan?"

Moss leaned down and wiped the bloody blade clean on my suit jacket. "Yes, it is. He was a fool, too, Mr . . . What is your name, little man?"

"Polo. Nick Polo. Ask your girlfriend. We had dinner the other night."

Moss backed away and barked out an accusation at Anna.

She barked right back at him.

Alexander was sprawled in his chair, lips trembling, the *paitza* clutched in his lap.

Moss held the Beretta in his right hand, his arm extended, his left hand cupped under his right elbow. The tip of the barrel was no more than three feet from its target—my head.

He did that thing with the side of his lip again.

When I was in seventh grade, the nuns guaranteed me that if I made Holy Communion ten times in a row and didn't commit any mortal sins during that time period, I would have time to recite a final Act of Contrition before I died, thus guaranteeing me a trip to, and through, the pearly gates.

I didn't have time to say, "Forgive me" before the first bullet shattered Moss's skull. At first, I wasn't even sure it was a bullet. There was no bang, just a soft coughing noise, and the front of Moss's face turned into a bloody gargoyle.

He spun around and took the second and third shots in his chest. He fell in a thud, landing alongside me.

My Beretta was still clutched in Moss's fingers. I was reaching for it when Colonel Colby nudged my arm away with his foot.

"You don't want the gun, Polo," Colby advised. "You might hurt someone."

He slipped his foot under what was left of Jonathan Moss's head. "He killed Tommy, huh?"

"Yes, he admitted that, Colonel. Would you mind calling an ambulance? I'm bleeding a little."

"Yeah. Good idea. Rickard, call an ambulance."

Detective Rickard's face came into view. He knelt down, checked my wound, then scooped up the Beretta in his white-gloved hand.

"You need an ambulance all right. I'll make the call."

Colby said, "Better tell them there're going to be two customers, Al. The old man doesn't look too good."

Rickard went out to the front of the shop while Colby nodded toward Anna. "Ah, the lady in the photograph."

Anna was frozen in place, her arms hanging straight down along her side, like a prisoner waiting to be led to the gas chamber.

"Right. That's Anna, Tanya, Irina. Moss's partner in crime."

"Was she involved in Tommy's murder?"

"I don't know."

"Let's find out," Colby said in a calm, conversational tone. He crossed over to Anna, yanking at her hair to get her attention.

"Girly, your boyfriend admitted he killed Tommy Dashuk. Tell me about it. You were there, weren't you?"

Anna kept her eyes riveted on Moss's body. I turned my head and took a peek, then jerked my eyes shut.

"Girly, tell me about Dashuk," Colby pressed. "Were you there?"

Anna's lips were moving, but no sounds were coming out.

Colby reached out and grabbed hold of Anna's right wrist, shaking her hand as if it were a fan. "We found a lot of fingerprints in the van, girly. Yours and his are bound to be there. Tell me now and it'll go a lot easier for you."

"Yes. I was there. I . . . I didn't think that Jonathan was going to . . ."

"Slice his neck from ear to ear," Colby provided.

Rickard bounded back into the room.

"An ambulance is on its way."

Colby nodded. "I think this time we better call in the local cops, Al."

"Let's get all we can before we do that, Colonel. Has the woman confessed?"

"Sort of," Colby disclosed. "You saw him—Jonathan, is that his name? You saw him do it, didn't you?"

Anna covered her face with her hands. "Yes. Yes, I saw him do it. I didn't want it to happen. We were just there to talk. But the man . . . the man wanted money. He knew . . . he knew about the coin, and the *paitza*. He knew how much they were worth. It . . . it happened so quickly." She began sobbing heavily, stumbling backward, leaning against Rostov's desk.

"What about that ambulance?" I asked, watching the stream of blood course down my fingers.

"It should be here any minute," Rickard announced.

Colby was shaking his head back and forth negatively. "I don't know if it's going to get here on time, Polo. You don't look too good. But I've got to thank you for all your help. I never could have done it without you."

I jammed a handkerchief against the wound. "How did you do it, Colonel?"

Colby smiled at Alexander, who was still slumped in his chair. His eyes were glazed, his face the color of boiled rice.

Colby watched as Rickard pried the *paitza* from Alexander's hand, then said, "I followed Joseph Vallin here to this shop. Now Vallin, at first, he looked like a heavy hitter. But when Al and I went to see him, he came apart. Especially when I brought up your name, Polo. He doesn't like you. Not at all. And Vallin's houseboy, Nathan, he's all busted up. Was that you, Polo? Did you get rough with the guy?"

"We had an argument," I admitted.

Colby grunted a response, then said, "So I followed Vallin here. Why here? To this dump? Old Rostov looks like he's ready for the woodpile. I was going to walk away from him, but then I asked about you, Polo. Rostov starts sweating. He gave me some bull-shit line about 'Polo? Like Marco Polo?' I knew he was putting me on. Then I noticed his phone. His speaker was on while I was interrogating him. Someone was listening in. Was that you, Polo?"

When I didn't respond, Colby leaned down and pressed his fingers into my cheeks. "Hang on there, Polo. Was that you listening in?"

I closed my eyes, hoping to hear a siren. "Yep, that was me."

"Well, that's a relief. I wasn't sure who it was. But I'm glad it was you, pal. It got me thinking. First Vallin stops by to see the old man; then I'm getting vibes that old Rostov here is your client. The one you refused to tell me about. Both you and Vallin hooked up with Rostov. There had to be something to it. So I decide to stake out the shop. Sure enough, you came waltzing in." He sighted his pistol on Moss. "Then this sap shows up. In a Buick with diplomatic plates, no less. Who is he, Polo?"

"His name is Moss. Jonathan Moss. He's a cultural attaché with the Germany embassy."

"Was a cultural attaché," Colby corrected. "He's dog meat, now. Rickard and I saw him come into the shop. There was someone waiting for him in his car." He smiled at Anna. "Cutie pie here. Then she hops out of the car and you open the door for her. Al and I decided it was time to join you all." He dug his ring of skeleton keys from the pocket of his trench coat and shook them at Alexander. "You need a better lock, old-timer. Good thing we came in, Polo. Otherwise, your German friend would have shot you dead. You owe me, Polo. I saved your life." He bent over at the waist and stared into my eyes. "Maybe I saved you."

The blood was seeping through the handkerchief. "What about Lily Wong, Colonel? Moss and Anna didn't have anything to do with her."

"How do you know? Maybe they did. Or maybe it was one of those old farts Tommy and the whore were blackmailing."

"None of those old farts ever saw Dashuk."

Colby shrugged his shoulders. "So? No big deal. She's a whore.

The whole investigation will slip through the cracks." He started to grin; then the grin turned into a full-blown smile. "A whore, slipping through the cracks? Get it, Polo?"

"I get it. I also think that you killed Lily."

Colby knocked the silencer against his chest. "Me? Are you kidding? What reason would I have to kill a whore?"

"Maybe she knew about you. You and Dashuk, old army buddies working together. You supplied Dashuk with the surveillance equipment. And you ran the unlisted telephone numbers. You used the MI computer to get the DMV information on the suckers. You—"

Colby was smiling widely as I made the accusations. "Sorry to disappoint you, Polo. But it wasn't me."

"Then who was it? Someone was helping him. How about Rickard?"

"No, you've got to—" Colby stopped in midsentence and started to turn around.

Al Rickard jammed the tip of my Beretta into his back. "Drop your gun, Colonel."

"Listen, Rickard, I—"

"Drop it."

Colby opened his hand, and before his gun hit the carpet, Rickard pulled the Beretta's trigger three times.

Colonel Colby straightened up as if he'd been electrocuted, quivered, then sank slowly to his knees, finally keeling over on his side at Anna's feet.

She let out a loud scream and Rickard slapped her across the face, then picked up Colby's silenced pistol, aimed straight at her, and pulled the trigger.

A mushroom of blood sprouted on Anna's blouse and she was thrown backward by the force of the bullet.

Rickard calmly pulled the trigger twice more and she did a slow slide, leaving a trail of blood streaks on the wall.

Rickard next pointed the weapon at Alexander, who was sitting as if in a trance. Or as if he'd had a stroke.

Rickard wheeled the tip of the gun in my direction.

"I'm getting the feeling you really didn't call an ambulance, Detective."

"Right you are, Polo. How are you feeling? It would be better for me if you just bled to death, but if necessary, I'll shoot you."

"How are you going to explain all this carnage?"

"Simple. You and the old man were involved in buying stolen merchandise. When you learned that the merchandise was phony, a fight took place. Moss knifed you; you fell to the floor, and shot back, hitting poor Mr. Rostov. Colby came in and fired, killing Moss and the woman. You in your confused state then shot Colonel Colby."

"That's a little complicated, Al."

"It will work. The police will find all of you tomorrow, maybe the next day. The phony *paitza*—that was a nice turn. I can leave that here. It will add a little more confusion."

He kicked out at my wounded shoulder. "Maybe that will speed things up."

"Why?" I winced through the pain. "I know why you killed Colby. For the *paitza*. But why Lily Wong?"

Rickard pulled the *paitza* from his coat pocket. "Beautiful, isn't it?"

My blood was spreading across the Persian carpet like an incoming tide.

"Why Lily, Al?"

"She saw me once—in Tom's office."

"You knew Dashuk?"

"Sure. We were army brats together. We went to high school in Fort Dix. He went into the army, I chose the marines." He showed me his teeth. "They wanted a few good men. I ran into Dash in Berlin. I was a guard at the U.S. embassy. We kept in touch. When I got the job with the Park Police, I checked him through the computer. I found him in Oakland. Can you imagine that? Right across the Bay. He wanted out. He was tired of it all. Especially tired of that prick Colby. He took the test for the Park Police, but he didn't pass."

"Too bad. I'd feel a lot safer with both of you protecting us."

Rickard pushed back his coat sleeve and checked his watch. "Another minute, Polo. If you're not gone by then, I'll have to shoot you. Another notch on the colonel's gun. Then, if the old man isn't dead of a stroke by then, I'll put your gun in your hand and you can finish him off. How's that for a happy ending?"

"Lily. Lily never told me she recognized you," I said, feeling like I was talking in slow motion. Rickard's image appeared to be moving in slow motion.

"No. It's a shame really. When I saw her, she looked right through me. It wasn't until I talked to her for a few minutes that I could see the light go on." He looked at his watch again. "Speaking of lights, it's time to turn yours off. So long, Mr. Polo."

Then there was another of those coughing sounds and my chest felt as if it had exploded.

Everything started to go black. The last thing I heard were shots—gunshots. No coughing sounds. They were loud, terribly loud. Then nothing.

CHAPTER 33

Jane Tobin once did a series of columns on near-death experiences. Interesting stuff. Parapsychologists had interviewed hundreds of people who had reached the well named "big sleep," only to come back to the so-called real world.

The stories lucky stiffs, so to speak, told were amazingly similar. They'd wake up in a hospital and their view was from above, as if they were floating just below the ceiling, looking down at their own bodies, and those of the doctor, nurse, and visiting loved ones.

Then there was a feeling of entering a dark tunnel, speeding along and finally emerging from the tunnel into a clear, brilliantly white light.

When my eyes focused, however briefly, I definitely wasn't floating in air. I was looking upward, seeing snatches of human beings: an arm, a hand, faces that were nothing but pale flesh-color smudges. There was no pain, no discomfort, just an uneasy queasy feeling; then everything went fuzzy gray, like a TV screen switched to a channel that had signaled off for the night.

The images became clearer after awhile. I recognized the hands and arms as belonging to doctors or nurses, angels of mercy. Angels—no gender gap there. You can be a boy angel, a girl angel, a young angel, an old angel. The angels tending to me were a full mixture—men, women, young, old, black, white, Latin, Asian.

One of the nurses told me that the reason I was still alive was because of the cigarette case. The bullet had penetrated the case's metal and into my flesh, but it hadn't gone in too deep. The knife wound was the main concern because of the loss of blood.

Paul Paulsen stopped by and told me about Detective Al Rickard. Alexander Rostov had fired off all six shots from his old revolver. Two of them hit Rickard in the chest. He was dead. That's what he got for not having Errol Flynn's cigarette case to protect him. Rostov suffered a stroke and was in the same hospital, one floor below me. He was expected to survive.

At some point, I woke up and saw Mrs. Damonte, her beautifully aged features just a foot or so from me. Her black eyes were shiny with tears and I could see a reflection in them. I didn't like what I saw—a pale-faced man, tubes in his nose and mouth, turbanlike bandages wrapped around his head.

I tried speaking to her. I could hear gurgling sounds coming from my throat, but no words.

Mrs. D moved from sight, her place taken by a man's face: handsome, gray-haired. He was wearing a Roman collar. Monsignor Heaney. He smiled, his lips moving. I concentrated on my ears. Listen, damn it. Listen. What's he saying?

The grayness fuzzed in again. My eyelids felt as if they were lined with sandpaper. I felt movement. My vision was clearer now. A ceiling, an acoustical ceiling above my head. A man in a green gown, a green cap on his head, leaned over and stared at me. I saw my reflection in his glasses—the tubes, the bandages. I shuddered involuntarily. I looked like hell.

We were moving fast; my stomach was churning. It felt warm, a seasick feeling. I hoped I wasn't going to vomit.

Suddenly, we came to a halt. The green-capped man gave me another probing look. He nodded his head rapidly before disappearing from sight.

The ride started up again, then came to an abrupt halt. Another face. Jane Tobin's! Her skin tanned, her hair sun-bleached. She looked beautiful, even though she was frowning, her eyes wet, tears rolling down her cheeks. Her hand came out to me. I felt the touch on my forehead. Her hand moved away. Her left hand. There was a ring I hadn't seen before—a glittering diamond.

Movement again. The ceiling racing by, then it got dark—we were out of the hallway, into a tunnel. Darker, then black. Then light. Damn, they were right. Brilliant, clear white light.